PENGUIN BOOKS

Dear Dr Stopes

Born in 1933, in Sheffield, Ruth Hall is the daughter of Jack Clark, a holloware buffer in the local steelworks, and Ethel Ford, a miner's daughter. She inherited a musical talent from her father, but there were no facilities for a training in music available so she took a scholarship to a grammar school, followed by another to Nottingham University where she read English. After teaching for a year, then working as Public Relations Officer for the Calico Printers' Association in Manchester, she became a reporter for the *Glasgow Herald*, first in Glasgow, then in London.

For a time music drew her away from journalism, and she went to study harpsichord with Rafael Puyana in Paris. Finding herself not quite so gifted as she had believed, she returned to working for newspapers – the *Sunday Times*, the *New Statesman* and the *Observer* colour magazine which, with its series on British history, first stimulated her interest in Marie Stopes.

She now divides her time between music and writing. Her biography of Marie Stopes was published in 1977.

EDITED BY RUTH HALL

Dear Dr Stopes

SEX IN THE 1920S

PENGUIN BOOKS

Penguin Books Ltd, Harmondsworth, Middlesex, England
Penguin Books, 625 Madison Avenue, New York,
New York 10022, U.S.A.
Penguin Books Australia Ltd, Ringwood, Victoria, Australia
Penguin Books Canada Ltd, 2801 John Street,
Markham, Ontario, Canada L3R 1B4
Penguin Books (N.Z.) Ltd, 182–190 Wairau Road,
Auckland 10, New Zealand

—

First published by André Deutsch Ltd 1978
Published in Penguin Books 1981

—

Copyright © Ruth Hall, 1978
All rights reserved

—

Made and printed in Great Britain by
Richard Clay (The Chaucer Press) Ltd,
Bungay, Suffolk
Set in Monotype Plantin

CONTENTS

INTRODUCTION 7

1

THE LOWER CLASSES 11

2

THE UPPER CLASSES 47

3

THE CLERGY 59

4

THE MEDICAL PROFESSION 81

5

OVERSEAS 112

6

THE ARMED SERVICES 146

7

THE MIDDLE CLASSES 158

8

POLITICS 201

9

LITERARY 208

STATISTICAL APPENDIX 219

INTRODUCTION

Marie Stopes was the first person to whom large numbers of men and women wrote freely about their sexual and marital problems. When she came to prominence in 1918 with the publication of *Married Love* and *Wise Parenthood* the correspondence was naturally limited to the bookbuying public, overwhelmingly middle class. But with the opening of her first controversial birth control clinic in 1921, and the wide coverage given to her sensational libel action in 1923, her ideas and influence spread to all classes of society. She became as accustomed to the pencilled scrawls of desperate polyparturitive women in the London slums as to disapproving deckle-edged comments from episcopal palaces.

Few people at the time – George Bernard Shaw was her nearest rival – were quite so well known. Any pronouncement she made was widely reported, her advice sought on everything from the nature of dictatorship to the probable winner of the Derby. Her correspondents expected her to be a combination of doctor, priest, abortionist, pharmacist, nursery-maid and marriage-broker.

Married Love was published in March, 1918. At first Marie Stopes answered every letter personally. Six months later her correspondence had increased so much she began to charge fees in an attempt to reduce the flow – three guineas for a consultation by letter, ten guineas for a personal interview. She soon gave this up. Her doctorate was in fossil botany, not medicine – a fact she often failed to mention to her correspondents. To charge fees, sound though her recommendations might be, would have laid her open to criticism from an already suspicious medical profession.

By 1921, her correspondence was becoming unmanageable. A fortnight after she opened her clinic in March, she wrote triumphantly to her publisher: '. . . all together I have had nearly a thousand letters this week – 150 by one post alone at the Clinic'. She now employed several secretaries and was obliged to devise standard replies to the commoner queries, occasionally scribbling a postscript if the case particularly interested her (for this reason some of the replies included in this collection consist only of a postscript).

Realizing its unique value as a social record, Marie Stopes kept intact this vast and heterogeneous correspondence. The British Library, to which she left most of her papers, was unable to accommodate the whole collection. Some of the letters asking for advice were abstracted, but will not be available for inspection until the year 2008. Fortunately Dr Harry Stopes-Roe, Marie Stopes's son, was able to house the bulk of letters from the general public and it is on these, to which Dr Stopes-Roe generously gave me full access, that this selection is based.

I have limited it roughly to the years 1918–28, the decade when Marie Stopes's impact was at its strongest, and when, sexually, society was in its most interesting transitional stage between post-Victorian reticence and repression and today's more permissive attitudes to sexual matters. The extent of prejudice against birth control was still considerable. Advice on sexual and contraceptive matters was rarely available, and many of those who wrote to Marie Stopes explained that they were far too embarrassed to go to their own doctors for help. Another striking feature of the correspondence is the prevalent feeling of guilt at the mere mention of sex and birth control. Almost without exception, correspondents felt it necessary to plead, almost as before a judge, the special circumstances that prompted their requests for advice.

I have tried to avoid commenting on the letters, preferring to let the public speak for itself. The mere fact of selection, of course, implies some editorial bias. But within that limitation – and also that imposed by the desire to avoid repetition – I have tried to make the book as representative as possible. Many sexual problems are common to all groups of society: premature ejaculation, frigidity and impotence are no respecters of class barriers. Given the much more hierarchical nature of society in the 1920s, however, I felt it permissible to divide the letters into sections based on such structural groups. For those interested in a more numerical survey of sexual life in that decade, Christopher Stopes-Roe, Marie Stopes's grandson, kindly undertook the preparation of a statistical study based on the correspondence. This appears as an appendix. I am also grateful to the Duke of Bedford for permission to quote from his father's correspondence, though he points out that these letters bear no relation to the truth except as seen through his father's eyes.

Those who would like to place the letters in a wider context might find useful a short summary of Marie Stopes's life during those years when her crusading vigour was at its height:

1918   Publication of *Married Love* and *Wise Parenthood*. Marriage (her second) to H. V. Roe, aviator and co-founder of the Avro aircraft company, her first marriage having been dissolved in 1916 on the ground of nullity.

1919   Publication of *A Letter to Working Mothers*, 'on how to have healthy children and avoid weakening pregnancies'. Birth of first (stillborn) child, at the age of 38.

1920   *A New Gospel*, claimed by Marie Stopes to have been dictated to her by God, circulated to all the bishops attending the Lambeth Conference that year. *Radiant Motherhood*, 'A Book for Those Who Are Creating the Future'.

1921   Opening by Marie Stopes of Britain's first birth control clinic (the Mothers' Clinic) and formation of the Society for Constructive Control and Racial Progress. Publication of *The Truth About Venereal Disease*. Questionnaire sent out to parliamentary candidates.

1923   Hearing in the High Court of Marie Stopes's libel action against Halliday Sutherland, a Catholic doctor who had accused her of 'experimenting on the poor'. Judgment went against her but she won on appeal. Production on London stage of first birth control play, *Our Ostriches*, and of the first film with a contraceptive message, *Maisie's Marriage*. Publication of *Contraception, Its Theory, History and Practice*, aimed at the medical and legal professions.

1924 Birth, at the age of 43, of her only surviving child. Legal action against Sutherland, who had appealed to the House of Lords, finally resolved in Sutherland's favour.

1925 Publication of *The First Five Thousand*, a report on cases seen at the Mothers' Clinic. London stage production of her play *Don't Tell Timothy*.

1926 Publication of *The Human Body*, *Sex and the Young*, and *Vectia*, a play banned from public performance, recounting the insuperable problems of her first marriage.

1927-8 Organization of world's first travelling birth control caravan; various lawsuits against abortionists, Catholics, etc.; publication of her first novel, *Love's Creation*, and of *Enduring Passion*, a sequel to *Married Love*.

1929 Publication of *Mother England*, a short collection of letters from working-class women.

CHAPTER ONE

THE LOWER CLASSES

Britain in 1918 was still a society in which the rich got richer and the poor got children. Unlike the upper and middle classes, the working classes had still not made the connection between relative prosperity and the use of family limitation. The 1911 Census revealed that among married men under the age of fifty-five, unskilled labourers had a birth rate four times that of doctors or members of the Anglican clergy. The general misery of those with large families and inadequate incomes was exacerbated by widespread unemployment – over two million in 1921 – and by an acute housing shortage, no new houses having been built during the First World War.

Nor was it fair to blame the working classes, as many commentators did, for this improvident self-propagation. Not until 1930 was birth control advice even grudgingly available at the ante-natal and mothers' welfare clinics under the control of the Ministry of Health. Until then the burden was borne by the few voluntary birth control clinics; and, as the less hidebound recognized, it was surely foolish to expect those of limited foresight, initiative and intelligence – precisely those most in need of contraception – to exhibit, by visiting a clinic, qualities they did not possess. Outside the clinics (and in 1930 there were still only thirteen throughout Britain) family doctors were rarely helpful. Among the many thousands of letters to Marie Stopes from working-class women a depressingly large number complain that doctors have advised a patient to have no more children, but refused to give any information as to how this might be accomplished.

At one level, Marie Stopes argued, along with many of her

generation and background, that the lower classes were polluting the purity of the best British stock by their reckless multiplication. On a more personal level, however, she responded warmly and generously to individual pleas for help – indeed, her personality is revealed at its best in her genuine concern for those submerged in what she labelled, with typical flamboyance, 'a bog composed of the bleeding and tortured bodies of women and children'.

The problem was how to reach the working classes. She published A Letter to Working Mothers *in 1919, but many health visitors whom she asked to distribute the pamphlet refused to do so, and her attempts to deliver it house to house in the London slums were more often than not greeted with downright hostility. Her first real breakthrough occurred as a result of her libel action against Halliday Sutherland in February, 1923, widely reported in all sections of the press. She took on extra staff to deal with her enormously increased correspondence – also necessary in 1926, when her series of articles in the popular magazine* John Bull *brought in, over a three-month period, 20,000 requests for abortion alone. Abortion then being illegal, she either refused to answer these or, in particularly pathetic cases, sent a sad refusal. She used the* John Bull *letters for her book,* Mother England, a Contemporary History Self-written by Those who have had No Historian, *published in 1929, a compilation of letters received from working-class women in 1926 whose names began A–H. I include in this section a short selection from* Mother England, *now no longer in print, in cases where the problems described are not available elsewhere in the correspondence. Spelling and punctuation have been left uncorrected.*

23 DECEMBER 1918, WILTSHIRE: MR EG TO MCS ...
Regarding the 'killing of the sperms' would you kindly write me in what way this is done – how the vinegar or quinine is administered and the exact quantity and mixture? Also, are you not of opinion that at certain times coitus is *quite* safe for fertilization and what is this time? Is it better for the man to let the spermatozoon pass into the womb? I think you say so. During five years I have restrained myself from this except

when we desired our only child (now 5½) ... yours ffy, p.s. I have only had *involuntary* emissions 2 or 3 (at most I think) times in the 13 months. Anyway its been a lesson in self control!

25 SEPTEMBER 1919, LONDON: MR CJ TO MCS. Is it a desire to put bank notes into your pocket that you wrote such stuff as 'Married Love'? You seem to have set out with the conviction that all married people being on a similar low moral level to your own, are anxious to pay fabulous sums for this kind of book. Do you really think that my wife and I and our poverty-stricken friends (though none of us can afford to have more than two or three children) are sadly in need of such dirty advice as you offer? ... You deliberately misrepresent Malthus, who advised moral restraint ... Alas, is there not proof everywhere in this ghastly modern world that a large house, a large income and the superior education beloved of H G Wells have little to do with the creation of a genuine artistic let alone moral sense ... And really some of the things you propose in your book might have emanated from the brain of a Kaffir woman. CJ (a lover of Shelley)

3 MARCH 1920, LONDON: MRS MH TO MCS ... I have managed to get enough courage to write to you on a subject which has been most bitter to me throughout my five years of married life ... It was that I had nothing to show my husband I was a virgin girl. Of course my conscience is as clear as the sky in summer ... My dear mother kept me so very much in hand; and he knows that also ... A long time after we were married, he told me he was disappointed. He also gave me more than one reason how it would be possible to lose my hymen; but in none of these was there a solution to the problem, except once when I was very ill (poisoned I think) I had so much vomitting that I saw no period that month and it was said I had probably brought them upward. My husband and I have both been puzzling our heads whether you are old or young. Whichever you are you have won our hearts and admiration not that

it is worth much for we are of the real working class . . . Yours faithfully

5 MARCH 1920, MCS IN REPLY (UNDER A STANDARD PRINTED LETTER). P.S. You see what I have to send to most people, but your letter interests me particularly. You need have no such feelings of distress as you describe, because it happens – though not commonly – that girls are born without the hymen (the membrane generally broken at marriage). With best wishes

22 MARCH 1921, SOUTH WALES: MRS RGH TO MCS. I hope you will excuse me for taking the liberty of writing to you in this way as I know no other way of doing so I was reading Lloyds News on Sunday and I read about what you were going to do and about the Mothers Clinic that you have opened what I would like to know is how I can save having any more children as I think that I have done my duty to my Country having had 13 children 9 boys and 4 girls and I have 6 boys alive now and a little girl who will be 3 year old in may I burried a dear little baby girl 3 weeks old who died from the strain of whooping cough the reason I write this is I cannot look after the little one like I would like to as I am getting very stout and cannot bend to bath them and it do jest kill me to carry them in the shawl I have always got one in my arms and another clinging to my apron and it is such a lot of work to wash and clean for us all and it is such a lot you have got to pay for someone to do a day's washing or a bit of scrubbing if I was only thin I would not grumble and as my Husband and myself is not so very old I am afraid we should have some more children . . . I was 19 when I married so you can see by the family I have had that I have not had much time for pleasure and it is telling on me now I suffer very bad with varrecross veines in my legs and my ankles gives out and I jest drops down. I am please to tell you I received one of those Willow plates from the News of the World for Mothers of ten, so I think I have told you all my troubles . . . yours truly

16 SEPTEMBER 1921, NORFOLK: MRS SE TO MCS. (*To summarize a sixteen-page letter, Mrs E, 41, wife of a farm labourer,*

has had six live-born children, one still-born and two miscarriages.
Her husband accuses her of unfaithfulness, criticizes her for not
preventing conception, but insists on his marital rights, though
refusing to take precautions himself, and complains of her last,
near-fatal, confinement, and what it has cost.) . . . On Dec 3,
1920 we had a stillborn daughter, this was the worst confinement which I have ever had, my Docter was with me 2 hours,
before applying the instruments (I had never had instruments
before) and then the instruments were on over another 2 hours
and then my Docter said, well my girl we can't go on like this
any longer. I must send out for some more help . . . I was
cholorformed and the Docter told me several days after that
it was impossible to get my child until he had inserted his
hand and forearm as my baby's head was stuck fast in my
bladder. It was my dear Docter's boast that during his 53 years
practice he had never lost a mother. He said that my child had
been dead several days and he very much hoped that I should
never have another child. I was so very weak and ill that I
never got off my bed until January 16th. I had to lay with my
legs propped up over a month as I had Flebitis. I am not
certain that is the correct way to spell it but that was how I
understood my Docter to pronounce it. I never once heard of
it only in my case . . . The third day after my confinement my
husband came to my bedside and said it served me right that I
was so bad, other women could prevent having children and so
could I if I tried and he was so angry he never came into my
room once more for 2 months . . . since then he has been very
cruel to me because that I will not submit to his embrace. he
has often compelled me as he had done very very many times
before to submit with my back to him. He says if you wont let
me at the front, I will at the back. I dont care which way it is
so long as I get satisfied. Well Madam this is very painful to
me, also I have wondered if it might be injurious. I feel that I
hate my husband and cannot submit for fear of having any
more children and then again be accused of unfaithfulness but
when all is said and done I am still his wife and although I do
not like just to be used for his pleasure and then abused when
I am pregnant, still unless I do submit, he declares he will ask

other women. Can you please give me any advice . . . Thanking you in anticipation

17 JUNE 1922, LONDON: MR MC TO MCS . . . I beg to be allowed to trespass on your time on a most delicate matter and sincerly hope I may be excused if I should not. The position is this: I am 30 and my wife 21. Now for some reason I seem to lack desire for intercourse. When we come together (I have never Succeeded in Making Entry) altho there is a discharge yet my penis will not keep stiff to allow of pressing into my wife. Can you tell me anything to do: it is really a terrible thing for me . . . I used to become sexually excited on little or no provocation, but have never had intercourse with a woman. Trusting you will help me all you can, yours sincerly

6 DECEMBER 1922, LONDON: MRS NG TO MCS . . . Could you be kind enough to tell me the safest Means for Prevention of Children as my age is 37 I have had 14 children nine living the Eldest is 17, the youngest 6 months and as you know I am likely to have more at my age we are very poor People I have my last at the Maternity home the Matron and Dr told me I have a very Weak Heart if i have any more it might prove fatal my inside is quite exausted I have Prolapsed Womb, its wicked to bring children into the world to Practicly starve and be a burden to the ratepayers as that is what it Means in my case as my Husband is only a jobing Gardener his work is most uncertain I cannot feed baby myself I realy must try something as my Husband is not a careful man in that respect I dont want any more if I should sink with having another what would become of all the other little ones my nervs are getting quite bad worrying from one month to another its a splendid Idea the Birth control clinic where Mothers can write confidentail trusting a reply Yours Faithfully

JANUARY 1923, LONDON: MRS GA TO MCS. (*This letter was included by Marie Stopes in her brief to Sir Patrick Hastings for the Stopes–Sutherland libel action, February–March, 1923.*) . . . I think it is wicked and scandalous to call Dr Marie Stopes

Birth Control method an experiment or even to suggest that we women are her victims ... Can any of these people imagine what it is, or means to a woman like myself my last 2 children I had in 18 months. My husband being out of work I had to leave my children to be looked after by their father while I had to go into a poor law institute to have my baby because I did not have the means of providing for it at home ... I have many of my friend working class women who need and are grateful for the kind help Dr Marie Stopes has given them. I feel it a great injustice and unchristian like to think that rich women should have this knowledge and a poor woman should live in ignorance of it ... Well Dr Marie Stopes, if I expressed my feelings I would stop up all night. So will conclude now, wishing our Cause a great success ...

18 FEBRUARY 1923, LONDON: MRS ET TO THE MOTHERS' CLINIC ... I have had five living children and have been seven times pregnant. I belong to the working class and know only too well how bitterly the working classes need the kind of help Dr Marie Stopes is giving ... I thank God every day that I visited the Clinic when I did. I think it is wicked as well as ridiculous to call Dr Marie Stopes Birth Control method an experiment, or to call the poor mothers who go there Victims – very willing victims and very grateful too. I only wish I had become one sooner. I think us poor Mothers was more of a victim by suffering the strain of constant childbearing year after year. what do our lives become we get broken in health, have sickly babies and too often have to go out to work to make ends meet. and our Poor Husbands have to suffer for it you nag at them and then they pay toll at the nearest public house I wish Dr Marie Stopes was a Mult Millionaire so that she could open clinics in every town in England for the benifit of the working class ...

22 FEBRUARY 1923, BOLTON: MRS RM TO MCS. In sincerity I write to wish you the best of your luck in your Action of which I have just finished reading in the Daily Mail. To the

men who do condemn you, I would like to give one month as a mother in a working man's home, Four rooms bedrooms and scullery with whitewashed walls, stairs devoid of carpet in an obscure corner. The kitchen which serves as dining and drawing room, nursery drying room, bakehouse and bedroom when the mother is ill, can boast of papered walls and gas light. The men who condemn you would have to run this house. The weekly wage would be £3 (that is more than average) have two babies 1½ years and three years and prepare for the third. You could not possibly administer to them the terrible pains of travail which women endure under such conditions nor could you make them realize what it is to crave for a bit of food out of the ordinary (a good cup of tea, a bit of best butter, a 'snack' costing a few coppers which looks tempting in the cook shop window or one of the many other little treats for which a woman's condition make her long). They would have to feed that family, wash for it, bake for it, clean for it, make a good big dinner for 1½d each, make old clothes into new. This would be fairly hard but 'God Help Them!' what would they do if they were handicapped with pregnancy. You wouldn't have one enemy, they would all commit suicide ... Yours truly, an admirer

26 FEBRUARY 1923, HAMPSHIRE: MR JH TO MCS. I am an ex service man and unemploid suffering from Tubercolosis I get no pension my wife and child are at present in the workhouse my wife caught Pulmonary Tubercolosis but my child was born before that and am pleasd to say is sound and healthy he weighed 9 lb at birth and it is my ambition to get a Carravan and travel with them as we have no home for I spent my last penny to buy this paper and I wish to carry on the work of spreading practicle Religion. My wife dare not have any more children so I may have cause to thank your book later on my own behalf. I do not wish my name in this case but if its necessary then use it I trust you will be a Victor in the Battle. I will close now believeing I have given you a line of Thaught to fight on ... Faithfully yours

27 FEBRUARY 1923, KENT: MRS BR TO MCS. I have read your articles in Penny Magazine with the greatest interest. And I am writing to see if you will help me. I cannot afford to buy one of your books at present but I hope to be able to do so later.

I am 36 years of age and have been married for just over 14 years. My baby was born one year after my marriage and it was a failure. through fright either before or at birth she is paralysed all down the left side and the brain is not strong ... I had to undergo an operation after wards and they told me not to have any more children but they never told me how to avoid it, however nothing has happened since. my husband thinks too much of me. but we would like a little pleasure out of life before its too late. If you will help me I shall always be grateful, Yours respectfully

28 FEBRUARY 1923, BIRMINGHAM: MRS GD TO MCS. I have followed your action for libel in the Courts with great interest ... We women of the working classes only know how the horrible servitude, poverty and constitutional undermining excess of child bearing means, with the consequent lack of means to educate those surplus children and to equip them with knowledge with which to secure posts and positions of the sciences, letters and art of this land, relieving them of the nightmare of serfdom and slavery the mass of the lower orders are condemned to. I am the mother of two children and desire no more. My ambition is satisfied, but with the recent knowledge of my sufferings with them, another would drive me mad. I am asking you to forward the names of your books and prices that I may be one of the fortunate ones who have the superior knowledge of contraception ... The poor people of this land cry out in anguish for this knowledge which the aristocracy and capitalists would have withheld. Believe me, Yours very respectfully

MARCH 1923, BRIGHTON: MR SJ TO MCS. I wish to inform you that owing to the way you speak I would like to know what

kind of medson you offer them as I think it is not Right. Now
I wish to ask you these questions.

(1)   What did Christ put you on this Earth for?

(2)   What is a Womens Comfort? What did Christ make in
his Commandments? Did he say, did he make birth Control?
Well Madam No Women can have a Child without Gods help?
No law in England can make Birth Control. Nor you either.
If the better Class wont have Children they dont know the
Comfort they bring with them but if some one would go
through the pain they soon have them though? Well Madam
I would Like a letter with the true facts, as I have sent a
writing Address. I Reamin, a Married Man, and a Lover of
Children

12 MARCH 1923, GLOUCESTERSHIRE: MRS DE TO MCS. seeing in the newspapers I saw your address and I thought I
would write to you about Birth control, Dear Dr, I think you
are a Grand Lady and it would be a Great Blessing if thaire
was more in this cuntry like you. I am a mother of 12 children,
9 grown up I have 3 married daughters, I have had 4 children
in 6 years I would be please for you to Let me know what
would be the cost of your Trement and what to do I onely
wished I have known when I was having my children what I
have sufferd I have a Drunkerd Husband and have had to work
hard to pay my way I think what you have said in the papers is
quite true conserning the poor I hope God will Bless you all
through life I will let my daughter know when you do let me
know as we are all poor peopel and there is more than us like
us. I remain Yours truley

12 MARCH 1923, NORFOLK: MRS KE TO MCS. (*Marie Stopes
did not usually reply to letters asking for abortion, but here,
obviously moved by the woman's plight, she made an exception.*)
Please could you give me some advice about preventing my
self from becoming pregnant again, I had my first child in 1910
and it was 7 months but after a lot of expense we have managed
to rear Him. then 1 year after I was pregnant again and suffered

terribly could not get about by myself after the first month and could do no work and had a very bad time all through with this awful Pain and after that one was born could not sit down properly for 7 years, and was doctoring all the time (and my husband is only a cowman so its been an awful drag.) at last I went to Hospital and they said I must have an operation I was in a month and they said I must on no condition have any more children but did not tell me what to do and the consequences was I got pregnant again and had an awful time and the baby had to be removed last March to save my life it lived 7 weeks and died an awful death it lay in agonies for a fortnight, We tried for it not to happen again but I am now 3 months and having an awful time, always in pain, and have to diet myself on Benger food, brown bread, no Tea and no meat, and I am loosing off and on rather badly I sometimes bring up blood and when that stops it come the other way and this last week I have had to keep my feet up as much as possible, I have gone and tried to end my life and should have done so if my husband had not prevented me, as it sends me out of my mind with the pain ... Trusting you will do your best to help me ...

16 MARCH 1923, MCS IN REPLY. P.S. I am terribly sorry you have been allowed to become pregnant again in ignorance, but as you are pregnant I cannot do anything to help you. You should see your own doctors and see if they will not on medical grounds clear the uterus, but as you know it can only be done by two doctors who agree. You must not do anything yourself ... After the birth of this child though you need have no fear for the future if you will take all the precautions which I advise. Sad as it is you must just go through with it and console yourself with the hope that it will be the last time. With every good wish, Yours very truly

13 MARCH 1923, HAMPSHIRE: MRS HA TO MCS. I have seen the article you have written for the People Sunday Paper on the subject of Birth Control and I am taking the liberty of writing to ask you if you will send me some information about it, for I so dread having any more, I have five children three

of them I had in just over 3 years it seemed that no sooner did I give in to my husband than I was in a certain condition. Our wages are not sufficient to have and keep a lot of children farm Labourer's wages today are 26/- a week about here and there is 3/- to take out for rent and 2/4 for coal, what is left to feed, clothe man, wife and children and pay club and insurance the 8th commandment says Thou shalt not steal but I think to have food and clothes and not have the money to pay for it is another form of stealing I have known of Familys who have had a good place (as far as masters go) on a farm give notice to leave at Michelmas and get another place some miles further on all because they have been up to their ears in debt for food and saw no way of paying then start on with some fresh tradesmen just simply because the babies would keep coming, that is I think just another form of stealing. If its wicked to prevent children from coming its also wicked to bring them into the world and not be able to keep them. On Saturday last there was a man and a little boy about 9 years old was stone picking on our farm from 8 o'clock in the morning till 5 p.m. and all the food those two had was a slice bread and margarine each for all day, they have a family when they've got 1/- they can have a bit of food when they have none they just have to go without, isn't it wicked to bring children into the world to that existence so if you would kindly send me some knowledge I shall be so glad I could not come to your office as we have no money my husbands money is not enough to keep us properly let alone come to London hoping to hear from you soon I remain yours truly

12 APRIL 1923, LONDON: MR TB TO SISTER ROBERTS, AT THE MOTHERS' CLINIC. Last week I met Dr Stopes, and she told me that if I came across any youth who would care to earn money by selling your News, I could send him to the Clinic for 27 papers for 1/6.

I know a little about a rough lout named George — aged 17. His father has been out on relief for a long time and this son has done nothing much for almost as long, previous to which he did costering. He has recently fractured his thumb and is under the Northern Hospital. I saw him and his mother yesterday, and she took rather kindly to the suggestion that George should sell the papers. She had the good fortune to be relieved of her youngest unwanted child last month by death . . . Yours very truly

14 MAY 1923, KETTERING: MRS L TO MCS. I wonder if you will think I am presuming in writing to you of a very peculiar and tragic case. The case is of a woman who is blind through her husband coming home from the War with venereal disease. She has a dear little girl of 2 years who has inherited the loathsome complaint. Her lips are covered with sores. Now the mother is again pregnant. Cannot anything be done? Her Mother who has to look after her is 74 years of age. They are too poor to pay for help, The Husband having been unemployed for two years and if she could afford to go to a Dr he would do nothing for her. She tried last time . . .

Your book came up for discussion at our Psychology Class and the Dr said it was a very good thing to have in the hands of Drs and Scientists but he strongly advised none of us to read it which of course made us all very keen. We almost unanimously agreed that if it was for Drs and Scientists it was good for us so most of us ordered it at once. Yours sincerely

6 NOVEMBER 1923, STOCKPORT: MRS M TO MCS . . . I was at the lecture at the armoury of Sunday night what I think was very good and usefull. There is one thing that I cannot understand how you place this cap inside to make it safe and firm fitting And also how does one pass there water with the cap in there inside Will you please let me know the full instructions how to place them in And also how shall I go on for making water in comfort I enclose stamp for your kind reply PS I have had thre children

4 DECEMBER 1923, MANCHESTER: MRS SE TO MCS. I am deeply grieved at having had to receive a letter, asking for my

subscription, but believe me, it is not wilfully that I have not paid. When I joined your Society in August, 1922, I honestly thought I should be able to pay regularly. But by the time I had saved enough money to send to Lambert's for the things you recommend, I have received my Doctors bill for the last confinement, and to my dismay it was £3 12 6, and the Midwife's fee was £1 10. My sister who kindly looked after me, paid these bills for me and gave me twelve months in which to pay her back. I am thankful to say I have now done so, and am hoping to pay all my arrears in the New Year, if you do not mind waiting till then.

7 DECEMBER 1923, MCS IN REPLY. Dear Mrs E, I have had your letter explaining all your difficulties. Do not let the idea of the subscription worry you at all. Our Society exists to help people like you. We will be very glad to keep you as a member – to pay any time. If you find you cannot, never mind. Just go on letting people know about the work and hand on the paper. Yours very truly

28 DECEMBER 1923, NO ADDRESS: ANONYMOUS LETTER TO THE MOTHERS' CLINIC. If a married woman named Kennedy (Irish and slightly Irish accent) age 28–30, slightly below average height, slim, black hair, small face, from Camden Town area, brings to you an Irish girl (unmarried) named Miss MD (native of Co. Clare) age 22–24, average height, fairly plump, fair hair, full and round fresh-complexioned face, for the purpose of fitting your rubber cap on Miss D's womb, you will know that it is for an improper purpose. As the woman Kennedy is au fait with your procedure and knows that you take precautions as far as you can against abuse of the purposes of your Clinic it is of course certain that the single girl will pose as a married woman. A fictitious name will of course be used by the single girl who has a pronounced Irish accent but the married woman may or may not use a fictitious name. I am writing as one who thinks your Clinic is a boon for proper purposes and as one who knows that you guard as far as you can against its abuse for purposes of prostitution.

15 JANUARY 1924, SOUTH WALES: MRS GE TO SISTER ROBERTS. I would be very obliged if you could kindly tell me if there is any truth in the following. A woman I know of as been under an oporation recently. People I have heard, say that it as been to have these pessarys taken from their insides. Her back passage that *that* being in one after constant use of the contraceptives. Is it possible for this to happen? If that opening does not go right into our insides, how do they account for getting them inside. I would be very glad if you could confirm my mind on this, as it is not the first time I've heard these rumours between married people. Please excuse my seeming cowardice but I'm getting married Easter, and I'd like to feel safe and free from danger. I remain, Yours, And Oblige

16 JANUARY 1924, SURREY: MR LE TO MCS . . . I am a working man with 5 children the oldest 10 the youngest 16 months. my wife is three weeks over her time she is worrying herself so that she as made herself quite ill she as been taking difference kinds of pills people have told her about but of no use. I am under notice to leave my house owing to my large family and cannot find another to save my life what is coming of us I dont know my Wife is very deaf and dellicate nothing but a frame. I wonder if you would be kind enough to relieve us of this great wory I would bring my Wife up to you if you think you could do the needful or tell us what to do trusting you wond be offended and would do me the favour I remain yours Truly

9 APRIL 1924, NEWPORT, MON: MR TJ TO MCS . . . I myself am getting old, I had a large family, only four of which survived, Wife also gone, I married again 5 years ago, a Widow with 2 Grown Up Daughters, she had these two when she was only 21 years old, now she about 48. After I married her I found she resorted to a simple device, not to have children by me, I believe it has been effective in her case for many years, and if it will help you in your work and writing, and so help others,

I will give you details (free) what she does, and what I think has been the effect upon her: she uses nothing at all.

Now Sir what about us Men Is there anything in the shape of books, Or Medicine or Stimulant for us. I am in the same position as thousands more men, Getting Old over 60, Wife not 50, have led a good life, never had any disease, or Urinal trouble, I have a desire to give pleasure and receve pleasure in the sexual act as long as it is humanely possible for me, but several times lately have lamentably failed after trying, and this has set up a nervousness and depression and reluctance to try again, and she is not sympathetic in fact inclined to Bully me over it, as being an annoyance to her. Is there anything I can do, anything I can get that will enduce errection, without Injurious after effects, I see a number of Things advertized, and have tried Iron Jelloids and Damaroids. The worst feature about me, is when we retire, I don't want anything, but after sleeping a couple of hours, I wake feel myself in a certain condition and am so at times for a long time, but she absolutely refuses to allow me to disturb her, thus in the middle of the night, so I let it go and think I will do so when morning comes. But when it does, although In my mind I want to, yet no power to do so will come, and so I get down-hearted. She will never allow me to fondle her, or carress her or that might bring the power. But she absolutely refuses to be messed about as she calls it . . . Yours

25 NOVEMBER 1924, LONDON: MISS EB TO MCS. I read your case in the paper I felt very sorry to here that you lost. I went to one of your lectuers at the Queens Hall and liked it very much I think you are a very good woman. I have been ill all my life. My mother was ill before I was born. I am sure your advice to my mother would have saved me a life of pain. I was quite helpless till 5 years old could not go to school or work. I had the sence to keep single. I would not like a dog to suffer as I have. I love children. But you are no good on this world without strength and brains. if the Doctors are so keen on people having children, and a poor mother has a child and they

know you will be ill all your life they ought to make a law not to let you live. I have said it to my people time after time, they say wile there is life there is hope. My mother and father have been Dead about 20 years now. the Doctors did not think I would live but I have worse luck. I think a good woman like you would have saved children like me a lot of trouble. I feel a worry to myself and everybody else that helps me. Yours truly

10 JUNE 1925, LANCASHIRE: MR DW TO MCS. Enclosed is ten shillings for a supply of letters to working class mothers ... Since I commenced a ruthless war on poverty and distress by advocating the principle of scientific birth control, my employers have hurled me into the surplus labour army, and I appeal for help to carry this message to every working man and woman who are ignorant of their fecundity. Two years ago I addressed the local Parliamentry debating society on birth control and succeeded in convincing most of them, including ministers of religion and labour leaders of the urgent necessity of securing the sanction of the minister for health to allow information to be given at welfare centres.

The sequel to this is the unemployed army, but I am single, and energetic and willing to do anything and go anywhere to further the cause of constructive birth control, anticipating an early reply, Yours faithfully

30 OCTOBER 1925, WILTSHIRE: MR LH TO MCS ... My Wife gave birth to a second child and all went well untill complications set in towards the end of the 'lying-in' period. Some kind of Mainia My Doctor told me it was, but I didn't catch what name he gave it. On account of this sad mainia I was obliged to send my beloved wife to the mental hospital where she still is. I saw her today ... I am very eager to, yet cannot find out if there is any hopes of her ever recovering *permanently*. I am writing you this letter as I think you are the one person to whom I may appeal and on whose answer I may rely so please dear Doctor kindly tell me if these cases do recover and if so is there any possibility of a reacurence ...

And before I close Doctor several times lately when I have been with her, in a small visiting Room by ourselves she has pleaded with me for connections which I have refused her. Will you kindly advice me on this point also and very much Oblige Yours Very Sincerely

9 NOVEMBER 1925, YORKSHIRE: MR SW TO MCS. My wife and I for some time have been looking for a true preventative in conception ... Perhaps you may think me impertinent if I ask you a question or two. Knowing your works 'Married Love' and knowing you are married and have now given birth to a child, I naturally ask you was the child intended or was it a failure in your preventatives? ... Yours in service

11 NOVEMBER 1925, MCS IN REPLY. P.S. I consider your enquiry about our son incredible; of course he was planned and arranged for.

JANUARY 1926, NORTHUMBERLAND: MR GC TO MCS ... Here we have a population of some 30,000 packed into a fetid atmosphere arising from the excrementary deposits outside their larder windows of all this pitiful population. Smallpox and other diseases are of course being bred here and the death-rate of children is twice that of some 140 other towns. The job I am securing bread and butter from intimately takes me where even the nurses don't go or rather won't go without notice. Vermin fill the electric light fittings in some dens like a solid block, and the walls appear to have a pattern which is composed of squashed bugs in hundreds, beds and floors urine saturated. I have to strip and fumigate sometimes before going home ... Children are more like so many imps. Filthy in mind and body and on a dark night you can fall over big girls squatting in the roads (beastly bogs rather) not altogether because they are so brought up but through so called 'ash pits' having too many adult users. It is nothing for them to take a tea mug off the table, hand it to a child, and then fling urine anywhere, and put it back on table again for tea. The Cooperative meat arrives on a dirty lorry with livers hanging over bare side. In spite of the terrible conditions for childbirth no knowledge of Control is available. Some do know of quinine pessaries but believe that in every box they buy there is one dud to keep within the 'Law'. Gin and whisky are the more probable causes of failure . . .

I am wonderfully surprised at the homely unobjectionable manner your pamphlet deals with the subject in view of the libellous account generally circulated. It would be worth sacrificing the futile expense arising out of several hostile religious edifices erected here and allocate a fraction of their cost in circulating your information, particularly so if the Mine Owners' commendation here to sack 100,000 men materialises . . . Perhaps you would not mind definitely stating whether it is a fact that important particulars, essential to your Method's success have, or have not been deleted from your books by order of the authorities (whoever they may be).

(2) Whether you believe that Chemists are only allowed to sell Quinine pessaries conditional upon one 'dud' being included in every box sold. Yours very sincerely

26 JANUARY 1926, MCS IN REPLY. Dear Mr C, I am glad to know that the pamphlet has reached you safely at last.

I am indeed shocked at the social conditions you describe in your letter and urge you to do what you can locally by bringing the matter constantly before anyone up for Council election; attend their meetings and ask questions, also write to your local MP, telling him the conditions and demanding his support for Birth Control. In reply to your questions,

(1) Nothing has been deleted from my books; they are written without interference, exactly as I wish them to be written.

(2) I have often heard the rumour that chemists only sell quinine pessaries conditionally on one being 'dud', but manufacturers of whom I have enquired say this is not so . . . Trusting you will do what you can for the movement, Yours sincerely

1 FEBRUARY 1926, SHEFFIELD: MRS W TO MCS. I have read your letters lately in John Bull, you ask us poor women to

write to you. Well Dr i have had 5 children in 5 years, 2 are dead which i thank God for the 3 i have left are always ailing they seem bloodless. My husband who was in the Navy right through the war, i and my 3 children have to live sleep in one small room, my last baby was born 3 months ago it was night time and whil i was been seen my husband had to sit o the doorstep in the rain worse still my little girl age 4 sat up in bed and looked at me, she said next day naughty mamma dirty the bed, the Dr here is sorry for us, he gave me a note to take to the Mayor saying we were all ill with been herded together, but they are letting the new houses to people without Children, i should be glad for a letter from you Dr and do anything you advise i am yours respectfully

6 FEBRUARY 1926, SCOTLAND: MRS MCA TO MCS. I would like your Advise by telling me if there can be anything wrong with me. As the last Birth I had was twins a Boy and a Girl. But they came at seven months So they only lived three days. That was my second birth. The First Birth was a little Girl, she being only two years when I had the twins But I was very unlucky for the year after I lost the twins My little girl contracted Hooking Cough from which Pumion set in And she died at three years of age . . . the lost of my little Girl nearly broke my Heart for she would of been six years old if God had spared her and what a Comfort For I am hear all day long when I am not working and has no one to speak to. For my Husband has never took the same interest in the home owing to me loseing the children for you see we none at all now. And I feel very miserable. You know I had to go out and work in the Mill nearly all since my misfortunate. But I am idle now since Christmas time . . . I have noticed that for a week or so before my coarses that I feel chilly and a shiver all through me and I am always very wet. Just like a lot of Inflitation or whites comeing from me for about a week or so . . . I must tell you Doctor that it is not for the want of my Husband trying for he is very fond of children and so am I myself and it was a great blow to us two young people having bad luck with our little

family. But God work must be done So Doctor if there is anything you can Advise me to do, I would be very glad of the Advise As I am just a poor working woman and has very little Edcutation. But you must excuse me for writing to you or perhaps bothering you but I have no one to ask anything and I am very lonely here all day long So I seen a little Column of yours in the John Bull. And I just thought I would seek your advise and see what I would do. As I am very unhappy.

16 FEBRUARY 1926, MCS IN REPLY. I sympathize with you very much for having lost your children and desiring that you should have another one. I think, however, from what you tell me that there is something a little wrong inside that wants clearing up, and that once you were treated properly, you should be pregnant again. I am sorry you are so far away . . . but would advise you to go to the nearest Welfare Centre or Ante-Natal Clinic – there are several in Glasgow – and if you ask at the Post Office for the address of the nearest Welfare Centre they will tell you. Go there and ask for the Lady Doctor and say I told you to ask her to examine your womb and cure the discharges and to give you advice . . . Do not be afraid of the Welfare Centre, they are there to help, and if the first Welfare Centre does not understand your case, find another one and say I told you to go and they ought to be able to help you. With every good wish

20 FEBRUARY 1926, HAMPSHIRE: MR SW TO MCS. I beg to apply to you for advice. Last year I met with a very bad accident. Both my tisticles were badly injured matter formed and they had to be lanced to let matter out. Two doctors advised me not to marry. I feel not able to take a husband's part do you think I should not marry. Would my children be healthy if I was to have any I should be extremely gratefull for your true Opinion.

27 FEBRUARY 1926, MCS IN REPLY. I think there are many women that would be perfectly willing to marry without the thought of having children or sex relations, but I agree that you ought not to marry expecting to take your part as a husband. If, however, you wish for the companionship of a wife

and the home comforts of a married life, I think you should be quite frank with any lady you know . . . Yours faithfully

9 MARCH 1926, SCOTLAND: MRS MCM TO MCS. (*Mrs McM, daughter of drunken parents who beat her daily, escaped at the age of seventeen by marrying a much older man. He insisted on sexual intercourse twice a night – even four days after the births of her numerous children. After an operation for cancer, she returned home from hospital, still pregnant, and went on having children, in such pain that she became addicted to the laudanum her doctor had advised her to take – he did not mention contraception.*)

. . . I came home from the hospital before ready and of course started to do my washing and so forth untill after my baby came I started to take Laudanum thinking no harm for the pain was bad before the operation but nothing to what it was afterwards so our own Dr gave me it still he warned me to be carefull but did not explain what for and to my horror Dr when I tried to beat it off I was weak and done up and I was glad to send for that course never thinking where or what it meant for years now I have been taking it Dr and its keeping me in poverty, it has risen in price 1/- oz and it takes 2 oz every day am like a millstone round my family neck they dont grudge it but I do feel it badly Dr and Dr I once had a good home plenty to put on The Salvation Army took me to a home at Edinburgh but Dr it meant death as I would of done myself harm taken it off all at once god knows am afraid of what I would do to myself Dr do you hold out any hope Dr after all these years I know Dr if I had means I would of put myself under a professer . . . you know Dr the posision am keeping my family down I see there suffering yet they don't grumble my married sons has children of their own dear Dr for God sake do something . . . the chief in Edinburgh hospital says I should go to a mental hospital what say you I am anxiously awaiting your reply, Hoping to hear from you soon, Dr am trusting you yours faithfully my only regret is your too long of comming on this world for my sake as god has sent you

ammongst our womanfolk and god bless you I am yours
sincerely

(*In a long and sympathetic reply, Marie Stopes advised Mrs
McM to first cut the dose by half, and then go on gradually
reducing it.*)

11 AUGUST 1926, GRIMSBY: MRS MCD TO MCS ... I am a
married woman with six children and my husband has got into
trouble with a young lady, but I'm very doubtful about it myself.

This other woman is putting the blame on him for her baby,
which he doesn't think is his, but he admits knowing her. She
has admitted misconduct with other men, but this is the
question I would be grateful for if you will enlighten me. 'How
long can a woman's period of gestation go?'

My husband says that misconduct occurred on August the
9th 1925 and the baby, a fine healthy boy, was born on April
21, 1926. Has the baby is 3½ months old and she won't take it
to court to prove as we have invited her to, make me more
suspicious. As you will see the baby is about 8½ month child,
and being a boy I am a bit doubtful. My husband remembers
the day quite well, because it was on this woman's birthday ...

I would be very pleased if you will kindly tell me if it is
possible for her to only go on for this period, and the baby to
be born exactly as my children, which have all gone the full
period 9 months. Please forgive me for taking up your time for
writting to you, but please try to set my mind at rest one way
or the other and I shall be very grateful. Thanking you in
anticipation, I remain Yours Faithfully.

p.s.   I have already forgiven him on account of my children
but the thought will linger in my mind, if it is his child, but if
it is not, I shan't think any more about it.

13 AUGUST 1926, MCS IN REPLY TO MRS MCD. (*Under a
standard printed letter about how impossible it has become for
Marie Stopes to answer letters personally.*) P.S. It is, of course,
just possible that the child should be born at 8½ months, but if
everything was quite normal in the child's appearance and

birth and it was not brought on in any way by the doctors help, etc, I think you are right in feeling that it is much more likely to have been some other man a fortnight before your husband's misconduct with this woman, because in the usual way a child comes more nearly the ordinary nine months, although there is no exact rule about it. I think as the woman admits misconduct with other men, you can set your mind at rest that it was some other man two, or even more weeks before your husband. I am glad you are forgiving him for the sake of your home and family. Try now to forget it completely and encourage him to be a good father and husband. With every good wish.

16 AUGUST 1926, GRIMSBY: MISS BD TO MCS ... I am at present looking after all five of Mrs McD's children whilst she is away and having accidently come across your letter, it is breaking my heart. It is all a lie, but to get himself in his wife's favour he has disowned my child and because I have loved and always shall love him (there is nothing between us now, but I felt I owed it to her to look after them) and I would die for my baby boy, I have not summonsed him, as I knew very well he cannot pay – in trying to protect himself, he would slander my child to right and left. I am a public schoolgirl and have never known what it was to want until just lately and I feel that I could not trespass on my Mother's goodness again and so she keeps my baby boy and I send so much a week. Until I have made good once more, I shall never be able to face my boy. I told his Grannie to tell him his father died a hero's death, please God he will never know any different. He is the image of his own children, I was only 17 then, and I last saw my courses on the 18th July, I was caught on the 9th of August, my birthday. My little son was born on the 21st April. He allowed me to call him David (McD) D. If he had never thought it was his, wouldn't he have prevented it? ... I loved him doctor and I trusted him. He is not bad, by a long way, and he has time after time said, if I will tell him the truth, he will forgive me, and help me fight for him. I have sworn before 'God' doctor, on my bended knees that it has nothing

whatever to do with anyone else ... Can I prove that he is his son, without money, as you know every penny that I get goes to my baby and I never earn more than 10/- a week ... The other man mentioned about was my Father, but he interfered with me a long time previous to this.

If I had ever thought that he would have let me down like this, I would have killed myself. It is nearly driving me to distraction, please would you send me a reply as soon as possible and the price of the fee. I remain, Yours Truly.

6 JULY 1928, ESSEX: MRS TA TO MCS. I wonder if you can help me? I know there are no known methods of getting twins, but do you know of any methods which we could try out, on the off-chance

The Walthamstow woman who has just given birth to twins four days apart, longed for twins and seemed determined to have them. How do you account for it? Concentration alone does not do it, and yet there was no mention of twins in the history of the family. My mother's sister had twins, but they were one of each sex. Help me if you can. I will try anything. We have two of your books and they are very useful. Yours sincerely

10 JULY 1928, MCS IN REPLY. P.S. Sorry, there is no possible way of obtaining twins known to science. All best wishes

16 AUGUST 1928, NOTTINGHAM: MR RA TO MCS. I bought your book on Birth Control and persuaded my wife to do as you suggested. The very first time using was sufficient to cause my wife to be pregnant.

We thought it was because my wife was not fitted correctly. After 2 months my wife started with what the doctors (3 of them) thought was a miscarriage but no embryo came away.

Now after 2 month of suffering I have to have a specialist in and to all intents and purposes she has to be operated upon for Extra Uterine Pregnancy the pessary having directed the seed into the wrong tube.

I have been married 12 years and have always used the withdrawal method with success so I must hold you responsable
for my wifes illness. Yours

22 AUGUST 1928, MCS IN REPLY. I feel much sympathy
for you and your wife in her experience of that terrible mistake
of nature, an extra uterine pregnancy. I should explain that
when the pregnancy is thus in the wrong place it means that
the egg-cell has not come down into the womb as it should,
but has been fertilised before it reaches the womb ... The
Pessary *cannot* 'direct the seed into the right tube'; that is a
fantastic anatomical impossibility.

I can reassure you that you need feel no sense of personal
responsibility towards your wife in having suggested the use
of a pessary to her and can assure you that no human agency
can possibly cause the extra uterine pregnancy from which she
is suffering ... Yours sympathetically

6 MAY 1929, BALDOCK: MRS MJ TO MCS. I have had 3
children all boys which carry the bleeding decease, two I have
buried one it got to the age of 7 my second I lost at 2 months
through Circumcition I have one still living eight months
old ... I feel I cannot stand keep seeing these children come
into the world to suffer as they have ...

17 SEPTEMBER 1931, LONDON: MR MS TO MCS. I believe it
would be possible to practice birth control by mechanical
means, and as you are an authority on the subject, I am writing
to you hoping you will find the idea of some interest ... To
put it as plainly as possible, I believe it would be possible in
the early stages of pregnancy to remove the embryo from the
womb by means of suction, using an appliance something
after the style of a syringe. The suction would be caused by
withdrawing a plunger or piston ... if in your opinion there is
a possibility that it might be practicable, I should be very glad
to meet you in London at any time and discuss the matter ...
Trusting my project will not appear ridiculous to you, I am,
Yours faithfully

18 SEPTEMBER 1931, MCS IN REPLY . . . what you suggest is not birth control at all but its direct opposite, namely criminal abortion, and I should strongly advise you in your own interest and that of women in general whom you might mislead, to correct your knowledge and to drop all thought of considering the practice of abortion. Yours faithfully

The following seventeen letters were used by Marie Stopes in her compilation, Mother England, *based on requests for help that she received from working-class women in 1926.*

I am a young Mother of two beutiful children a Girl, born January first 1925 and a Boy born December 21st 1925 both born in the same year. I had terrible times for both, having to have instruments and chlorform and the dear little mites cut about. The Dr told me whan my baby boy was born I wasnt to have any more children as I should never deliver them myself, I am now dreading the thoughts of having any more children, My husband is only a working man and we feel we cant aford any more children on our money it would mean misery. Could you please give me some advice how to prevent any more little ones coming. I am yours truly

I have had 7 children lost my eldest girl 11 with consumption about three months since and have six children living my youngest 11 months three of them are consumptive my husband is only a labur and as been out of work 4 years. I dont want any more children and it seems how careful I try I seem to fall wrong I am just three days past my time and I feel worried I am 43 in October of course it might be change but I feel I want to be on the safe side so I thought I would write and ask you think it is a shame that pore people should be draged down with families fed up with life keep having children hoping you will oblige me by writing return of post Yours sinculy

I am forty one and have been married twenty one years I have three children all girls the eldest is nineteen the next eleven and the youngest will be five in June. We were quite comfortable and I thought I should have no more children as I had passed my fortieth year, but last June 16th I was washing blankets and after putting the line out my little girl put a toy on the steps the consequence was I stepped on it and had a nasty fall twisting my foot and breaking both bones at each side of the left ankle in fact one inside bone was both broke and right out of the socket. I thought I would try and put it back while awaiting the doctor so you will see I was not at all nervous but after the doctor came and set it properly and put it in splints, I had to lay in bed a month with it when he put me a plaster leg on for another month and still kept me in bed. When he took the plaster off he still put me another one on and when he took that one off he said it was not at all satisfactory as the inside bone had not knit properly but the outside one was all right. Well he ordered me to the Infirmary and they put me under ether and broke and set it all over . . . But to get to the point I should have been unwell on the day I fell and broke my ankle the 16th June 1925 but I never saw any colours or anything. I told my own doctor the second week but he did not attach much importance to it and I mentioned it at the Infirmary and they said it was the shock with the fall and I should be alright when I begun to walk but you can imagine my horror when I felt a movement in the body, in fact I was so unerved that a friend of my sisters took a sample of my water to a water doctor and he said there was no sign of pregnancy but the kidneys were in a poor condition . . . I should reckon about a month now to being confined. But you have no idea the state of mind I am in   I can not throw the depression off   I get no sleep and break down many a time because I wonder will the child be allright in brain and limb also I suffer agonies at Birth and have to have instruments as I am very narrow and have big children . . . Also will you send me your birth control method so I will have no more if God spares me to live. I remain yours

I should be more than grateful if you would enlighten me. I am nearly thirty seven and my husband ten years my senior and he is partially crippled with Rhumatoid Arthritis. We have three children, eleven, nearly ten and the youngest two yrs and ten months. Sixteen months before my baby was born I had a full time still-born child. Then last April I had (what the Nurse Judged to be a seven months miscarriage) although I carried it the full time, but it was in bad state and fell to pieces when touched . . . On November twentieth last I had another miscarriage of about four months Now the doctor tells me I have tumours in the womb and must have an operation as soon as I can arrange a bed and someone to see to our family. In the meantime we are terrified lest I get pregnant again. Also Doctor would the tumours have any effect on my husband. We are anxiously awaiting your reply. Obediently Yours

I am a Mother with 4 little children, all of whom are yet young. The oldest is 6 years and 1 month and is always ailing. I have to attend the childrens hospital regularly with her as she is so frail and suffers with her bowels. My husband served in France during the war and besides being wounded twice was also gassed, and had to undergo operations for frost bite in toes and feet . . . I am asking you for help upon the subject you write about, because we are both so ignorant like many thousands of poor people, as we find it a hard task to make ends meet and keep a roof over our heads, as my husband suffering as he does from gas bouts, neurasthenia, and bad feet, cannot attend his work as regularly as he would like, and knowing that another increase or more in our family would mean dire poverty and starvation, I take the liberty of asking you for your help and advice . . . Your Grateful Friend

I am writing on behalf of my wife to see if you would enlighten her on Birth Control. She has had nine children of whom three are alive only her sisters keep tell her to stop having Children but they wont give her any knowledge they just say they can stop from having them i have asked there husband and they say they dont do anything my wife has two sisters each has one Child only so if they have any knowledge they keep it to themselfs so i appeal to you for the sake of the Children we have and my wife to let us have the knowledge we ought to have. I am yours in unity

I would like to know if you can advise me what to do. I am a married woman with a family of small children, I was very ill over my last baby I was under the Doctor here all the time I was pregnant with my heart, and not only that I started with hemorage from the mouth, the consequence was I had not strength to bring the baby, my life was despaired of for quite a while but thank God I came through after a struggle. Now the Doctor has advised me to have no more family but did not give me a remedy, please Dr, can you tell me what to do, I am terribly afraid, not because of children, but of my other little ones I have, they are all such Babies, if anything should happen to me over bringing another one in the world, as I have had 9 and 6 are boys, I dont think I have done so bad, and I really think it is enough for any woman to have, my husband goes to sea, he is what they call a Deck Hand on a trawler and gets £2 2 per week my rent is 11/- a week, my oldest boy is turned 14 at Christmas and has managed to bring me a few shillings working on the Docks amoungst the fish, I really cant give the children all they should have to make them fine and Healthy ...Yours Truly

My Wife and I are married 20 years now, she being 40 years of age and I 42. I may say I have never read any of your books never having had enough cash, but I have read all about you in the Press, also in John Bull of which we are registered readers. She has had 7 children all living except one, who died at birth, and it was the last one, as the Doctor said she would never survive another, she now finds that her (menzes) have stopped since First Week in November, I keep telling her that as she is now 40 she will now not be so regular in her (Menzes) as she has been very regular all her life, but she has got the wind up completely and I find she has been taking (Salt Peter) (Carbolic Lotion) 8 Beecham's pills at once and so on. I pointed out to her the Danger of it all, and forbid her to take any of those Drugs for her own sake, as Well as mine and the children, but she says she knows the symptoms too well, and says she will never live to have another child, after what she suffered at the last one. Can you give her any advice and oblige me. Yours sincerely

Could I hear from you personally. I sorely need advice concerning birth control I have only been married Four years and have just given birth for the Fifth time and it has made us desperately poor financially as my husband's wages are but small. It is through my weakness of body that I become pregnant every single time we submit to Marital Rights. I would be grateful to the end of my days if you would save me any further distress. Yours Very Truly

I feel I would like to express my gratitude to you for the way in which you are trying to instill into the minds of the working class mothers what your birth controll realy is as for the ministry of health they would rather learn us how to have them rather than tell us how to avoid it. I am 43 years of age and I have my courses regularly I was told I couldent have any more when I had my 8th child that is 5 yrs ago I had another 2 yrs and 6 months ago do you think I could have more I have only known about your birth controll 12 months I have to watch my husband very closely or he would deceive me and not put it on We use the paragon sheath as I have a dropped womb I would use the combined pessary and Sheath but I fear it would be no use to me the health visitor seemed disgusted with me when I asked her about it . . . The health visitor said it was very wrong to do any thing to stop yourselves from having children so when I told her what I was useing she simply ignored me and has never been near me since and I dont care if I never see her again . . . I remain yours very sincereley, MB – A Working class Mother. We have 6 doctors in B— 5 of them have 2 children each the other only 1 the upper class have had Birth controll long enough they would

like to make it appear it is only the working class man and wife
who come together but are not so bad as depicted.

I have been married 5 years and have 3 children a fine strong
little Girl who will be four in April if God spares her, and two
boys the elder is two and baby is four months old they are all
fine healthy children but you will understand, because you are
a mother, how hard it is to keep them so, when I tell you my
husband after being in the Army from 1914 until the end is
unemployed. I have 29/- from the Exchange and after paying
10/- rent, 4/- coals 1/- Light and 1/- insurance 2/- sundries I
have 11/- left for food you can understand I want to bring no
more babies in to the world for their own little sakes My
babies are all the world to me, doctor, and my husband is an
Ideal daddy since little Reggie came he has had no connections
with me at all for he is afraid of my becoming pregnant again
. . . and doctor I will tell you something I dare tell no one else.
I have found out my husband is *abusing himself* You know what
I mean. It is worring me terrably because I am afraid to let
him have anything to do with me. I am, although ignorant of
such matters, sure he will do himself some harm and I told
him so but he seems to think other wise . . . thanking you in
advance for your kindness and thought I am dear doctor,
Yours most gratefully

I wonder if you can help me. I am married and the mother of
five children, and I live in a dread of having any more children.
My husband who is a Catholic does not believe in stopping
life by any means when I say I do not want any more he gets
very nasty with me he wont try and keep me right and I feel
now that if only I can manage to keep myself right life mite be
worth living as it is one horrable dread, my youngest is 2 years
old and before he was born I had to lay in bed for two months
I got viens all over my body . . . Can you let me know what I
can do if possable unknwon to my husband. Yours truly

I am 38 next birthday and I have had 3 children, the first was
born with terrible pain for me, and he although a beautiful

child, only lived half an hour, owing to his head being crushed it was a case of either the Baby or me ... The second boy, alive, and 7 years and a half of age, a fine healthy boy. I had a bad time with him, but nothing to be compared with the first and the last one, which had he lived would have been 5 years. Their was a growth, preventing the Baby being born, and when the Dr was trying to help Baby into the world, the instruments caught in this growth and came down in rags and hung there, and the Dr did not know for a few days if it was the womb or what it was, but I had diapers wrung out in Boiling water with mercury in and eventually it dried up and fell away, after that I had to go to London as I was to use the Dr's description, in rags, they told me I must have no more children, and yet when I asked them how I could prevent it they just shrug their shoulders and smile ... Yours sincerely

... I married a man in the year 1912 at the age of 18, he being 22 years older   year after I found I was to become a Mother (the child was still born which Was cause throught fright 3 or 4 days before   And that nearly corst me my life)   My Husband having to chrilder of his own at the time boy 3 and a girl 7, which are now 18 and 21. After that it was not till 1917 that I was in London and there waiting to go in the City Rd Hospital to be confined. (I was a lone in Lodging and had to Walk a mile in Angoing while the Air Raids was on. I just got to the Door and Callopsed, the Child beining bone almost at once. 13 months after I had a nother girl bone a hour before I could sent for help. 2 year later a boy, and 2 year later a nother boy, this last boy have shutter my nerves (for 2 months before he was Born I had nurses from the Guild Hall to dress my Varcass Vain. The last month I walk on Sticks and they came trice aday (the Weaight of the child cause the Vain to come to such a terrible size that the chair bottom had to be removed) I had to sleep with legs up he was born on the 6th of Oct and 24 hours after I found I had got to be sticthed. When I got up I had a large lump form in the Brest. I went to the Hospital and they operated 16 stitches I had. I was there 4 weeks all my chrilen being in the Wookhouse I cam out to fetch the chrilden, and 2 months after the other brest was very bad I went up at 1 oclock to have to opration 12 stiches and walk home at 5. I could not have a days rest I still had to keep on, after I had to go for the Dressings Twice a day pushing 2 kiddies in the pram till at the week end my leg gave way and I had to stay four hours and wait for a letter, to say that I could go in the Calvassing Homes. I said yes, I did not go; the worry brought on a groth in my ear, I have to have it Lance. My troble are my own, I have no simpathy hear the last day I saw was 15th of Dec; It was on Boxing Night I conceived I have tried many Pills but Have not seen the desired effect. Please Help me! I have Had my share ... My life is only a living Hell. Yours truly

... Before my marriage nearly 7 years ago I was a healthy girl and a Nurse at the — Hospital. Now I am little more than a nervous wreck. I have only one child aged 5. A few months after my marriage I had Gastric trouble, supposed to be caused by eating inferior bread. I recovered from this and all went well until I became pregnant. Almost from the first week sickness set in, then gastric trouble became acute ... I was fed through my bowels, not even water passing through my mouth, yet the sickness kept on. After 4½ months of this, it became a case of life or death and a Specialist called in promptly ordered an immediate operation. This was performed and the Ulcers removed from the Stomach. The acid green sickness ended but pregnancy sickness continued throughout the 9 months. I lay for weeks on end in a darkened room with ice on my head and morphia to relieve the dreadful pain I was in. Turpentine poultices or pads I should say, were applied to my stomach when needed. I had on two occasions a fallen Womb which the doctor corrected also had my inside painted with Iodine. To finish all this I had a dreadful time at the birth. Chloroform and instruments had to be used. The after birth seemed fixed and sometime after I was round from the Chloroform this was removed ...

Do you wonder after all this agony neither myself nor my

husband *ever* want more children ... This last two months or rather two monthly periods I have had two shocks. The first time after being overdue a week I took, at intervals, 19 female pills and a bottle of medicine before I became poorly. Almost the same thing happened during my last period, I was 13 days overdue. My husband swears he will kill himself rather than see me suffer with child again, and I myself would prefer death first. Can you help us? ... I fear my letter is longer than I meant it to be, but I am an orphan and so you are the first I have unburdened my very soul to. My age is 32 and my hubby's 33. Please do help me. Sincerely Yours

Please I hope you will excuse the liberty I am takeing in writing to you it is about my daughter it wont be six years till the end of August since she was married and she has had four children and she has always been very ill and the youngest is one year and 3 months old and she is makng herself ill afraid she has any more   it is not the babies she objects to but She is unfortunate in having a bad husband he has put her out repeatedly and sent her home and he is very ready in useing his hands to her we took her home when her first baby was less than a year old and she applied for a seperation order in the sheriff court she was told by the sherriff that he did not count it illtreatment for a husband to put his wife out unless he marked her she had five witness with her stating the kind of life he led her also a line from the Dr stating the condition off her health but the sheriff told her she would have to go back to her husband or loose her baby as the husband got full controll of her we read your articles in John Bull about birth control so I wondered if you would help her   the night before her last baby was born he would not allow her to go to bed she had either to walk the floor or sit in a chair so you will have some Idea what sort of man he is she dare not let him know we are writing to you and he is always worse to her whenever he knows she is pregnant they live in a kitchen and it will be rather acward if she has to use anything ... Please do not put anything of this in John Bull as my son-in-law reads it   I remain Yours

... I have been a Mother of 14 children well 11 full born and 3 carried so far through and then had a very bad miscarriage and I have had 3 more little ones since the last miss. And I had such an alful time since having my baby of 2 yrs. and my Navel used to protrude like a child's 2d. ball nothing would keep it back in place and I was examined in Hospital and it was supposed to be rupture of the Stomach and I was told they'd send for me when they had a bed vacant   so I waited in agony for about 3 or 4 months and then on August 1st they sent for me I went in and went under a serious operation ... I was told I had my womb and all taken away, well about in november I came flooded one night in bed of course my husband was very worried as he thought I shouldnt seen anything again after undergoing this operation, well Dear I went to the hospital after a day or 2 as I couldnt possibly make the journey before as I was so terrible faint and bad and the Dr told me after he examined me they only took one side out or the swelling, I was thoroughly cross at the time   I ask him what he meant he wouldnt tell me, and I ask him if it was possible for me to have any more family he would not tell me he only told me I had a slight touch of hemorage and to go home and go to bed, I told I wanted to know as it was only right me and my dear husband should know, as I had such a terrible time with our last little one, they have taken my navel right away and I've been opened from there nearly down. Now dear I am writing to ask you a serious question which means so much to me and my dear man, do you possibly think I could get pregnant again, or carry a child through the 9 months of waiting, I am asking you as I would a dear Mother and I trust to the Dear Lord and you for my answer knowing we are all sisters in his sight ... Please answer it your dear self to me I shall be most thankfull so will my dear one. We are, Yours thankfully

CHAPTER TWO

THE UPPER CLASSES

From the beginning of her campaign in 1918, Marie Stopes never ceased to bombard Britain's kings, queens, princes and princesses with copies of her latest book, but they were rarely accepted. The only exception was the Duke of Windsor who – though not until after his abdication – wrote to her encouragingly and even sent an occasional cheque to help with the running expenses of her clinics.

The number of letters to Marie Stopes from the upper classes is understandably much smaller than from other social groups. In general the upper end of society had both the money and the know-ledge to obtain whatever specialist help was available. As Lady Constance Lytton observed, the principles of birth control had been used in her own family and by their friends for generations, and she saw no reason why the knowledge should not be given to everyone who wanted it.

There were exceptions, of course; and several of the most energetic fighters for birth control were those who – even coming from fairly liberal upper-class families – had themselves suffered as a result of ignorance and prejudice.

In his autobiography, Bertrand Russell recalled the family quarrels preceding his first marriage, to Alys Pearsall-Smith. Having been told that any children of the marriage would almost certainly be either imbecile or epileptic, Russell and his fiancée decided to marry anyway, but to use contraceptives. 'Birth control was viewed in those days,' Russell later wrote, 'with the sort of horror which it now inspires only in Roman Catholics. My people and the family doctor tore their hair. The family doctor assured me that, as a result of his medical experience, he knew the use of contraceptives to be almost invariably gravely injurious to health.

My people hinted that it was the use of contraceptives which had made my father epileptic. A thick atmosphere of sighs, tears, groans and morbid horror was produced, in which it was scarcely possible to breathe.'

Bertrand's elder brother Francis, the second Earl Russell, also supported the movement in the House of Lords, in the press and in correspondence with the various women's organizations who attacked his stand. Judging by their resolution, he replied coldly to the St Joan's Social and Political Alliance, 'it appears that this strange body, consisting almost exclusively of unmarried women, is pleased that married women should continue to bear children that they don't want, who are likely to ruin their health and to be themselves unhealthy, whenever the caprice of their husbands makes this inevitable.' He also notes the satisfaction expressed at the fact that information available to all the wealthier members of the community should be denied to the poor.'

21 MARCH 1920, GIVONS GROVE, LEATHERHEAD: MCS TO QUEEN MARY. Madam. Knowing the profound and gracious interest your Majesty takes in the homes and virtuous happiness of your subjects, I humbly crave the honour of your gracious acceptance of the accompanying book, *Married Love*. It was written as a result of scientific research, inspired by art and the love of beauty and of health and it was published in the interests primarily of your subjects the British, but ultimately of the whole of humanity . . .

It is my profound conviction that only *happy* homes are truly healthy and of full value to the State, and that such knowledge as I place for the first time before the world is essential in the present if homes are to be true nurture-spots of love and peace and healthy children. On such homes the stability of our Empire rests.

A word of encouragement or advice from your gracious Majesty would greatly strengthen one who is wholly devoted to the service of your Majesty's state, and who hopes in her life time through knowledge to *stamp beauty* on the deepest facts of life that the human race may be transformed and

glorified. Your loyal and devoted subject, Marie Carmichael
Stopes

10 AUGUST 1921, TELEGRAPH HOUSE, CHICHESTER: EARL
RUSSELL TO MCS. *(John Francis Stanley, second Earl Russell,
whose brother Bertrand Russell succeeded to his title in 1931, was
a staunch supporter of Marie Stopes. The Russell family had
long been connected with the birth control movement, partly as a
result of the 'Amberley Affair'. Viscount Amberley, father of
Francis and Bertrand, stood as Liberal candidate for South
Devon in 1868. Perhaps unwisely, he allowed his favourable
attitude to birth control to become known. His opponents made
much of it, and one current lampoon addressed him:*

> *If you could, my Lord, change your baptismal name,*
> *You might indeed the name of Onan claim,*
> *That being now the name through Devon flown,*
> *By which hereafter you will there be known.*

*The second Earl Russell had a rather scandalous reputation,
having been tried for bigamy by his peers in the House of Lords and
sentenced to three months jail following his American divorce. He
was later exonerated by the King.)*
 ... I will be a Vice-President of your Society with pleasure
if you think it won't do you harm. I am told to my amusement
that I have an entirely undeserved reputation as a profligate
roué, and it might be said was controlling my own lapses! But
I think serious people know me better ... Yours sincerely

3 SEPTEMBER 1921, MCS TO RUSSELL ... From your very
charming and modest note I feel that you will understand my
regrets – but when your name came up two of my most useful
supporters threatened to resign if you were *prominently* associated with us, though all would be delighted if you were an
ordinary member. You will understand I withdrew your name
rather than make a controversy. We need to be united in this
world of opposers ... Yours sincerely

10 JANUARY 1922, RUSSELL TO MCS. I opened the matter
of the Vice-Presidency to my brother and very much to my

surprise he did not turn it down. On the contrary he is much interested in your work and a few words from you personally will get him. He seemed to think having a baby was against him but I pointed out the meaning of the word constructive. Am I not a good messenger? Yours sincerely

13 JANUARY 1923, 31 SYDNEY STREET, LONDON: BERT-RAND RUSSELL TO MCS. (*Initially, Bertrand Russell was an admirer of Marie Stopes and accepted her invitation to become a vice-president of the Society for Constructive Birth Control. They soon quarrelled, over the Aldred affair. In January 1923, Guy Aldred and his wife, Rose Witcop – both Communists – were prosecuted for selling Margaret Sanger's pamphlet,* Family Limitation. *The magistrate found the pamphlet obscene and ordered its destruction. Bertrand Russell asked Marie Stopes for help in organizing their defence but – possibly because her own libel suit against Halliday Sutherland was pending – she refused, and Russell resigned from the CBC.*)

I suppose the CBC is doing what is possible to support the Guy Aldreds in their case – I read the pamphlet in question carefully and found nothing in it that could reasonably be objected to; certainly nothing which, if it is declared indecent, will enable your books to escape legal condemnation. There will of course be considerable expense connected with the appeal; I have subscribed to the necessary fund myself and I hope everybody prominently connected with the CBC is going to do likewise. Also couldn't you encourage some of the more respectable of your members to give evidence for the defence? Conservatives, if possible. Dean Inge would be ideal.

Would you mind letting me know what steps you are taking to help the Aldreds? I feel it important that all who stand for birth control, should hang together, if only for fear of hanging separately. Yours sincerely

24 FEBRUARY 1923, LADY CONSTANCE LYTTON TO MCS. (*Lady Lytton, a Suffragette, whose health had been permanently damaged as a result of forcible feeding, was one of the original*

patrons of the Mothers' Clinic. Marie Stopes's libel action against the Catholic doctor, Halliday Sutherland, had opened two days previously in the High Court, on 21 February.) ... If there is anything I can do to help you, please call on me. I am a spinster without children and not the sort to do much use. It [birth control] has been practised in our family and by their numerous friends for generations. It should be known, by those who crave to know it, in every class ... Yours sincerely

23 AUGUST 1923, SCOTLAND: SIR MC TO MCS. I have gone through the whole of your interesting book – Married Love – but have failed to find what I want – I am over 70 and have never had any connection with women. My brain being set on other matters. But now I would like to have heirs to carry on the line and title. Would you kindly tell me if a man over 70 is likely to have heirs? If not too late, can you guide or give advice as to the Mode to proceed by to have sons? ...

11 NOVEMBER 1923, ESSEX: SIR SJ TO MCS. A maiden lady of 30 years of age, one of my relatives, whose ideas on the reproduction of the species are exceedingly primitive, is firmly convinced by the 4th and 5th paragraphs on p. 81 of your book, Married Love, First Impression 1918, that conception is possible where only one of the two parties concerned experiences an orgasm.

This belief, after search through encyclopaedias, and the testimony of married friends who know from experience, is unshakeable, and is based on the following extracts from your book. 'He was manly and sufficiently virile to feel the need of sex intercourse, but he was unaware ... of the woman's corresponding need; and he did not give his wife any orgasm. Very shortly after marriage she conceived, and a child was born ten months after the wedding day.'

At first sight it is obvious that the untutored stubborn mind construes these paragraphs to lay down as a definite article of fact the possibility of a woman who experiences no orgasm in the sexual act conceiving and bearing a child.

As I and all my friends are weary of much striving to teach this relative – who looks forward to marriage in the near future – the fact that in order for conception there must be *mutual* orgasm, we have decided to ask you to write to me stating in plain non-technical language what are the actual facts.

I am sure that as a fellow-seeker after more perfect knowledge in all fields, you will not be averse to correcting this misapprehension and teaching the lady what I call the ABC of reproduction. As she gains her unshakeable opinion from your writings, and particularly from the two paragraphs referred to, it will be an act of charity on your part to tell her what are the true facts and perhaps thus save her in the future much guessing . . . Yours faithfully

12 DECEMBER 1923, MCS IN REPLY . . . In reply to your letter, on the contrary, the lady whose advice you so much despise is perfectly correct. In a very large number of cases, the woman conceives without any orgasm on her part, the male sperm being capable of living 17 days and penetrating from the outside though this of course is not usual. You will find full details in my new book *Contraception* . . . I hope as you are interested in these matters you will join our Society of which I enclose membership form and some papers. Yours truly

5 JUNE 1926, CORNWALL: LADY KM TO MCS. I have just been reading your *wonderful* book Married Love, and I am writing to beg you to help me. I am 61 years old, I was married in 1907 to an old man of 73 years of course he could do nothing. Last December I married a man of 58. My husband has not yet been able to consummate our marriage, he seems anxious to do so, he lies all over me and nearly smothers me, I don't think it is my age for other men have been very passionate if I would let them, my husband never tries to get me ready he just gets into bed and is on the top of me at once he never kisses me or touches me first, and I *do* want it so much I have longed for it all my life. Can you help me? Yours sincerely

12 JUNE 1926, MCS IN REPLY. I shall be only too pleased to help you, and should advise you to get your husband to read

the book, and after that you might suggest to him that you should try union, lying each on your sides. You will find if you put one leg under his waist that this position is very easy for both, and in the circumstances you describe should, I think, be useful and make matters possible for you. Perhaps if you knew more of the structure of the body it might help. Perhaps the book I have just published, *The Human Body*, might be of assistance. With every good wish, Yours sincerely

27 NOVEMBER 1929, HEATHERBANK, HINDHEAD: MCS TO KING GEORGE V. (*In December 1929, Marie Stopes published* Mother England, *a harrowing collection of letters she had received from working-class mothers over a period of six months in 1926. She sent copies to – among others – King George, Queen Mary, the Duke of York, and Princess Mary. The Duke of York accepted his. The others did not.*)

Sir, May I humbly ask your most gracious Majesty to accept this advance copy of a limited edition of a chapter of Contemporary History? I do so because the lives of your People have always been a matter for your gracious interest and solicitude. I remain, With profound veneration, Sir, Your Majesty's most faithful subject and dutiful servant, Marie Carmichael Stopes

28 NOVEMBER 1929, BUCKINGHAM PALACE. The Private Secretary presents his compliments to Dr Marie Stopes and regrets to inform her that he is unable to lay before the King the copy of her book *Mother England*, as, in accordance with rule, works on medical subjects can only be submitted through one of His Majesty's Physicians or Surgeons. The book is consequently returned herewith.

3 AUGUST 1930, B— CASTLE, SCOTLAND: MISS SB TO MCS. I have among my tenants a woman who at the age of 34 is the mother of six children. Just recently, a serious miscarriage probably brought on by the taking of pills to avoid a birth, has nearly cost her her life.

Her doctor advises her not to have any more children as her

last baby weighed 13½ lbs and nearly resulted in the death of mother and child. But the same doctor is of the old school and will not tell her of anything to avoid pregnancy.

I have read some of your books with great interest and should be grateful if you would tell me what I could advise this working woman to purchase (also where) which would be a *perfectly sure* stop to any further pregnancy.

Unfortunately her husband does not consider her as she would wish – but I would like to feel I had been able to advise her by your help and to be sure she could look forward to a happy future without the constant dread which up to now has always been before her . . . Yours truly

23 JUNE 1933, DEVON: LADY CF TO MCS. (*Lady F was married to a bishop, who frequently expressed his abhorrence of birth control.*) My husband has received a good many letters condemning his attitude regarding childbearing on the score that he, as a man, knows nothing about the suffering entailed on the woman. But I do – and yet I very heartily endorse all he says. I am the mother of many, having had nine confinements (twice twins) and I quite agree that having babies is intense agony . . . As in time we were to be bereaved of three of our sons in the Great War, while others were lost at birth, it is easy to understand how thankful we are that we did not limit our family . . . Yours faithfully

29 DECEMBER 1933, SCOTLAND: SIR CR TO MCS . . . A young friend – I am 73 years of age and old enough to be her grandfather – has confided in me that she is in great trouble. She has been fooling with a fellow, as girls seem to do now-a-days, and her monthly period which generally occurs in about 3 weeks has ceased during the last six weeks. She assures me, and I am confident it is the truth that, while there has been familiarity outside, there has been no insertion of the male organ. Is it possible for a girl to get in the family way without actual connection? I am ignorant of these matters, but I understand there is some sort of protection in the female which must

be pierced before contact has been established ... Marriage in this case is out of the question ... Yours very truly

2 JANUARY 1934, MCS IN REPLY. Your letter grieves me very much. It is such a sad thing that young people should eat forbidden fruit for the consequences are so terrible. I have tried so hard in my work to look on marriage as a serious and beautiful thing and the physical side of marriage ought not to be tampered with except in marriage.

In answer to your question about the possibility of pregnancy without actual entry: yes, it is possible though very rare, yet nevertheless it is perfectly possible and a girl can become pregnant who is actually, technically a virgin if a man plays familiarly with her outside.

Anxiety by itself, however, may cause the cessation of the menses. I know of one case of a very innocent girl who was so frightened at being kissed by a man, although it was merely a kiss by the mouth, that menstruation ceased for nine months although pregnancy was utterly impossible ... I am afraid this letter will not be very encouraging for her, but I cannot emphasize more than I do that there should be no physical tampering with sex until marriage. If only young people were taught elementary physiology how much anguish would be saved! Yours very truly

30 DECEMBER 1933, SIR CR TO MCS. Will you please cancel the letter I sent you yesterday. My young friend informs me her long-delayed visitor arrived last night, and I think she has got a lesson she will never forget ... Yours very truly

19 OCTOBER 1934, NEWTON STEWART, SCOTLAND: THE MARQUESS OF TAVISTOCK TO MCS. (*The Marquess of Tavistock, later Duke of Bedford, wrote at great length to Marie Stopes about his marital problems and about the upbringing of his two sons, Ian, the present Duke of Bedford, and Hugh.*) ... Eton, where I was, was perfectly appalling. Skill at games was considered the greatest of all virtues; slavish deference was paid to public opinion and the observance of trivial and often foolish customs ... Sodomy was very prevalent and dirty and

foolish discussion of matters of sex extremely common . . .

To give you a full and helpful idea of the progress of my own experiment up to the present, it is unfortunately impossible to avoid references to rather painful and personal troubles. I feel, however, that it is only right to do this, partly because a stage has now been reached when most of what I shall tell you is likely to become to some extent public property and partly because something enormously important – the welfare of your son – is at stake and it is my duty to give you all the help and information I can to base your judgment on what is best for his future.

My original *plan* was to educate my children at home with private tuition until they were old enough to go to the University . . . I meant them to see as much of other children, especially nice children, from good homes, as the boarding school education plans of my neighbours permitted . . . I do not know what your views are on matters of religion but it has been my experience that the *very* best and most useful people in the world are invariably sincere Christians belonging to one of the various churches that permit a liberal and tolerant school of thought. I am afraid, anyhow in my younger days when bitter experience of human frailty had not made me as cautious (and perhaps as uncharitable?) as I am now, I had rather an invete-rate habit of regarding the geese among my friends and acquain-tances as swans and in the first tutor I got – an anglo-Catholic clergyman a few years younger than myself – I made a most unfortunate choice. His work for the children, to do him justice, he did tolerably well and I think he was really fond of them but the effect of his influence on my wife proved utterly disastrous. Previous to his coming we had been gloriously happy, but in time he not only gained complete ascendancy over her in all matters affecting her religion and outlook on life, but eventually there is no reasonable doubt that she developed for him a feeling much stronger than that of ordinary friendship. Like many anglo-Catholics he was very intolerant and could see little good in any religion but his own and he succeeded in prejudicing my wife not only against the Christian social work in which we had found such a deep bond of common interest, but also against all the people she had met in the course of that work and against all our own friends whom he disliked on religious and personal grounds, with the result that practically all the people and influences I had relied on to give my children the right outlook and ideals were cut completely out of our home atmosphere. When I got rid of Squire my wife showed plainly that her attitude to me had changed to one of definite dislike and after more than four years of growing unhappiness . . . I have recently, in the children's interests and for the preservation of my own health, been compelled to leave her and I am endeavouring to arrange a separation . . .

My elder boy – now 17 – was always 'difficult'. He was a war baby and I am afraid was somewhat harmed in early childhood by a nurse whose faults we did not discover for some time . . . It became evident that the teaching I gave him on matters of religion and matters of sex made no impression on him although similar methods with many other young boys had produced most gratifying results . . .

In desperation a few months ago I sent Ian to a gathering of the Oxford Group Movement . . . one of the group leaders helped him enormously by inducing him to make a frank admission of various bad habits into which he had got . . . I mention these points because they seemed to me to teach a most useful lesson viz. that where the will and the atmosphere are not right the most natural and careful imparting of information can be perfectly useless. I do not think that even a critic of your experience and ability would have found much to disagree with in either the matter or the manner of the sex teaching I gave Ian, yet for all the good it did him I might just as well have been an early Victorian parent . . . Yours sincerely

18 NOVEMBER 1934, ST JAMES'S COURT, LONDON SW1: MARQUESS OF TAVISTOCK TO MCS . . . If you will forgive me for reverting to my domestic troubles it would be very helpful and interesting to me to know – (in view of your suggestion that my wife's age might have had something to do with the change in her character and attitude) – how far a woman is

able to control such a change in her character encouraged by physiological causes? Is she absolutely at the mercy of the effects of these physiological changes and as irresponsible for her altered conduct as an insane person; or is it rather that these changes make it more difficult for her to continue to regain high standards of thought and behaviour much as it becomes more difficult, though not impossible, to remain cheerful and good-humoured when one is ill? Yours sincerely

CHAPTER THREE

THE CLERGY

For Roman Catholic priests the question of birth control posed few problems. Celibate, and bound by the edicts of their Church, they had no option but to recommend, if family limitation were sought, either total abstinence or the use of the safe period.

Anglican priests were under much greater strain. In 1908 the Lambeth Conference of Bishops of the Anglican Communion unanimously adopted a resolution viewing 'with alarm the growing practice of the artificial restriction of the family' and earnestly called on all Christians 'to discountenance the use of all artificial means of restriction as demoralizing to character and hostile to national welfare'. Only twenty-two years later, in 1930, the Lambeth Conference decided that where there was a clearly felt moral obligation to limit or avoid parenthood, and where there was a morally sound reason for avoiding complete abstinence, 'the Conference agrees that other methods may be used'.

This relatively sudden volte-face created enormous confusion among the Anglican clergy – usually married, but having somehow achieved a birth-rate considerably lower than that of the population at large. The crisis of conscience was amply reflected in their letters to Marie Stopes after the publication in 1918 of her first book on sex, Married Love. Unsolicited, they sent requests for help on sexual and contraceptive problems, how to advise their parishioners and how to find a suitable wife. Solicited, they responded with even greater enthusiasm.

In 1920 every bishop attending the Lambeth Conference received a copy of the pamphlet, A New Gospel to All Peoples, claimed by Marie Stopes to have been personally dictated to her by God and advocating 'artificial' birth control. Later that year, *incensed by the bishops' failure to heed Christianity's latest prophet, she sent out a questionnaire to members of the clergy, asking for details of their marriages and contraceptive techniques. While a small proportion of those who replied rejected her request for information – one vicar merely scrawled 'What abominably impudent questions!' across his form and another, with nine children, commented 'Thou shalt do no murder. If God sends the babies, he sends their breeches' – the majority were only too eager to discuss their problems.*

The clergy's low birth-rate, it was obvious from the replies, had been achieved only at the cost of much marital misery. One vicar, in Durham, had practised total abstinence for twenty-nine out of his thirty-eight years of marriage. Another, married twenty-nine years, wrote plaintively that he had enjoyed 'only two unions in whole married life' – both of which resulted in the birth of a child.

When Marie Stopes and her husband H. V. Roe opened London's first birth control clinic and formed the Society for Constructive Birth Control and Racial Progress, she invited eminent churchmen of various persuasions to support her – but with little success. Mrs Florence Booth, wife of the Salvation Army leader, wrote that 'I should greatly deplore anything which induced the poorer people to use the means for the prevention of conception which are now so prevalent amongst the middle classes'; the Bishop of Willesden returned the platform ticket he had been sent; and the Archbishop of Canterbury feared 'he would not find himself to be sufficiently in sympathy with what you probably desire to say'.

The Anglican Church's change of attitude towards birth control was due in part to its support by one or two eminent divines – notably W. R. Inge, Dean of St Paul's, and Russell Wakefield, Bishop of Birmingham. Their motive in promoting population control – the preservation of middle-class values, which they felt were threatened by the unhindered multiplication of the lower orders – would today be considered questionable. But it was largely to Marie Stopes that the Church owed its recognition that, as the Lambeth Conference of 1930 acknowledged, 'intercourse between husband and wife as the consummation of marriage has a value of its own within that sacrament, and that thereby married love is enhanced and its character strengthened'. This change of emphasis is perfectly summed up by the last letter in this section from the Archbishop of York.

11 DECEMBER 1917, LONDON: FATHER ST JOHN, SJ, TO MCS. I have read with interest 'They Twain' [i.e. *Married Love*] ... Your wonderfully clear exposition of the rhythmic curve and of the want of understanding on the part of most men of what they call their wives contrariness should of itself bring deep happiness where there had been misunderstanding consequent on ignorance and want of thought ...

So far we are in complete agreement, but our ways part when you treat of preventives. You write as a scientist occupied mainly, if not wholly, with the facts of earthly life. I, as a Catholic, look on life as something which stretches out beyond the grave into Eternity ... to take the example of the worn-out mother of twelve, my belief is that the loss of health for a few years, diminished strength in the later children, would be a very small price to pay for the joy of seeing these children with her in happiness for endless ages. To my mind it is not the destruction of one spermatozoon that is the question, but the deliberate prevention of an eternal existence which in the supposition would result from its life ... Believe me, dear Dr Stopes, yours very truly

26 JANUARY 1918, ST PAUL'S: DEAN WR INGE TO MCS (*who had sent him an advance copy of* Married Love *in the hope that he would write a preface to it*). I am much obliged to you for sending me your very able and interesting book, which contains advice for which I have no doubt that many married people will be grateful.

But I am afraid you will find it impossible to get any clergyman to associate his name with it; I could not do so myself.

There is no doubt that public opinion has changed greatly and rapidly about the morality of chemical and mechanical preventives. But the weight of moral and religious authority against the use of them is still very considerable . . . I have a good deal of respect for authority in ethics, and for this reason I neither practise nor recommend these methods . . .

The idea of artificial impregnation is to me most repulsive and will be received with horror by those who have not heard of it before. I believe you will be wise to expunge this paragraph.

I must also protest against the statement that 'very few' men live in perfect continence . . . I have had long experience of public schools and universities; and my opinion is that in that class and at that age the proportion of those who entirely abstain from illicit relations with any other person is between 80 and 90 per cent. It is quite common for a man's passions to remain dormant till he falls in love with the girl he wishes to marry; I have had curious cases of men who were shocked at discovering these instincts in themselves; they have consulted me as to whether they were fit to marry a nice girl . . . Yours truly

29 JANUARY 1919, LONDON: REV CA TO MCS. I am in touch now with two elderly married women whose lives have been wrecked by lack of knowledge in reference to their marriage relations and after they have read your book I will see what can be done. One of them is a lady past the 'change' whose whole nature is crying out for the satisfaction of 'love-play' which her husband fails to give, while she has been condemning herself for having such desires. I do not want to encroach on your time but otherwise I could run down to see you some afternoon by train from Streatham . . . I should greatly value a talk especially in relation to unmarried women whose natures have been greatly stirred from one cause or another. I remain, Yours sincerely

1 FEBRUARY 1919, MANSFIELD: REV BLF TO MCS. May I first of all thank you for your little book, *Married Love*, which I have just been reading . . . Yet there are some points on which, after a second reading, I am not yet clear . . .

(1) p. 21, line 25, 'her husband's lips upon her breast melt

a wife to tenderness' – Before reading this, we had already discovered the great joy that might come from it, especially for her. Yet I have always been afraid to indulge in it, lest it should do her physical harm. Your words seem to quell that fear – yet I still wonder whether the *sustained* holding of the nipple with my lips is covered by your statement, or whether it might be injurious to her . . . Yours gratefully

NO DATE, DERBY: REV JW TO MCS . . . Is it unnecessary to use any safeguard against conception until penetration of the hymen is complete? Perhaps it would be of value to you to know of this true case of ignorance which came to my knowledge a week or two ago. A young woman of 22 admitted to my fiancée that until just before her wedding last year, when her prospective husband lent her a book, she had always thought that children were secured as the result of prayers offered at the marriage ceremony . . . Yours truly

27 MARCH 1919, LONDON: REV TH TO MCS. Having read your book 'Married Love' with a great deal of interest, so much so that I am going to send it to the lady I am shortly going to marry, may I ask you this question? From your book it seems that at times the use of preventives are not only permissible but desirable from a point of view of the health of the wife. And it is secured by the use of vinegar. What I want to know is in what manner is the Vinegar administered. Yours very truly

1 APRIL 1919, SURREY: REV CA TO MCS . . . I myself 17 years ago had to stop using means (syringing) and trust God with results, but inasmuch as we did not want more children I only had intercourse when my wife requested it. This led to conception and an almost painless delivery, with no rise of temperature afterwards. I have known other cases where what I believe to be the result of the Fall (Gen. iii, 16) has been removed by the Cross of Christ as in 1, Tim., 11, 15 (Dr Weymouth's translation). 'Yet a woman will be brought safely

through childbirth if she and her husband continue to live in faith and love and growing holiness, with habitual self-restraint'. Yours sincerely

27 MAY 1919, YORKSHIRE: MRS DE (A VICAR'S WIFE) TO MCS ... I have only a few very few times looked at that part with the aid of a mirror – and then only for a minute and I cannot describe the horror and dread I have of putting a finger in anywhere there ... I shall *never* forget the terrible torture when the doctor examined me before Baby came ...

16 AUGUST 1919, DURHAM: REV CANON TG TO MCS. There is another common question, wide reaching, in the consideration of Birth-Control and the ability for a man or woman to 'keep themselves pure'. It is the question of what used to be called self-abuse.

I am now an old Priest and I have pondered this question very deeply and widely. It cannot be discussed in public prints. I believe now that 'self-abuse' is an exaggerated term and shd only be applied when the practice is too freely resorted to. If it is only availed of for *relief* and *self-regulation* (like the bowels, as an eminent London man once said to me) say once a week or in 10 days, I not only see no sin or fault in this but an act of self-denial, of escape, and probably of unselfishness towards another. It is certainly better than either seducing a girl, or availing of prostitution.

24 AUGUST 1919, MCS IN REPLY ... *Regulated* self-relief is without doubt the least undesirable method for a self-controlled man who has a sweet disposition and can remain loving to a *real* woman ...

23 SEPTEMBER 1919, GALWAY, IRELAND: REV SB TO MCS ... I am a 'mere man' who for 30 years has worked in Ireland as a Clergyman and before then in the slums of London and other places in England. I was a lover of the Medical as all my people were medical ... You stated that some wives were virgins to death. I know of one such case where both slept in

one room but after 30 years she was as she was before marriage but the life was not ideal for either and she took to horses and got so 'horsey' if you grip my meaning, she, well he, went wrong – a miserable rotten ending – he was a medical man.

I have been struck by watching girls in London outskirts riding cycles, you did not refer to this in your book – they elevated the peak of the cycle saddle and put it too high, in riding, it necessitated an overstretch of the leg at each downward stroke of the pedal, which rubbed the peak of the saddle where it should not be, those girls were always inclined to be fast – I have found decent girls who did it and tried to show how injurious it was and being a cyclist myself lowered peak and saddle ... I myself have twice met in Railway carriages ladies (women) one would prefer travelled in a 'Ladies only' – sad to say over here in the last few years girls have largely lost the 'honour' they used to possess ... they do things today that 12 years ago would never be tolerated – and today are winked at. I have written a very queer letter for a man but somehow I felt drawn to your brave attempt to help the ignorant and guard the steps of men and women who all unwittingly pave their paths with sorrow. Pardon the outspokenness of this letter, it is done with no wrong motive, I assure you. Yours sincerely

7 OCTOBER 1919, ROEHAMPTON: FATHER FM DE Z, SJ TO MCS ... I consider it most useful to pray to God that your writings may not do as much injury to morals – to the *souls* of the ignorant poor especially – which they are calculated to do. Nor to their mere *bodily* interest which you seem alone to consider – For, as I am instructed by competent medical men, some of your counsels to mothers are fraught with bodily ruin also, as experience has proved.

When people in discussion start from fundamentally different *first principles* no common ground exists upon which usefully to discuss. I am a Christian and a Catholic priest accepting wholeheartedly the teaching, regarding sexual matters and moral conduct generally, given by the Catholic Church.

You, on the other hand, ignore, in your writings and advice, that same teaching and even that of many non-Catholic Christians – indeed I find no sure evidence in your books that you hold any *definite* Christian doctrines at all. It appears to me that a pagan might have written as you do – though he would probably not have quoted the word of God in the sense in which you – to any sincere Christian, shockingly – quote 'He giveth unto His beloved sleep' (*Married Love*). A friend has lent me *Wise Parenthood* and *Married Love* – from your pen. I had hoped no woman would write such books ... Yours faithfully

11 OCTOBER 1919, MCS IN REPLY. Thanks for your letter. You say you are a sincere Christian and accept wholeheartedly the teaching of the Catholic Church – I should therefore be most truly grateful if you would explain to me a point which has much puzzled me and about which I desire *honest* instruction. For you do me a wrong to conclude that I am not a Christian, I am – a Quaker or, as I should say, a Friend.

Will you therefore oblige me by telling me *how* my book is 'unchristian' and in what detail does it conflict with any of Christ's teaching? As there is but one basis of *truth* I cannot see your point that discussion is fruitless between those of different creed. Yours very sincerely

15 OCTOBER 1919, FATHER FM DE Z IN REPLY. Dear Madam ... In what, then, do your views conflict with Catholic ethics? For one thing ... in that you advise the mother to prevent the natural effects of coition by artificial means. That is a grave and unnatural sin – a grave sin against Him who fashioned the sexes. The temporal benefits you expect therefrom do not justify such conduct. *Please notice* this statement by a *Jesuit* – who is popularly supposed to teach that a good object justifies the use of corrupt means for obtaining it. Catholic morality allows of no middle course between carrying out the design of nature honestly and *abstention* from the animal gratification attending its execution. Married couples may not have it both ways ...

In other words, where limitation is mutually desired she

(the Catholic Church) *enjoins Flesh Control,* or restraint of sensual appetites. If abstention from use of marriage is mutually agreed upon and yet this arrangement leads either party into solitary irregularities – then marriage should be used (and *naturally* used): And a truly Christian wife will face very much rather than be a stumbling block to her husband's soul by refusals. Yours faithfully

10 JANUARY 1920, SCOTLAND: REV NJ TO MCS ... I feel that *Married Love* and *Wise Parenthood* go far to meet a great need. It seems to me that the latter might be improved by specifying the amount of quinine to be used in the home-made, gelatin pessary. Would it not do as well to use a strong mixture of vaseline and powdered borax – injected with a small syringe? This would be oily but would be easily prepared and inexpensive – very great considerations among the poor as we have them here. Yours for wiser parenthood, not fewer but better citizens.

7 FEBRUARY 1920, ESSEX: REV SH TO MCS ... I cannot believe that it is in accordance with the Will of God that those joined together in the holy Ordinance of Matrimony should accept the pleasure of the sex act and yet set themselves to thwart what He has ordained as its outcome. This is why I am so determinedly opposed to any and every device for the prevention and control of conception. As to your impression that the Church advocates 'withdrawal' when it speaks of self-control, I never heard of such a thing, and I certainly refuse to believe it. Yours faithfully

9 JULY 1920, ROEHAMPTON: FATHER FM DE Z TO MCS (*after reading her allegedly God-dictated booklet,* A New Gospel). I beg to acknowledge receipt of your pamphlet ... Reading what you have put in cold print, I regard it as a most profane compound of imaginary mysticism and pornography. It may perhaps serve the purpose that type of young medical student who needs a veneer of religiosity to dignify his sexual pruriency,

but could only revolt anyone with a real sense of religion – whether Catholic or non-Catholic.

I do not know on what ground you speak of your production as 'delivered' to the Lambeth Conference. At all events one would need to have stated the exact hour and date on which that assembly of gentlemen listened to the 'prophet' before regarding the description as anything more than a figure of speech.

But I know from some experience of life that when a woman gets to the point of saying 'I spoke to Christ yesterday' but has no idea of submitting her imagined inspirations to the judgement of any recognized spiritual authority, it is waste of time to reason. She is too self-satisfied to listen, much less to submit. I remain, Madam, Yrs obediently

10 JULY 1920, MCS IN REPLY ... I should like to ask whether your Church does know its own mind. It is only a few hundred years since they were torturing people for accepting the truth that the world went round the Sun and not vice versa ... I think you will agree that it is the truth which has conquered and not the Roman Catholic Church, for I suppose you do not maintain today that the Sun goes round the world – or do I wrong your logic, perhaps you do? If you do not, then I do not see how you can maintain your position of blind belief in the 'clear and uniform Teaching' of the Roman Catholic Church. I remain, Sir, Yours very faithfully

12 JULY 1920, FATHER FM DE Z in reply ... As far as I am concerned, this discussion is closed ... It only remains for me to offer my poor prayers to God that He may enlighten your ignorance of His Law, remedy your self-complacency, and prevent your doing the amount of harm to others – in body and in soul – which your experiments are calculated to produce. I remain, Madam, Yrs obediently

20 AUGUST 1920, NORFOLK: REV LD TO MCS ... You emphasize the importance of conjugal intercourse being a *joint* act, i.e. the gratification of the discharge should not be confined to the male; but should be shared by the female – There is

a wide spread ignorance of this fact, if fact it be . . . But the difficulty must often be that the discharges do not coincide in time. If that of the woman is late, it is difficult to see what ought to be done, as to prolong coition would be for the man a serious strain . . . Yours faithfully

13 SEPTEMBER 1920, DEVON: MISS DM (*about to marry a church missionary*) TO MCS (*after reading* Married Love) . . . Owing to ignorance we had both looked upon the sex-life as something rather degrading and a kind of necessary evil. I had looked forward to it as the least joyful part of married life and he, being an infinitely unselfish man, had thought it absolutely unsatisfactory since he could only see it in the light of a sacrifice of the woman to the desire of the man.

2 NOVEMBER 1920, NOTTINGHAMSHIRE: REV CD TO MCS . . . the third point is how best to arouse. I have had no instruction in what you call the Art of Love . . . This Art of Love is so often referred to, p. 42 'romantic advances', p. 50, 'charming love play', p. 100, 'the love play', p. 82, 'ardently to woo her', p. 84, 'a passionate return' – these and other passages seem beyond me. They raise pictures I long for, but do not know how to attain to. After the poetry of your book what actually has happened? We go to rest, my Wife always lies with her back towards me, I make a 'tender advance' and suggest that she turn round that we may chat and cuddle – the end of the poetry is 'I do not like your breath in my face!' . . . I fear that my loved one has not known rapture. I know nothing of the transport (p. 54) which prostitutes simulate . . .

THE ANGLICAN QUESTIONNAIRE

In November 1920, Marie Stopes took the then unusual step of soliciting personal information about marriage. Her questionnaire was sent out to 2,000 Church of England incumbents, chosen at random from Crockford's Directory. In addition to the fairly straightforward questions – length of marriage, age of wife at

*marriage, number of children born, the intervals between births
and/or miscarriages – the form went on to ask 'whether after the
children desired had been born any method of preventing undue
increase of the family had been adopted'. If some means had been
adopted, the clergymen were asked to specify whether they were:*

(a)   *Total abstinence from sex relations for — years*
(b)   *Limitation of unions to 'safe periods'*
(c)   *Use of withdrawal – 'coitus interruptus'*
(d)   *Use of quinine or other pessary*
(e)   *Use of rubber cap or occlusive pessary*
(f)   *Use of sheath*
(g)   *Other means.*

*The following fifteen communications came in from recipients
of the questionnaire.*

NO DATE, NO ADDRESS, NO SIGNATURE: *a vicar's wife, aged
thirty-nine at marriage, married eleven years.* There has been no
consummation of a marriage which is a byword for happiness
– but my own share is not even now easy for, though a hard
brain worker, sexual life is still vigorous with me, and Sarah's
condition is a long way off apparently.

There are several reasons for the state of affairs – my husband, affectionate and quickly moved, had so severe a training
in chastity as to amount to inhibition – The doctor who knows
me best is distressed at the state of affairs but though I envy
women to whom the night brings more than rest I have much
for which to be proud and thankful – But there are times when
the false position and my husband's ignorance of the nature
of my suffering are very trying – I fear however there is no
help.

13 NOVEMBER 1920, STOKE: UNSIGNED . . . I got a copy of
your book *Married Love* not long ago, because I understood
from *The Commonwealth* that it contained a letter by a Jesuit
priest. But I found no such letter in my copy. The book raised
many questions in my mind I am not sure what the effect of it
will generally be. My own conduct in life, I am thankful to say,

has been kept perfectly regular in such matters. But for all that I have been far from pure in heart – I am still – though I am 54 and a married priest. My reading of your book gave me an uncomfortable day or two – I seemed to suffer from an inflammation of the sensual animal part of myself. Does it not tend to concentrate attention too much on that side of a man's nature – and is it not rather perilous for any reader who may be in any degree 'over-sexed' – as most men are nowadays perhaps. There are not many people into whose hands I should think it safe to put your book ...

18 NOVEMBER 1920, NO ADDRESS: REV HS *curate to a vicar too senile to read or fill in the questionnaire, and addressed to H. V. Roe, Marie Stopes's husband.* Dr Stopes apparently uses no care or discrimination to whom she sends her rotten communications – for no decent man could read such papers without loathing – If Dr Stopes could use her energies to prevent people marrying who were not fit and by having lunatics and weakminded castrated before leaving an asylum she would be doing a more useful work – leaving healthy young people to have children as a wise nature intended them, instead of having six or seven means of prevention plonked before their eyes by a person who unless strong evidence is brought to the contrary Mr S must believe to be an old whore.

20 NOVEMBER 1920, H. V. ROE IN REPLY ... It is quite evident you have rushed off your letter without giving it any Christian thought, otherwise I am sure it would not have been worded in so insolent and objectionable a fashion ... That you may differ from Dr Stopes in your opinion is quite permissible but to write as you have done, makes it evident that you are unacquainted with the wonderful work she has done in making married life more sacred ... If you do study her work you will, as a gentleman, suitably apologize to her for your disgusting letter. Yours faithfully

26 NOVEMBER 1920, REV HS IN REPLY ... Can you not feel that if a man wrote to you on such topics, you would travel a long, long way to thrash him?

29 NOVEMBER 1920, NO ADDRESS: UNSIGNED. Having read your wonderful book, *Married Love*, I have filled in your form received today – I do indeed believe you are making thousands happier and I am very happy to think our children will have your books to help them in their married lives – I felt every word you said in *Married Love* was the exact truth – Judging by our experience during a glorious happy life – you are indeed a blessing to mankind.

30 NOVEMBER 1920, REV CY, *in reply to the question on contraception*. Yes – occasional – rubbing 'stuff' out of erect penis by hand – self – wife – and middle-aged widowed cook in absent of wife.

Dear Madam, In reply to your note and request for sex particulars. Under your pledge of secrecy I rather reluctantly give them fully – they will so I gather be of more use. You will understand I know it is injurious to often rub 'stuff' out of my penis by hand and I have never done it regularly. I can never see it harmful or wrong occasionally. I naturally do not like to ask any doctor I know about this. If ever you found time to tell me whether this is morbid etc I should be grateful. I enclose a cheque for two of your books as marked to be sent by post. I do not care to order from local bookseller. Yours faithfully

30 NOVEMBER 1920, HERTFORDSHIRE: REV DB . . . I should very much like to find someone whom I could love and be capable of bearing healthy children. Situated as I am here I have few opportunities of suitable introductions. Although 57 years of age I am healthy, strong and vigorous and belong to a long-lived family. My wife I suppose should be not more than about 30 . . . For the sake of comfort the wife should have some means, although they need not be large if she were willing to share the work of the house with me and do without servants. This is a pleasant healthy neighbourhood. I am an abstainer and a non-smoker. I have been the Rector here for 12 years and am very happy and comfortable in my surroundings but I feel I could be more so, if married to a congenial companion of

Church sympathies, gentle and refined, good walker and cyclist, content with a quiet country life, intelligent, agreeable and sensible. A few good families live in the place ... Yours faithfully

UNDATED, BATH: A VICAR'S WIDOW. My husband would have considered *all* these suggestions absolutely *criminal*. He religiously confined himself to once-a-week unions, but was quite rampant during the month of abstention during childbirth and I always thought inclined to be 'off his head' – I *never* felt any 'orgasm' but he didn't seem to notice that.

UNDATED, UNSIGNED. I am a clergyman who has a travelling appointment. I was married in 1915, a son was born in 1916, a girl was born in 1919. We cannot afford another one now and my wife's health (nerves etc) would not stand it. I am usually away three nights of week. For purposes of your work I give a record of my 'nights' for five months:

Novem	21 (Sund)	away	abuse
	26 (Fri)	home	abuse
Decem	2 (Thurs)	away	abuse
	12 (Sund)	home	abuse
	24 Frid:	home	abuse
	30 Thurs	M: member withdrawn just before ejection – gave wife manual climax.	
Jan	5 Wed:	M: sheath used – no 'feeling' for wife, although I tried with hand.	
	9 Sund:	away	abuse
	20 Th.	home	abuse
	25 Tues	home	abuse
	27 Th.	home	abuse
	30 Sund.	M: (wife 'had it', I did not except as a nocturnal Omission afterwards in sleep)	
Feb	3 Th.	away	abuse
	7 Mond.	M: (sheath used, no 'feeling' for wife, I had omission afterward also)	

	20 Sund.	away	abuse
	26 Sat:	away	abuse
Mar	3 Th.	M: sheath used. wife had no 'feeling' (although attempt after)	
	18	home	nocturnal omission
	25	home	nocturnal omission
	27 Sun	away	abuse
April	14	home	noct. ommission
	15	away	,,
	16	abuse	away
	24	,,	,,
	25	M: wife only – apparent desire, she had it immediately contact was established.	

Wife has tried two of your pessaries which do not fit and give discomfort, and sheath never satisfies her: so we have decided to abstain altogether (or me).

The suggestion in your book that it is natural for man to 'desire' three times a week is, I think, an exaggeration. Also your remarks on sleep led one to adopt this as an artificial help to sleep which I do not think is healthy, for by good and interesting and varied thoughts or by reading, the thing is done much better.

UNDATED, DURHAM: REV BH. I am a Bachelor though desire Married Life though if married fear I could look for no seed. As my own seed has left me an inadequate supply. Had a discharge last night but only a little came.

UNDATED, UNSIGNED: *a vicar, aged fifty-six, wife fifty-four, four children, who has practised abstinence for many years* ... I consented somewhat unwillingly to the last and permanent separation. I now regret the separation and think it has been bad for the happiness of our married life. I suspect that such separations require great compensating devotion ... I now think that I ought to have asserted more than I did my rights as a husband. I deliberately at a later date on the very highest grounds and after much consideration requested union and was refused. I think the separation has led to real suffering in my case.

UNDATED, UNSIGNED QUESTIONNAIRE, POSTMARKED BRADFORD: *addressed to 'Dr Marie Stopes, Doctor of German Philosophy, Munich'.* The only contribution which seems likely to assist the spread of German philosophy of bogus Dr and increase the profit from pornographic productions that I can supply is the Maiden Prayer:

> Holy Mary, Queen of women,
> Who conceived without sinning
> Help thy little child believing
> How to sin without conceiving.

UNDATED, KENT: REV AH. I am interested as a clergyman of the Ch. of Engl, in the matters you name; and have thought over and discussed them with such friends as did not think them indecent subjects for years past. I have also read carefully Malthus' book, with which in the main I agree . . .

By my first wife I had no children. She died in 1905 and in 1907 I married again. The lady I then married was a fine amateur pianist who had spent many years in Leipsic under the best masters. This, I think, indisposed her to the affections of married life . . .

As a clergyman I hold that all means to prevent conception (except abstinence from sex relation) are not only dangerous and disgusting but against the laws of God and the Church. I have never myself suffered physically or mentally from abstinence. The best work of my life was done before 40 years of age when I first married . . . I am quite alive to the other side of the question. The professional and cultured classes are at the moment being gradually submerged under existing economic conditions. There arises civil war between a vulgar plutocracy and an ignorant democracy . . .

Meanwhile the old live too long – I am speaking economically, and I think the time is not far distant when we shall have to

consider seriously what we are to do with the insane, the hopeless invalid, and all irredeemably degraded in mind and body.
They are already a burden such as the community can scarcely
bear; and a painless extinction seems to me the only remedy.
Nor do I see anything anti-Christian in such action . . .

16 JANUARY 1921, LINCOLNSHIRE: MRS B. Your questions
vide other side were sent to a friend of mine who was disposed
to destroy the paper but it has occurred to me that without
answering your questions I tell you in strict privacy and confidence my own case.

I was married at 20. My husband was 24. We have been
married 15 years. My husband is a well-to-do farmer, educated
at a public school and owns his own farm so we are very comfortable. He hates children. Before we were married he told
me that he did not intend to have any damned kids who would
spoil our amusements and cost us a lot of money which we
could use better to enjoy ourselves. When once married he at
once put into practice what he intended. He told me immediately that he intended always to 'pull back' – what you call
coitus interruptus. He did this on our first night together and
has done so ever since and he has never spared himself any
connexion with myself. I have never known anything else but
this pull back of his and therefore as a consequence none of the
joys of motherhood. I am stinted in nothing and my husband
is kind and affectionate, but I have never, never had anything
else from him but the pull back. I am healthy and so is he. I
suppose most wives would have resented this and gone elsewhere. I have not. My husband assures me he has never touched
another woman in his life; he is strictly moral, never misses
Holy Communion. His selfishness consists in the above. Pray
keep this strictly private. *Don't* write to me, simply read this
and you will know or not whether this is an abnormal experience.

9 FEBRUARY 1922, NOTTINGHAMSHIRE: REV RA TO MCS
. . . You may be interested to know that a mother of ten, in
great fear of early death like *her* mother, from over-childbearing,

has enjoyed a respite now of three years since I told her to sit up and cough after an embrace.

15 JUNE 1922, IRELAND: MRS RW, WIFE OF A CLERGYMAN, TO MCS. I got the check pessary and quinine pessary you recommend and thought at last I had found just the thing I needed. Well, the first month I used both, I got caught and had I not taken *four* doses of a certain drug I would be 'off' again . . .

*

6 DECEMBER 1923, LONDON: REV TD TO MCS. As a member of your audience at Battersea Town Hall last Monday evening I was very surprised at your statement that Baptist ministers have an average of only 0·9 children each. I happen to include a large number of Baptist ministers in the circle of my acquaintance and have just made a list of all those concerning the number of whose children I have direct personal knowledge. I find that 41 Baptist ministers and missionaries have 101 children among them – only four are childless. My personal knowledge on this subject is so different from the statement you made in public that I venture to enquire what authority you have for your statement . . . Yours faithfully

8 DECEMBER 1923, MCS IN REPLY . . . The statement I made about the Baptist ministers was based on a statement made to me by a Baptist Minister while I was a member of the Birth Rate Commission. You will find the clerical profession as a whole included in the Government reports although the different sets are not separated out. The fact that you happen to know a number of Baptist Ministers with large families does not interfere with the total statistics of the country . . . Yours truly

(*In 1924, Marie Stopes was approached by the deaf-and-dumb father of four deaf children for help in getting one of his sons admitted to a special school run by the Royal Association in Aid of the Deaf and Dumb. In reply, she not only chided him for his irresponsibility in fathering such children, but also wrote to the chaplain superintendent of the association.)*

10 OCTOBER 1924, MCS TO REV A. SMITH . . . I note that he is one of four children who are all deaf and dumb. I also note that his parents are both deaf and were educated at this Institution. I should be much obliged if you could tell me how it came about that two persons educated at the above Institution were permitted to marry and bring forth children, all of whom are still more imperfect and a burden on the community . . . Do you think it advisable that two defectives, both brought up at public expense, should be permitted to produce four defectives to be brought up at public expense, and where is this geometrical progression to stop? . . . Yours very faithfully

14 OCTOBER 1924, REV A. SMITH IN REPLY . . . The purport of your letter appears to be censure on me for strongly recommending the admission of a Deaf child to a residential school for the Deaf. Ought I, then, to have recommended the lethal chamber? Or is there a third alternative known to you which could save this child from becoming that burden on the community you presume and so much fear?

17 MAY 1926, ABERDEEN: MISS GE TO MCS. Can you help me any in the matter of the unmarried problem? You may be able to advise; or even put me in touch with someone, not the usual spinster philanthropic worker or even the usual type of Christian worker. I am a Gospel preacher; I am President of a Mission. Aberdeen teems with girls. I *love* them – they know it and feel it. I seek to lead them to Christ. I enter into their difficulties all I can. If they care to give me their confidence I honour it, but never force it. Very naturally sex, love and emotion is one of the biggest. They may love someone else; they may love me! I prefer them to, to loving someone worse who might unscrupulously play on their tender feelings. I respect those feelings and honour the body. I a little bit understand the suffering of repressed nature and sympathize instead . . . consequently I have had some most cruel persecution from

my fellows – who evidently would prefer to let a girl have *hours* of cruel suffering in body at night instead of sleeping rather than let her have some little outlet. If I do I am 'feeding her evil nature' or 'encouraging sin' etc, and many a girl goes down in health for no other reason than *repression*. Oh! the struggles! – I do not mean, to keep pure; but *because they are pure* and have no intention of being anything else by God's grace; but the struggle with life and sex-nature within is an *agony*. I have lately been attacked by a body of Christian people on this point and am seeking information to help all I can to make them desist and withdraw some evil imputations they have put out against me because of sympathizing in this matter ... They call it 'psychic' hypnotism in me and have nearly blasted my character by insinuating evil ... I *live* for the Gospel and to help others to know God – especially do I get into touch with young girls. Yours sincerely

20 JANUARY 1927, HAMPSHIRE: REV HOB TO MCS ... Do tell me how I can train my body to defer the climax so as to coincide with the orgasm of my mate. I am so easily influenced that I fear to be unable to defer the ejaculation till she has also attained her climax, being very susceptible to sex-life ... I may mention that I generally run through J. P. Muller's Physical Exercises on rising in the morning and pour cold water over my sex organs in abundance – so as to brace up and strengthen the parts concerned ... Yours sincerely

22 MARCH 1927, INTERNATIONAL HQ, SALVATION ARMY, LONDON: GENERAL BRAMWELL BOOTH TO MCS ... I have given serious thought to your letter of the 15th March. In the present state of my mind with reference to Birth Control, I do not think I ought to accede to your request to become one of the Vice-Presidents of your Society, although I am honoured by the suggestion. Yours sincerely

17 APRIL 1928, IRELAND: REV CR TO MCS. On p. 67 of your *Married Love* you write ... 'have revealed that the woman

did not know that it was not only her arms which should embrace her lover.'

This seems incomplete. 'not only her arms'. but what else? Should it be legs as well? Perhaps you would kindly inform me. Thanking you in anticipation. very truly yours, Is the sense 'arms alone' or is there some other position such as embracing at same time with legs?

9 OCTOBER 1929, NORFOLK: REV LA TO MCS . . . Prohibitions come thro' our consciences. The conscience of the serious-minded people is against contraception for reasons sometimes too deep to be explained. Dr Andrew Clark, Mr Gladstone and Hutton of the *Spectator* all said at once, 'It is wrong and loath-some'. Again those who advocate it almost always show they mean only for specially urgent cases, slums, etc, knowing that in 99 out of 100 cases it is used for self-indulgence; and that you cannot spread the knowledge of it without making it general. Conscience is also against it because of its inevitable consequences, the spread of promiscuity and presumably of unnatural vice. As ordinarily practised, C^n is a flat contradiction to the central ethic of Xtianity since it is an attempt to elimin-ate the Cross from a life which professes to be a following of Xt.

30 NOVEMBER 1929, BISHOPTHORPE: ARCHBISHOP OF YORK TO MCS. I have received your book *Mother England* for which I desire to thank you. I have long considered that the traditional attitude of the Church on this question is unwar-rantable, and have (I think) done something to prepare the way for a modification . . . For myself I desire that doctors in such cases as you describe give the information which you show that they commonly refuse; and while I dislike the establishment of Birth Control Clinics, I desire the establishment of Family Welfare Clinics at which information on this as on other subjects should be given . . . Yours faithfully

CHAPTER FOUR

THE MEDICAL PROFESSION

'Dear Dr Havelock Ellis,' Marie Stopes *wrote in April 1920,* *'I often seriously contemplate publishing* Letters to Marie Stopes, *everyone containing a pretty revelation of doctors' incompetence!'*

Relations between the medical profession and Marie Stopes were not of the most cordial. Dr Stopes, as she insisted on being called, resented the fact that her doctorate was in science, not medicine – a weakness of which opponents were quick to take advantage when she talked of medical matters. In return, she accused them, often justifiably, of ignorance, incompetence and bias.

This last, in the decade 1918–28, was certainly true. Though some medical authorities, among them Lord Dawson, the King's physician, were supporters of birth control, many doctors still considered it an issue to be decided on moral rather than medical grounds. In 1921, the year in which Marie Stopes opened Britain's first birth control clinic, Dr Mary Scharlieb, a distinguished gynaecologist, wrote to the British Medical Journal: *'The people and the nations who practise artificial prevention of conception and who therefore have no restraint in their sexual passions are likely to become effeminate and degenerate. The removal of the sanction of matrimony and the unhindered and unbalanced sexual indulgence that would follow would war against self-control, chivalry and self-respect.'*

Dr Scharlieb's condemnation was typical of a large segment of medical opinion. Two years later, The Practitioner *brought out a special issue devoted to birth control. Of the ten consultants invited to contribute, only one was unequivocally in favour of it. Three argued that it would lead to sterility. Sir Maurice Abbot-Anderson argued that the rubber cap would 'inevitably lead to a nervous breakdown, and may finally land the victim in a lunatic asylum'; for Professor Anne Louise McIlroy, the cap was 'a most dangerous appliance'; and Dr J. S. Fairbairn, obstetric physician at St Thomas's, found it 'too nasty and unhygienic to be sanctioned by medical opinion'.*

A different picture emerges from Marie Stopes's own correspondence with doctors. The vast majority of those family doctors who wrote to her, particularly from slum and rural areas, expressed nothing but gratitude for her books, and regret at their own ignorance. They were only too ready to ask for advice, both for themselves and for their patients, and to offer distillations of their own experience in a world where contraceptive problems could not yet be solved by scribbling a prescription for oral contraceptives, nor sexual difficulties be any longer ameliorated by cold baths, willpower and guilty masturbation. Birth control technique was not taught at any of the medical schools and, The Practitioner wrongly forecast in 1923, 'it is safe to predict that it never will be'.

It was to counteract such unwilling ignorance that Marie Stopes set up her own training sessions for doctors and medical students at the Mothers' Clinic; and that she never failed, despite her distrust of the medical profession, to answer a doctor's request for help – even if her reply were no more than advertisement slips for her books.

3 FEBRUARY 1919, DUBLIN: DR LD TO MCS ... I was wondering if you have published any book or leaflet embodying your theories that would be suitable for distributing amongst the labouring classes. Because here there seems to be a tremendous need. My work as helper and visitor in Baby Welfare work brings me into touch with many of these poor families and my heart bleeds to see the overburdened mothers struggling on under the strain of a far too rapidly increasing family. I am one of a great many others who have tried in all the first class chemists in Dublin for the appliances you recommend and have been met with an indignant denial of stocking any such things

(in the very best chemists in Dublin I was told that they were not allowed to stock anything of the sort) . . . Yours sincerely

6 FEBRUARY 1919, MCS IN REPLY . . . As regards your question about a leaflet for the labouring classes, I have all along been conscious that that was the most urgent and necessary part of my work, and I have delayed publishing it only in order more securely to establish my general propaganda first . . . You confirm my general impression of Ireland when you tell me how particularly urgent it is in that country. As regards your difficulty in obtaining the pessaries, I am interested and surprised at the treatment you receive in Ireland. I should be very glad if you would let me have the names and addresses of the firms that told you they were not allowed to stock anything of the sort. I have already had more than half a suspicion that the authorities, who dared not attack me openly, are trying to counter the result of my propaganda in this way . . . Yours sincerely

7 DECEMBER 1915, WIMPOLE STREET, LONDON WI: SIR T. BARLOW TO MCS (*after reading the first version of* Married Love, *three years before its publication*) . . . 1st as to the need of your propaganda of enlightenment. I don't think I can admit the necessity. It is open (1) to a young prospective husband to go and consult his family doctor about the duties and risks of matrimony and it is open to the prospective wife to consult her own mother or better perhaps her married sister and also to consult a good lady doctor . . . (2) as to the objection of your method of enlightenment. Your treatise – for it is a treatise, so far as it goes on the branch of sexual relationship dealt with – puts the prospective wife into a position of criticism, an attitude of the wife on absolutely equal footing with the husband – I am not concerned to deny your contention but I maintain that it is not a wise or prudent line to take under present conditions. Whether rightly or wrongly the conventions of ages have made the sex relations such that the husband is in some sense dominant and has the initiative in married life. It is a debatable thing how far that is ideal . . . I personally think it has been carried a

great deal too far . . . but whatever our hopes and fears may be on that question we have to take the established convention as a big fact that has to be reckoned with . . . Yours very truly

15 NOVEMBER 1917, THE MALTHUSIAN LEAGUE, LONDON S.W.I: DR BINNIE DUNLOP TO MCS. (*Dr Dunlop, secretary to the Malthusian League, first introduced Marie Stopes to her second husband, H. V. Roe, who financed in 1918 the publication of* Married Love. *A tireless worker in the field of birth control, Dr Dunlop was male, sixty, and a virgin.*) I am always sorry to hear anything, and I often do, against withdrawal; for what hope is there otherwise for the world's teeming and struggling millions? Thus, having no personal experience of sexual intercourse, I am prejudiced in favour of this method which requires no apparatus. Dr Robinson and other writers strongly condemn it. But some of our old members have told me they never in all their long lives used any other and had also satisfied their wives. One sexologist explained to me how the man could stop when nearing his climax, then resume, and so on until the woman had her orgasm. Indeed, the process could be played for an hour or more. I do most earnestly hope that this or some other inexpensive method may be recommended to poor people . . .

15 MAY 1918, LONDON: DR ARMAND AGATE TO MCS. (*About one of his patients who became a nervous wreck because her husband ignored her 'sexual curve' – defined in* Married Love *as occurring just before and after a woman's period and, to a lesser extent, midway between two periods.*) . . . I had not thought of any such curve as you have formulated, but my suggestion was that the husband should only approach his wife when she invited him by wearing a pink ribbon round her neck! It sounds silly, of course, but it worked all right, she became perfectly well, and they were quite happy . . . Yours truly

(*In the margin of this letter, Marie Stopes pencilled the terse comment: 'Mention in next edition, but say against the true ideals for a woman to advertize to her husband that she is wanting.'*)

84

29 MAY 1918, FRANCE: CAPT. ECB TO MCS ... I have just finished reading your interesting and instructive book, *Married Love*. Although a practitioner of twelve years and a married man with four children, it has taught me many things that I did not know before and concerning which many of our profession are ignorant. A question frequently asked in private practice is 'what means of prevention do you advise?' I have always advised 'coitus interruptus'. You are evidently of the opinion that this has harmful effects ... Yours truly

4 JANUARY 1919, CRAIGVARA, LEATHERHEAD: MCS TO MESSRS BOOTS ... Please supply me with one Medium Sized Occlusive Rubber Cap Pessary. It is, I think, sometimes called Mensinga's in this country. If you will let me know the price, I will forward cash by return. Yours faithfully, for Mrs Roe, Secretary.

6 JANUARY 1919, 182 REGENT ST, LONDON: MESSRS BOOTS TO MRS ROE ... In reply to your letter of the 4th inst., none of our branches stock the goods about which you enquire. If however the article in question is ordered in a prescription signed by a medical practitioner, the prescription, if sent to one of our branches, will be forwarded by the branch to our London warehouse for execution. Yours faithfully, p.p. Boots.

8 JANUARY 1919, MANCHESTER SQUARE, LONDON: DR AMAND ROUTH TO MCS. (*Dr Routh, Marie Stopes's gynaecologist whilst she was carrying her first – stillborn – child, 1918–1919, was initially an opponent of birth control. His reaction here – to* Wise Parenthood, *published 1919 – refers to Marie Stopes's contention that, if a rubber cap were contra-indicated, a small piece of sponge, impregnated with soap, might be just as effective.*) ... *Sponge*. Absolutely the worst possible 'preventive'. If left in 24 hours begins to smell and in a week is putrid. Much more difficult for patient to remove as it cannot be appreciated by an unskilled finger. I have certainly removed 20 sponges from ladies – putrid. One of these had 2 sponges in, was pregnant, and was having septic abortion when the Dr called me in to empty uterus. She nearly died.

To use *soap* would cause intense annoyance to the male esp. 'if she had filled the spores of the sponge with powdered soap'. A husband brought his wife to me some months ago, saying he wished me to examine her with a view to judicial separation, as coition made him so very sore and caused a urethral discharge. She had a good deal of irritation of vag. and she told me she wanted to avoid pregnancy, so had, unknown to her husband, done as you now advise, i.e., soap rubbed well into a sponge ... I have followed up 2 or 3 cases where a woman 'wanted' her husband during pregnancy, as much or more than previously, but he refused to acquiesce for fear of hurting the child, and the children have grown up restless, uncontrollable, and with unduly marked sexual tendencies to masturbation – I *think* this may have been due to unsatisfied desire in the mother. Yours truly

19 APRIL 1919, CITY OF LONDON HOSPITAL FOR DISEASES OF THE CHEST: DR GEORGE JONES TO MCS. (*Dr Jones gave evidence for Marie Stopes in her celebrated libel action against Halliday Sutherland, the Catholic doctor who had accused her of 'experimenting on the poor'. Erudite, a classical scholar as well as physician, he was much more liberal in his attitudes than Marie Stopes, advocating contraception for the unmarried as well as the married, abortion, and the enjoyment of sex whether or not 'sanctified by marriage' in the Stopesian sense.*) I have just read your book on Married Love and I have no doubt much of what you say is correct as to many women never having had a proper sexual orgasm. Herewith I send you some anatomical considerations of the matter. I have gone into rather minute details at the expense of being charged with 'pornography'. As it is the essence of success in a prostitute to induce her customers to return to her, a knowledge of some of the matters I have elaborated is no doubt more often found with prostitutes than with married women, though the more passionate of the latter are often well aware of many of these points, which after all were known to Ovid, and are elaborated in the *Ars Amandi*, and in the much greater poet Lucretius (*De Rerum Natura*) while

everything which I have written can be traced in Juvenal and Martial and was quite familiar to Roman women of every class.

I should be glad to see a fuller handling of the prevention of conception in its economic aspect of which those who have worked among the poor might say something and also how far repeated pregnancies are the direct cause of Phthisis in the mother and Rickets not to mention tuberculosis in the children . . . I have here one little ward of 4 beds all occupied by married women from 30 to 40. Two are utterly worn out. One, the youngest, is a very strong woman and may survive, and the 4th is near the limit of childbearing. To their families these 4 women are today worse than useless. If a copious douche of Quinine or Vinegar would have kept them from coming here surely the state would have been the gainer . . .

(The following extracts are from Dr Jones's enclosed essay):

Some Consequences of the adoption by Quadrupeds of the Erect position . . . In the coitus of quadrupeds the horizontal position secures (1) the stimulation of the clitoris by the erect penis before intromission. The clitoris when a woman lies on her face or is kneeling on hands and knees points downwards and forwards as in the lower animals, which during coitus stand with hoofs widely parted from side to side to steady themselves to bear the weight of the male. This separates the labia majora and exposes the clitoris which is stroked by the erect penis of the male as he makes his first efforts to mount the female . . . There may be objections to the knee–elbow position on the grounds of indecency but to coitus in bed with the partners on their Right sides, their thighs flexed, the wife bending hers up to her abdomen and the husband moulding his abdomen and thighs to her buttocks there can be none. It is almost impossible not to give a few preliminary strokes to the clitoris as the penis makes its way from behind forwards between the labia majora and the almost immediate result is that the wife will rapidly respond with quickened pulse and breathing, the vulval and vaginal secretions will be poured out copiously and with a few characteristic movements of the buttocks the wife herself will probably capture her husband's penis without any effort on his part . . .

It is true that in coitus from behind kisses are not easily given or taken . . . The writer is rather disinclined to pursue the subject, but logically he finds it hard to see why kisses on the lips should be thought proper, kisses on the neck tolerated, kisses on the breast scarcely decent and on the clitoris absolutely sinful, while the insertion of the tongue in the vagina is absolutely immoral. A little soap and water and a douche of warm salt and water would render the vagina much cleaner than a mouth with a lot of unstopped teeth, and if the object of kisses is to provoke the sexual orgasm then why not apply the lips to the part where they will be most effectual . . . I am, Yours truly

(*The publication of Marie Stopes's* Wise Parenthood *in 1919 brought another flood of letters from doctors, whose opinions Marie Stopes frequently solicited.*)

27 AUGUST 1919, LONDON: SIR AB TO MCS . . . I myself have always advocated limitation of families. Apart from the difficulties which beset parents who have more children than they can decently afford, apart from the dangers and miseries of over-population, there is the abomination of turning the world, now so filled with the splendid and irreplaceable products of evolution, into a market garden, which would happen if it were over-populated . . . Yours most gratefully

17 SEPTEMBER 1919, WILTSHIRE: DR H. O-B TO MCS. Your well-written book has given me much useful information, so I gladly accept your invitation to give my views. Now you forbid coitus interruptus, yet you believe in limiting the family, will you then give me a better remedy?

My experience gained from young soldiers in the army and women in civil practice teaches me that this is the general method, men adopt this practice to prevent pregnancy, they also say that many girls will not agree to intercourse unless this condition is carried out.

Women, married and single, say that intercourse is safer this way, far better than pessaries, and as they hate anything wet, object to douching – I notice they generally ask if withdrawing during the act can possibly harm their husbands. When asked, 'what about yourself?' the woman generally replies 'I don't allow myself to give way or become excited for fear of the consequences' (the fear of pregnancy prevents orgasm) . . . Yours truly

2 NOVEMBER 1919, CITY OF LONDON HOSPITAL, LONDON: DR GEORGE JONES TO MCS (*commenting on Marie Stopes's statement in* Wise Parenthood *that she would condemn any attempt to turn sex into 'an easy self-indulgence'*) . . . If you mean that neither man nor woman should indulge in intercourse to the point of exhaustion you must I think deal with the not very rare folk who are capable of quite surprising efforts in this way. Forgive my putting things plainly, but I remember a pair of people whose standard was '4 every night and one in the morning till he is 60'. Healthy too, they both were . . .

9 NOVEMBER 1919, CITY OF LONDON HOSPITAL: DR GEORGE JONES TO MCS . . . May I here make the criticism which is becoming more urgent as I think things over.

It is the prevention of unwanted children for which you are out, *not* the limitation of the families of the married. The illegitimate child has a very much worse chance of survival than the legitimate. Therefore the prevention of conception is just as important for a lascivious housemaid or milliner of 18 as for a married woman of 35 with 9 sickly children. The child of a prostitute is likely to have gonorrheal ophthalmia and become blind or to have congenital syphilis.

I do not see why you should deprecate the falling of your book into the hands of the non-moral or the lustful or the sensuous. No one is foolish enough to suppose that the girl who writes to you in *frantic* despair to say she is in terrible trouble is thereby improved, or likely to be driven back to a moral elevation to which she had never risen. Let your book pass into any hands . . . those who wish to be continent will remain continent even if they have a check pessary in place and a packet of quinine pessaries handy . . . Yours truly

8 AUGUST 1920, ROCHESTER, KENT: DR MJ TO MCS. My wife and I have just had the pleasure of reading your most interesting book – *Married Love* . . . Though a medical man myself, I must confess to a most woeful ignorance of all essential points bearing on a subject of such importance. The result has been that, to quote the inspired phrase in your preface, we *have* had 'years of heartache and blind questioning in the dark'. Now (thanks to you) we have a 'glimmering of the supreme art, the art of love' – but we feel that we need still further enlightenment.

My wife is a slightly-built woman – though of ardent temperament – and I am a heavy man and alas! getting heavier with approaching middle age! The result is that she seldom has an orgasm owing to that sense of crushing and suffocation in the 'usual' position, to which you draw attention, but such is our lack of knowledge that we are at a loss to know how otherwise coitus may be performed . . . With sincere apologies for troubling you, I am, Madam, Yours faithfully

18 AUGUST 1920, MCS IN REPLY . . . I am very glad my book is useful and only wish I could describe explicitly all you wish to know. I should try both lying on the same side, the wife in your arms and bending, you entering from behind, one of her legs being slightly bent and entwined round yours. Twist about and try all sorts of modifications of this; it is the very best way for lots of people. With best wishes, Yours very truly

24 AUGUST 1920, LONDON HOSPITAL MEDICAL COLLEGE, LONDON: MISS DS TO MCS. I don't know how you can possibly answer all the appeals that must reach you, but I would be so grateful if you would answer this one. I hope to qualify in a few months, and to get married soon after . . . When a boy or girl becomes aware of the sexual instinct before marriage, should he or she try to suppress it altogether, or is onanism

(self-abuse) a legitimate way out? Does this practice lead to pathological changes in the reproductive organs in addition to its bad moral effects? This question is also of a personal nature – I realized the possibility of it for myself 2 years ago (I am now 25) and was very unhappy at having done so – and set myself increasingly long periods in which to refrain, but only succeeded very partially ... My husband to be is also a doctor and you will wonder that we have not discussed it, but I think he has never given way to it, I don't want to confer just yet ... Yours sincerely

8 SEPTEMBER 1920, MCS IN REPLY ... As regards what you say about yourself you should not allow yourself to dwell on the past at all nor feel any unhappiness. I think your case is like that of many thousands of women and men too, and once the normal life of love has begun, these premature longings and reactions cease ... You must not, however, imagine that I am in the least advocating such a course and condoning it where it has taken place to excess, but in the small degree you describe it it is in no way considered seriously. With best wishes, Yours sincerely

31 OCTOBER 1920, WEST END HOSPITAL FOR NERVOUS DISEASES, LONDON: DR GEORGE JONES TO MCS ... The awkward thing is that they *look* better for it! It is common knowledge that many women of notoriously loose lives do look well, and are well, and can do a great deal of hard work both in mind and body, whereas the pale and saintly and chaste are often neurotic to a degree. Worse still remains. The neurotics and the hysterical women, who for my sins are fairly well represented in this place, suggest to me painfully that what they need is the stimulus of vigorous sexual intercourse such as shall produce a real and prolonged orgasm assuaged by a copious dose of semen! What is to be done for these folk! To keep them in bed is a waste of beds. To give them tonics makes them more mad for embraces than ever – as for Valerian and Bromides it simply amounts to getting rid of wind and making the poor things feel too low to do anything sexual!

Perhaps it is because I am getting old and somewhat

detached that I feel indifferent to both religious and ethical arguments on sex matters ... Two people meet and like each other and their liking matures into mutual desire for sex relations – why not let them alone to indulge what is after all only the closest possible friendship? To say they propose to administer the matter of a sacrament to each other is sheer nonsense. To say it is moral or immoral is no better ... There is no more immorality in the enjoyment of sexual intercourse, than in the enjoyment of mince pies (unless the pies are stolen). In the one case you waste gastric juices and muscles of mastication in trying to assimilate mince pies beyond your needs – not that people eat mince pies to support life, they don't, they eat them because they like them. In the other case they don't indulge in sexual intercourse to produce children. No one is foolish enough to assert that for it is palpable nonsense and against all experience ... They indulge because they enjoy it. Yours truly

15 DECEMBER 1920, 150 HARLEY STREET, LONDON: DR JANE LORIMER HAWTHORNE TO MCS (*Dr Hawthorne later became honorary consultant physician at the Mothers' Clinic*) ... I have had two cases today which I think you would have been interested in. One was a refined woman of 38 years who has never been personally interested in sex matters, nor had any love affair. She was 'Psychoanalysed' a month or two ago – and was evidently roused to such an extent that she is now in a state of acute misery trying to fight and subdue this excess of feeling ... Yours V. sincerely

11 FEBRUARY 1921, LONDON E3: DR IM TO MCS ... Would you give me your opinion, if you have time, on the following case, if so I would forward details, I enclose some which please return. Is a lady justified in bringing a charge of cruelty against the husband if she proves that he was addicted to peculiar habits? Yours sincerely

14 FEBRUARY 1921, MCS IN REPLY ... In the present attitude of public opinion, I think that not only would a wife be justified in bringing a charge of cruelty on two of the acts

you mention (not the third) but that it would really be something of a public service to bring such a charge . . . she should confine it to the two points which are really disgusting and cruel, namely oral and rectal coitus. As such a large number of men use hand masturbation, any mention of that in addition would be like a red herring dragged across the path because no judge would dare to base a charge of cruelty on such a point as it would involve too revolutionary a change. The other two points, however, namely the use or even the attempt to use oral and rectal coitus are acts of such gross indecency that they undoubtedly amount to cruelty mentally to any refined or sensitive woman . . . Yours sincerely

21 FEBRUARY 1921, BARONS COURT, LONDON: ETTIE A. ROUT TO MCS. (*Miss Rout, a New Zealander of considerable determination, was an authority on venereal disease, and had been connected with the treatment and prevention of VD among ANZAC troops during the First World War. In 1921, sent a copy of Marie Stopes's latest book,* The Truth About Venereal Disease, *she found Marie Stopes's attitudes generally much too conventional and mealy-mouthed. Unable to obtain official backing to go and cure VD in the Rhine Army, she nevertheless accepted Marie Stopes's offer of £100 to visit Germany, in return for which she agreed to advise the troops there to buy* The Truth About VD. *She refused, however, to acknowledge that all changes in public opinion about sex and birth control were entirely due to Marie Stopes; whereupon the offer was withdrawn and the correspondence ended in mutual recrimination.*) . . . All parts of the British Empire have become broader in sex matters in the last ten years – particularly in the last five years. Rationalism and socialism are partly responsible and Continental literature (Ellen Keys etc) and of course Havelock Ellis and Wells and Shaw and Carpenter and many others . . . The question should be a purely personal one. So long as men and women are not spreading disease and sowing promiscuous and irresponsible impregnation what harm are they doing anyhow? Whose business is it but their own? . . . Briefly, I think you take far too

high a view of modern marriage and far too low a view of prostitution. I've known prostitutes who were much finer than some members of the Married Women's Trade Union and many cases where monogamy was the extreme penalty of the law ... Yours sincerely

30 MARCH 1921, ETTIE ROUT TO MCS, *enclosing the Pledge Cards she intended to issue to the troops in Germany* ... I think these promises are better carried out if the signature is witnessed ... then we could check the names with the military register and parade any men who had not voluntarily signed and ask them *why*? ... This is the pledge card to be issued to troops:

FRONT

I PROMISE to do my utmost to refrain from dangerous and immoral sexual intercourse.

(2) I PROMISE to disinfect myself IMMEDIATELY if ever I do risk venereal infection.

(3) I PROMISE to seek medical treatment at once if ever I believe I have venereal disease and to continue such treatment till discharged by doctor.

Note: You are earnestly advised to purchase a copy of TRUTH ABOUT VD by Dr Marie Stopes and to study it carefully. PRICE 1/9 postfree. HQ: Dr Marie Stopes, Leatherhead, Surrey, England.

BACK

DIRECTIONS FOR SELF-DISINFECTION

MEN:

Before connection: Use calomel ointment (or lanoline or vaseline) to cover all over parts and to block entrance to 'pipe'.

After each connection: Urinate IMMEDIATELY and cleanse parts carefully with disinfecting lotion or with soap and water. Calomel ointment to be well rubbed in. If possible report to Prophylactic Station early and – Better Late than Never.

WOMEN:

Before connection: Syringe with disinfecting lotion, or wash parts thoroughly with soap and water.

After each connection: Urinate IMMEDIATELY; then syringe again, or wash parts.

Note: CARRY A LITTLE DISINFECTANT WITH YOU ALWAYS AS A CONTINUAL REMINDER OF THE GRAVE DANGERS OF IRREGULAR INTERCOURSE. AVOID RISKS.

---

18 APRIL 1921, MCS TO ETTIE ROUT ... I know you cannot understand how very deeply I feel that it is entirely mistaken and very dangerous to distribute disinfection information in so bold a form which will mislead the men into thinking they know enough about it, which they do not. I don't think it can be put more shortly than it is in my book ... Yours very sincerely

19 APRIL 1921, ETTIE ROUT TO MCS. I am ruling the matter right out so far as you are concerned. But I think that you should know that I gave out EXACTLY THE SAME DIRECTIONS to the Anzacs in Paris as you now say are 'entirely mistaken and very dangerous'. This is the result:

7 October 1918 ... During the last 22 days 57 v.d. infections have been recorded at Pépinère Barracks, Paris, among men on leave and reporting v.d.

NEW ZEALANDERS	0
AUSTRALIANS	0
CANADIANS	33
ENGLISH	24

The Canadians and English had the over-nice, careful, elaborate directions you have been misguided into thinking are necessary. My advice is DON'T consult anybody who hasn't emptied out of their minds the conventional lies of civilization ... rely on the evidence of those who like myself have SUC-CEEDED in controlling v.d. – not on the unsupported statements of those who have failed themselves.

20 MAY 1922, ETTIE ROUT TO MCS ... You are quite mistaken in thinking I under-estimate the value of the 'publicity' you have given to birth-control. But I am writing you next week, and we'll leave the matter over till then.

24 MAY 1922, ETTIE ROUT TO MCS (*after further quarrels as to whether or not Marie Stopes was the only truly important figure in the history of birth control. Not surprisingly, their correspondence came to a halt after this letter*). I have now been through the papers you kindly sent me.

(1) NEWSPAPER: I do not think it will do the B.C. movement much good, but no doubt it will serve to advertise your books ...

(2) PAMPHLET, 'THE MOTHERS' CLINIC': I had seen this before. Your priority to the Malthusian Centre [i.e. the clinic founded by the Malthusian League six months after Marie Stopes's clinic] is of no importance at all. There are many other clinics in different parts of the world.

(3) 'EARLY DAYS OF BIRTH CONTROL'. The 'early days' of B.C. go back to the dawn of history, and I think it is misleading to give this title to your pamphlet.

(4) APPRECIATION OF YOUR WORK: I greatly value the publicity you have given to the B.C. Movement, and I am sure both your husband and yourself have devoted much time and money and effort to the work. But it is disinterested field-workers that are wanted – not Museum Hypatias or Prophet-esses. You can write well, talk well, and I believe you could work well – if you would empty out the rubbishy emotionalism, the superstition, the vanity and egoism with which you becloud and degrade your work ... Yours sincerely

(*On 17 March 1921, Marie Stopes and her husband, H. V. Roe, opened Britain's first birth control clinic in Marlborough Road,*

Holloway, a poor district of North London. It was by no means universally welcomed.)

21 MARCH 1921, LONDON: DR WA TO MCS. I am obliged for yours of the 13th inst received this morning and for the enclosed pamphlet re the Mothers' Clinic.

The gospel you preach is in my opinion a pernicious one and I propose to deal with your pamphlet in an early issue of the *Medical World*.

12 APRIL 1921, YORKSHIRE: DR JB, MOH, TO MCS ... Personally, I have doubts with respect to your new Clinic ... in Bradford and the West Riding gross forms of birth control have given rise to the most grave abuse and the population is slowly controlling itself out of existence ... in a generation or two if things go on as they are here, the Bradford man and woman will be practically extinct. Bradford at the present time is not self-supporting in life. The population is aged, jaded and non-virile and materialistic to a degree. It is a population of married old maids and married old bachelors ... This is the sort of result that birth control brings about. Yours faithfully

14 APRIL 1921, ANTE-NATAL CLINIC, LONDON NW3: DR KM TO THE MOTHERS' CLINIC. I shall be glad if you will kindly refrain from sending invitations to my Nurses and Health Visitors here to send along our patients to your Birth Control Clinic – I entirely and utterly disapprove of Dr Marie Stopes action in setting up this clinic both as a doctor and as a woman and as a Christian – My health visitors therefore will do no such thing as to send my patients along to you, whilst I am the medical officer in charge here – and you can tell Dr Stopes so. Yours truly

JUNE 1921, CHRISTCHURCH, NEW ZEALAND: DR WS TO MCS. *This letter was headed* Licensed Houses v. Masturbation. *It read:* I consider that Licensed Houses are necessary, and that they should be managed by a trained nurse with no financial interest in it, and paid by ye Boro. A medical officer should be appointed with full authority and made responsible for disease contracted there . . . The abolition of these Houses has spread disease through ye community and enormously increased immorality. I look upon them as 'Moral Sewers' more necessary than ye street sewers are for preventing Typhoid fever and Diphtheria. Another evil result has been ye great increase of masturbation. I examined every candidate for ye Canterbury Police for 40 years from 1878 to 1918: averaging about 3 Doz a year, of whom about 1 Doz were passed. Before 1896 I scarcely ever rejected one for Varicocele, ye result of Masturbation. Since 1896, ye rejections for that cause increased from 1% to 25% . . . The number of young men crippled by Masturbation is appalling. The British Bluejacket has an intense horror of it. I was formerly Surgeon in ye R. Navy. We had on board 850 men, and 100 boys. If a boy was caught masturbating, 2 Bluejackets made a line fast to his feet and ducked him overboard after which, on reaching ye first port, they took him to a Tolerated House and put him into bed with a woman. That boy was cured . . . Yours faithfully

24 JANUARY 1922, 72 RODNEY STREET, LIVERPOOL: SIR JAMES BARR TO MCS. (*Sir James, a former president of the British Medical Association, was one of the original patrons of the Mothers' Clinic.*) . . . If there were early and suitable marriages with small families, there would be a higher sexual morality, more love and happiness, there would be less disease and death; parents would recognize their responsibility to bring into the world only healthy children, children whom they wanted and of whom they could feel proud, and not the mere accidents of haphazard sexual indulgence. A selective birthrate is the necessary complement of the abolition of Nature's selective deathrate and until we get a selective birthrate there can be no general elevation of the human race. The nation which most effectually adopts eugenic ideals is bound to rule the world. The sexual function should not be repressed in the subconscious mind, we wish to get rid of Freudian filth which degrades and debases

the human species. We may not at once be able to get rid of homosexuals, but an enlightened nation will have no use for them, and they will gradually disappear from the face of the earth which their shadow now darkens ... Yours very truly

THE MEDICAL QUESTIONNAIRE

The medical profession and the clergy enjoyed the lowest birth-rates of all social groups in Britain. At the end of 1922, Marie Stopes sent out questionnaires to doctors, asking for details of their marriages and birth control methods. Of the 128 who replied, three had used only abortion, then illegal, as their method of birth control – one doctor surgically aborting his wife no fewer than five times. Abstinence was used by fifteen doctors, for periods ranging from one month to thirty years. Of the fourteen wives who used the safe period, eight became pregnant (understandably, since the safe period was then commonly, but wrongly, held to occur in the middle of the menstrual month). Only eleven used the rubber cap, the method most often recommended at the growing number of birth control clinics in the 1920s. Most couples, of course, alternated between various methods, the two most often mentioned being the sheath, used at some point by forty-four of the 128, and withdrawal, practised by sixty-three doctors, and condemned by most of the medical profession and by Marie Stopes. Thirty used the soluble quinine pessary alone, eleven used a douche, and twelve couples used nothing at all. In addition to filling in the questionnaire, many doctors sent explanatory notes or letters.

OCTOBER 1922, UNSIGNED. Wife used a douche but conceived shortly after marriage. After birth of a child coitus interruptus for about 2 years. She however hated sexual intercourse from the beginning and after two or three years of struggling and utter misery all relations ceased. Later I became intimate with a professional woman. Was happy with her for about 10 years. She used a douche for first six or seven years – then douche and rubber cap. Twice in this period she went a week or fortnight over her periods and an instrument was used, but it is not clear that this was really necessary.

30 SEPTEMBER 1922, LONDON: DR B TO MCS. My firs
thought on receiving your circular letter re Married Love and
the use of 'preventatives' was to put it into the waste paper
basket – I have decided to send it on to our MP etc and ask him
if he gets a chance to get some legislation to prevent the country
being flooded with this rubbish you being a woman prevents
me from saying what I think of your use of knowledge in pan-
dering to the depraved sexual instincts of clergymen and
neurasthenics – and being a gentleman I refrain from writing
it – The only excuse apparently is that you make money out of
it. I am, Yrs

16 OCTOBER 1922, BRADFORD: DR BA TO MCS. I received
your circular letter this morning which I am refusing to answer
in the way you desire and may I say that in my opinion you are
starting on a crusade that is destined to failure because the sort
of response you are likely to get, I am convinced, will not be
representative, and you will draw a blank from the very large
majority of right minded individuals ... We as medical folk
know of the existence of sex, of parenthood, of bodies male and
female, of bowels, etc, there are legitimate uses and illegitimate
uses. There are things that happen that we all know but respectfully conceal. It is not that I am a prude I worked on the neo-
Malthusian platform for years, but being also some sort of
psychologist I know the horrible result of filling the so called
subconscious mind with sexual matter ... To put sex on a
pedestal is a social crime to the highest part of man.

I am not a disciple of George Bernard Shaw, but this I know
there are some regions of Hell that require neither investigation
or advertisement. I do not believe that it is necessary to show
the young minds the horrors of Hell so that they can avoid them,
for glorious Youth, 'God bless them' are well prone to be clean
and wholesome ... Yours respectfully

23 OCTOBER 1922, MCS IN REPLY. Thank you for your
letter. I agree with much that you say. Indeed I am very much
against the parade of unwholesome sex matters particularly by
the psychoanalysts, but I cannot agree with you that to ask

medical men about the use of contraceptives can do anything to harm their minds and it is of very great importance to the community that one should know of the methods used by the medical men as they have by far the lowest birth rate in this country and they presumably do not use methods which are harmful ... Yours faithfully

17 OCTOBER 1922, BIRMINGHAM: DR A TO MCS. I think your ideas are splendid. I enclose details of my own experience and have not signed it as I thought it better not to do so.

As a medical man I have had very considerable experience of the poor 'prolific' wife, whose life is one continual struggle against poverty, and the misfortune of having a baby every 18 months or possibly more frequently. I have had patients threaten to commit suicide and even have abortion brought on to prevent them having a large family of possibly weakly children that they cannot afford to rear or educate ...

31 OCTOBER 1922, STOCKPORT: MR S, MRCS, TO MCS. Mr S, MRCS, is acquainted with the writings of Dr Marie Stopes and her methods which he regards as more in the interests of pornography than of science.

He agrees with Mr Hilaire Belloc that 'the Catholic Church is an expert in man's nature and man's needs' that She has the wisdom of eighteen centuries with Her and the direct guidance of the Holy Ghost. When Dr Marie Stopes has these two qualifications, Mr S will be pleased to communicate with her again and to reveal to her the intimacies of his sex life.

8 NOVEMBER 1922, MCS IN REPLY. Doctor Marie Stopes notes Dr S's views, and would draw his attention to the Roman Catholic Church's failure in the recent interests of France as shown by the facts and figures in the enclosed paper. [Alarmed by its rapidly declining birth rate, France had recently introduced laws making illegal the sale and advertisement of contraceptives.]

19 NOVEMBER 1922, YORKSHIRE: DR WR, MEDICAL OF-FICER IN A LUNATIC ASYLUM, TO MCS. I am unable to

furnish you with any data as I am not married. I am, however, professionally interested in your subject as I am often asked by the husbands of women who have been under my care suffering from Puerperal Insanity what means they should take to prevent a recurrence ... The method of prevention you advocate, namely a pessary to fit on the cervix, I consider quite unsafe and have found to be quite impracticable even amongst intelligent women, much more amongst the lower classes. Every contraceptive method is open to some objection if it is to be really effective and not merely to diminish the chances of impregnation ... Bearing this in mind I consider that the stout washable sheath offers the best means of prevention. I have often wondered whether the Quinine pessary might not merely injure the sperm instead of killing it and so bring about the birth of a defective child ... Yours faithfully

11 NOVEMBER 1922, KENT: MISS BT, MB, TO MCS ... This is not sent to you from any motive of self-advertisement, nor from any morbid desire to write on sex subjects ... You may not think, as I do, that the facts are conclusive proof that a mother's subconscious mentality may, during pregnancy, impress characteristics on the coming child – nor perhaps will you think, as I do, that they indicate a very grave, and perhaps not fully realized responsibility for those who are homosexual.

I am homosexual, so far as I can tell, from birth – was conscious of homosexual feeling, though not then understanding it, before the age of six years. I have often, without intending it, roused sex excitement in both heterosexual and homosexual women. In the case of one girl this led to relations that were immoral and indefensible because she was really a normal heterosexual, and was several years younger than myself and the relationship included intense physiological sexual excitement in each of us. There were passionate kissing, caresses and embraces. There was no such filthiness as cunnilingus, nor was there any act comparable with the complete sexual act of a man and woman, nor was there kissing of the filthy tongue sucking type indulged in by some men and women. It therefore seems to me impossible that any cells having directive power on the ovum can have passed to her from me. Our relationship lasted for some 19 months, then came to an abrupt ending because she met and fell in love with a man and reverted to normal heterosexual feeling. She became engaged to the man, but he was a priest and got bitten with the celibacy craze and the engagement was broken off. Our relationship was not renewed, I was simply her friend. Some time later she learned to love another man, a very good fellow and they were married. As I had left the neighbourhood where she lived, it happened that we didn't meet for a long time. It was certainly more than fifteen months before the birth of her first child, a boy. Her husband assured me the time was two years and three months ... When the boy was about five years old, I happened to spend a day with them, and – it was rather disconcerting – her husband, who knew *all* about my former relations with his wife, asked me for a scientific explanation of how I had managed to impress on his son many of my characteristics. He pointed out to me some of them and I noted others for myself. They were tricks of manner and behaviour that are like mine, and are not like those of the husband and wife, nor like those of the wife's relatives, nor according to the husband, like those of his people. They are enumerated below.

Way of holding a teacup. Marked courtesy in speaking to persons of inferior social position such as servants. Complete absence of physical fear. Holding one's breath when kissing. Manner of caressing hair of anyone one loves (I had to grin when I saw the boy stroke his mother's hair) ... How they reached the boy passes my comprehension except on the assumption that hero worship of me had impressed a subconscious memory of them on the braincells of his mother and that she had somehow passed on that memory to his brain cells ...

In these days of my old age I do not sorrow too much over my responsibilities of (?) mental maternity or paternity, which is it? The other children of the marriage do not show any of my characteristics. No one of the three children seems, so far as I can learn, to show any signs of homosexuality, for which I thank God ... Yours faithfully

11 NOVEMBER 1922, BURTON: DR FW TO MCS. I have read and thought much about contraceptives and I cannot bring myself to believe that any method except abstinence is either right or moral. I am, Yours very faithfully

12 NOVEMBER 1922, MANCHESTER: DR AE TO MCS. I have your circular letter and also the enclosed questionnaire. I am quite aware that it is possible to argue on the limitation of progeny and with all seeming success, but I am also perfectly well aware that man and woman were not endowed with the instincts for procreation in order that they should indulge these without the natural results ... The amount of apparent benefit you do not know – you attempt to combat the evils of civilisation by artificial means: in point of fact you pander to the desires for parent's tastes for luxury rather than to his necessity to do justice to his offspring – God knows a great deal better than you do how to deal with vital problems ... Yours faithfully

NOVEMBER 1922, LONDON: DR FP TO MCS. As a doctor who is almost entirely engaged in psychotherapy, I am of the opinion that any form of prevention is *psychically* and *spiritually* injurous – and though quinine pessaries and coitus interruptus are to my mind the least objectionable of any form of prevention, it lowers the whole act to the physical plane which should be spiritual union as well as physical. This is impossible where any forms of active prevention are used.

*

1 MARCH 1923: MISS MH, A HAMPSHIRE MIDWIFE, TO MCS (*commiserating over the result of Marie Stopes's unsuccessful libel action against Halliday Sutherland, and describing conditions in her rural area*) ... Another woman took 12 Beechams Pills

every morning for a week (and was still alive to tell the tale!) another took gunpowder; while yet another was more succesful by passing a bone crochet hook up the vagina to the cervix and keeping it there with cotton wool padding till the abortion took place . . .

4 MAY 1923, GUY'S HOSPITAL, LONDON: GROUP OF MEDICAL STUDENTS TO MCS. Since the medical curriculum at this hospital contains no teaching whatever on the subject of birth control, several of us are wondering whether it would be possible to attend your clinic with a view to receiving some instruction on a subject on which advice is often sought from Medical practitioners . . . Anyone who has worked in the district attached to Guy's Hospital must see the necessity for some safe and simple method of birth prevention, other than the artificial abortion methods which seem prevalent in these boroughs. p.s. There are a very large number of men interested. We are, Yours etc

8 MAY 1923, MCS IN REPLY . . . I should be only too delighted to let you all come to the Clinic if it were bigger, but the truth is that we are most dreadfully crowded out. The rooms are very small so certainly not more than two of you could come at a time, and then you would have to take the risk of waiting until a patient was there who did not mind the process being seen. You will understand that we do not treat those we help at the Clinic in the same kind of way they are treated at an ordinary hospital as we create round the whole subject an atmosphere of confidence and trust on their part, but sometimes, of course, there are women who would not all mind a young medical doctor seeing the cap fitted on them . . . Yours sincerely

31 AUGUST 1923, DR GEORGE JONES TO MCS, *having recently set up a private birth control practice in the East End of London, to which MCS occasionally sent patients* . . . You would have been immensely amused with a charming pair who came this morning. She was 35 and he 27, both well made healthy folk:

married 6 weeks. She was a dancer, with beautiful limbs: her fingers were rather short and her vagina rather long. She had a very powerful sphincter and used it. At last as I could only just reach the posterior fornix myself and she couldn't at all, I suggested fetching in her husband. She didn't mind a bit and they both laughed over her valuable assets, the merits of which I explained to her . . . In the end his long fingers in a rubber glove for the sake of his nails, fixed the thing well in place and I taught him how to put it in and take it out. Repeated manipulations had given her at least one orgasm and I began to wonder whether I hadn't better fix things up and leave them for half an hour . . . Yours truly

14 NOVEMBER 1924, MCS TO DR M KERSLAKE, *one of the consultants at the Mothers' Clinic. The Society for Constructive Birth Control and Racial Progress (CBC for short) which ran the clinic, had also set up a medical research committee, which was frequently sent samples of new contraceptives. Only a few months earlier, at the age of 43, Marie Stopes had given birth, by Caesarean section, to her only living child* . . . I am sending you herewith a specimen of Dr D's new contraceptive, which he has been very insistent that he should be allowed to present personally to the Committee. Although it is not the function of our Research Committee to push any individual commercial product, I think that, as it is being privately said that I am jealous of him and blocking his entry to the Committee, it would be better for him to come up and say to our Committee what he wants to say . . . I may say that I tried this beastly thing on myself – a very special privilege, the extremely special nature of which I do not think he fully realizes, and nothing in Heaven or on earth would allow another one to touch my vagina. Not that it did me any actual harm, but the sticky, slimy feeling was so beastly, and it took so many days to clear the thing out that I would not dream of trying it again. It appears that he is incredulous and has been more or less implying that I am only out for my own things and trying to block his and other people's new inventions . . . Yours sincerely

21 JANUARY 1925, HARLEY STREET, LONDON: DR JANE L. HAWTHORNE TO MCS . . . I had a patient today who is evidently the wife of a 'Landed Proprietor' and she seems to interest herself in the welfare of the people of the district. She was telling me how she arranged for someone to come and address the women on Birth Control. It seems to have made a great sensation and to have stirred up a perfect Hotch-potch of 'Feelings' and now the Vicar's Wife, and the Bank Manager's good lady and even the doctor's Helpmeet all pretend they don't see her when she passes through the village! . . . Yours ever

21 MAY 1925, LONDON: DR SA TO MCS. Mylady, Referring to my last letter I beg to inform you that the bill over the Studs-Contraceptives is at my hands, which I send enclosed . . . I have brought two Contraceptives, which I have already got from Vienna, and have handed them over to your secretary. One of these specimens, the pessary 'Hygibe' is very characteristic for its shape and all the pessaries of this firm are out of sale. It was quite accidentally that I could still get one exemplar . . .

LIST OF CONTRACEPTIVES FOR THE DR STOPES-MUSEUM

1.	Stud after Struppek		1. piec.	aluminum	6/-
2.	"	"	2	rubbermass	8/-
3.	"	"	1	silver	17/-
4.	"	Fehling	"	glass	7/-
5.	"	"	"	rubbermass	8/-
6.	"	Braun	"	"	8/-
7.	"	"	"	silkworm with glass button	10/-
8.	"	Obstavit	"	alumin.	6/-
9.	"	Erlkönig	"	ivory	20/-
10.	"	Erlkönig	"	rubbermass with introducer	15/-

I beg to remain, honoured lady, your most respectful servant

27 MAY 1925, MEDICAL RESEARCH COUNCIL, LONDON: DR LH TO MCS. The department of chemistry, Kansas Agricultural Experimental Station, have recently issued a report which shows that ultra-violet rays not only stops rickets in chickens, but also influences egg production in adults. Breeders have told me that fertility of young bulls kept in stalls, for safety's sake, falls off. I believe this is due to want of sunlight. We have ascertained that arc-light treatment has restored sexual power in two or three cases of men, with the improvement of general health. The greater fertility of peasants, e.g. of French Canadians (average 10 per family) compared with city people must be more a question of diet and sunlight and air than of use of preventives, as the diminution of fertility occurred and occurs still in those who have not used preventives. Yours v. truly

29 SEPTEMBER 1926, PRAGUE: DR AKK TO MCS. Dear Sire, I beg your advice kindly. My best friend is a crippled man, he has a poliomyelities and both his legs are palsied. He is an artist, painter, a man of high intellect. I myself explained him often the perceptions, which I collect from the books of Dr Marie Carmichael Stopes and this friend entreated me for two things:

(1) He is 25 years old, and fell in love with the girl 20 years old, which is also in love with him, but that girl suffer from sexual neurasthenia. She is up to this time the virgin and she would be glad to marry him. He thought all over and entreated me for advice. His physical conditions is in such state that he is able only of very small number of the selection from sexual technique. Shall he to have the premarital union with that beloved girl? And when that woman will not have any orgasm, shall he the marriage with that beloved woman give up? I myself dont desire to determine that difficult case and therefore I entreat you for precious advice. If that premarital union will not be successful, then my best friend is fully determined to end with suicide in spite of all my dissuasions.

(2) I beg you for information, whether the poliomyelitis is hereditary or not.

OCTOBER 1926, MCS IN REPLY . . . Such a marriage as you describe should give some comfort to the sufferer but they should on no account have children.

1 SEPTEMBER 1927, ROMAN CATHOLIC HOSPITAL FOR WOMEN, SYDNEY, AUSTRALIA: DR KS TO MCS . . . Instead of coaching newly married young women with details they are too shy to listen to I tell them to go off and buy your *Married Love* and when they come back in a *week's* time you can see by their manner that they have suddenly *grown up*, as they have found your book a road guide, a child's guide and a Baedeker for sexual intercourse. I think you might call it the Honeymoon Baedeker – a guide to the *smallest place of entertainment* in the world, where there is *standing* room for one only . . . When your book first came out, I remember one tart old Minerva saying to me, 'I have read *that* book and all I can say is that *Miss* Marie Stopes obviously does not belong to the Society of Confirmed Virgins.'

4 FEBRUARY 1928, LONDON: DR BK TO MCS . . . This last pregnancy was a failure of a well-fitting cervical cap, *two* Semori tablets and a soap and water douche next morning. I think I told you that our last baby was also not deliberately intended, although fortunately the fertilization occurred at a time when we were both at the acme of physical fitness. We seem to be in a category all to ourselves and are faced with a difficult situation in the future as of course it is out of the question to allow my wife to run any more risks. There seem to be only the alternatives of total abstinence or vasectomy . . . Very sincerely yours

7 JUNE 1929, LIVERPOOL: DR AM TO MCS . . . You omit to mention in your books re Coit. Interruptus that working class women are sometimes disinclined to give up that method on the ground that they find it so conducive to habits of sobriety in those husbands that use it. Of a series of 100 couples using Birth Control in this practice only 4 have found the Prorace

[i.e. the small cervical cap advocated by MCS] satisfactory. I am, yours truly

10 JUNE 1929, MCS IN REPLY . . . Would you mind telling me more details about the 100 couples who did not find the Pro Race satisfactory? Have they been examined by an expert? How did they start using the Pro Race? What social class are they? What size cap did they use? But the most important thing is, who instructed them and how? If just self instructed I am not surprised because the working classes suffer so tremendously from lacerated cervix and a very large proportion of them would never be advised to use the cap at all by a responsible clinic where the staff knew its job . . . Yours truly

12 JUNE 1929, DR AM IN REPLY. Apparently my reference to 100 couples practising birth control has been slightly misunderstood. These people are chiefly working class and are using various contraceptive methods; but only 11 women used the prorace, 7 discarding it as unsuitable and 4 finding it satisfactory. One woman was over 15 st. and could not use the prorace properly, another was a nullipara who could isolate the os cervici but could not put the cap on herself, another could only put the cap on dome upwards; two women destroyed the prorace as they could only insert it halfway up the vagina; another found the cap came off in coitus and a second cap was found to be so tight it tore on being taken off. The other woman was disappointed on finding the cap tear after coitus . . .

B.B. [a gynaecologist] tells me that a teaspoonful of washing soda in a bottle of Stout was not known to him as an abortifacient. This method is sometimes used successfully by working class women when their contraceptive methods fail. The large majority of these 100 couples preferred to use some form or other of post-coital micturition as a contraceptive usually in association with coit. Interruptus.

24 OCTOBER 1929, HARLEY ST, LONDON: DR NORMAN HAIRE TO MCS . . . I think your reproaches against the medical profession are less justified now than they used to be. There are a great many of us, in this country as well as in other countries,

who are carrying out researches with different contraceptive methods and really doing our very best for our poor patients as well as our rich ones. At one clinic I used to see about 40 women in one afternoon and I worked there three afternoons a week without payment of any sort . . .

26 MAY 1931, NORFOLK: DR DM TO MCS. *Please* have my name struck off the list of those to whom your poisonous literature is sent. I am *ashamed* as a Christian married woman and mother to receive it into our home. You are *not* married and cannot understand. Yours very truly

CHAPTER FIVE

OVERSEAS

Returning from Africa in 1934, Professor B. Malinowski, the distinguished anthropologist, wrote to Marie Stopes that her name was better known among the Chaggas of Swaziland than that of any other British writer. While Malinowski may have exaggerated a little – it is rather difficult to imagine the middle-class nursery values of Radiant Motherhood, *for example, being of much relevance in a mud hut – her name was certainly known all over the world.*

Her fame rested on two factors. The immediate success of Married Love *in 1918, and of* Wise Parenthood *a year later, resulted in a flood of requests for translations. Within a few years* Married Love *was obtainable in fourteen languages other than English, among them Afrikaans, Arabic, Chinese, Czech, Danish and Roumanian – and also in Braille.* Wise Parenthood *appeared in twelve other languages, and* Radiant Motherhood *in eight.*

Also, with the gradual worldwide improvement in education, and in the popular journalism that catered for the newly literate, her cleverly-managed publicity campaigns were widely reported. These brought in further tides of letters particularly from those countries where her books were banned and the sale of birth control devices itself was a criminal offence, as in France. At various times throughout the Twenties, books by Marie Stopes were prohibited in New Zealand, Australia (where the first birth control clinic was not opened until 1933) and Canada where, as late as 1930, an eccentric Toronto lawyer left £500,000 in his will to the woman who had had most babies by 1936.

In America the Comstock Act had from 1873 made it an offence to sell, advertise or mail obscene matter, which included books on sexual technique and contraception. The first American publisher of Married Love, *Dr J. Robinson, was prosecuted and fined, even after having deleted much of what might then have been considered rather daring; and in 1930, judgment went against W. Paul Cook, a student who tried to bring a copy of* Enduring Passion *into the United States. The Customs Court judge found himself 'amazed and shocked at the boldness, yet withal subtle suavity of its language' and was quite satisfied that 'the average young man and woman would experience a certain loss of self-respect after reading its contents'.*

In addition to her books, Marie Stopes frequently wrote articles for foreign journals and newspapers, particularly in India about whose population problems she was, with good reason, most concerned. Many girls were married off at the age of eleven or twelve and started to produce children at puberty. In 1926 it was estimated that half the women in India prolapsed after the first delivery, ninety per cent after the second – largely due to early marriage and inadequate care. Not unnaturally, since he condemned all forms of birth control except abstinence, Marie Stopes developed a passionate distaste for Gandhi, accused him publicly of talking 'complete and arrant nonsense' and of being a 'slave-driver and bully of the most cruel and degraded kind'. Opposition to birth control in India was both religious and political. Rather as some Protestants in Britain were afraid of being numerically outbred by Catholics, Hindus were frightened of a possible Muslim supremacy. In 1935 the Delhi Municipal Committee turned down plans for a birth control clinic on the grounds that, since Muslims were enjoined by their religion to multiply, if Hindus agreed to limit their own growth they would be reduced to a minority, thus losing the political rights they possessed as a majority under the constitution. Letters from educated Indians form by far the largest national group in Marie Stopes's overseas correspondence.

21 JUNE 1919, QUEENSLAND, AUSTRALIA: MR ST TO MCS
... I might as well mention I study and believe in Theosophy – the making known of the hidden sides of Nature and the purpose of life. What I should like to know is: is the semen of

man (which I understand from medical books, 'lives' if left alone for about 24 hours and also has the tendency (consciousness) to rather work up into the vagina instead of dropping out of it) which is life, *sexed*? and is the woman's counterpart sexed also in its entity before being fecundated ... And could you tell me anything about that great secret: a woman's breasts? I take it, it is also the 'seat' of emotions, that some higher sphere works through them ... Your reference to kissing a woman's breasts (in *Married Love*) I think could be extended such a lot! Is the left breast (over the heart) exactly like the right! Would its produce (physically for feeding a baby's body, or superphysically, emotionally) exactly correspond with that of the right breast? And why must there be two and why do they so (on a beautiful body) draw – almost magnetically – something out of loving man that gives him an impulse to give – to caress? ... And you could also tell me how semen first of all gets formed in a human system. This letter will go over 120 miles by coach before reaching train! Yours sincerely

24 JANUARY 1920, MCS IN REPLY. The enclosed printed letter is what most of my correspondents get from me now, but I make an occasional exception ... The semen consists of various secretions, and the many myriad lives of each sperm. Each individual sperm in a healthy man may live as much as ten days, swimming about wherever it likes. The counterpart in woman is the single egg-cell, which lives for 28 days, and dies once each month ... Yours very truly

18 AUGUST 1919, BANGALORE, INDIA: FATHER BM APOSTOLIC MISSIONARY. I am a missionary priest belonging to the Foreign Mission Society of Paris, stationed at Bangalore, India. I have a poor parish where it would seem all miseries are gathered together. A mere enumeration will give you an idea. Besides the work of a large parish, I have to attend two hospitals, besides the Maternity Hospital. The segregation camp for plague, small-pox, cholera and other contagious diseases is in my parish. What an amount of misery I have met with there during the last few years! Moreover, there is the hospital for

the incurable, the lunatic asylum, the leper asylum and the central prison. May I not truly say that all miseries and misfortunes are gathered in my parish?

The chief object which for the present worries me is the future of my poor converts. During the last three or four years I have had about 2,000 conversions. Here are the results for last year:

Heathens baptized	402
Heathens baptized on their deathbed	5
Heathen children baptized at the hour of death	82
Protestant converts	15
	504

(*Not surprisingly, given her low opinion of the Catholic Church, Marie Stopes marked this letter 'No Answer'.*)

18 DECEMBER 1919, LAHORE, INDIA: MR BC TO MCS. I have read your books 'Wise Parenthood' and 'Married Love' with the greatest pleasure and shall be much obliged if you will let me know the following points:

(1) Have you read 'The Answer' by Chidley of Australia? In this book Chidley says a man's penis should not be erect but bent and soft and sucked in by the female in sexual embrace as in animals. The hymen should remain intact as, when a woman is sexually prepared, her vagina will open and close . . .

(2) What is the best position for husband and wife respectively in sexual embrace? On p. 90 'Mar. Love' – 'Men and Woman face to face' etc, does it mean standing?

(3) p. 93 'from ten to 20 minutes of actual physical union – hastiness due to mental ignorance alone can be conquered by persistent exerted will'. Can you tell me how a man can learn to prevent discharge for 20 minutes and what mental exercises are required.

(4) Can the clitoris be seen or can it possibly be absent? I

can see the prepuce in the case of my wife but not the clitoris I do not know why.

(5) I have been away from my wife for many years. She is now about 26. She shows great and unsatisfiable sexual desire. Do you think it is abnormal or it may be all right after some time? ... Yours very truly

14 JANUARY 1920, MCS IN REPLY. Thank you for your letter. I am very pleased to have your appreciation of my books ... No, I have not read 'The Answer' by Chidley. From what you tell me, however, of his views, I do not feel that they are natural for the average man, but I am increasingly coming to the conclusion that human types vary very considerably, and that what is natural in one is not so in another.

This applies also to your second question, namely, what is the best position? A pair must practise every kind of position until they find what suits them best. You have in India a very early old book that discusses this question with more wisdom than any other book I know. The title is: 'The Kama Sutra, or Vatsayana' translated from the Sanscrit, printed for the Hindoo Kama Shastra Society, Benares, 1883.

You will also find in this book the answer to your third question, giving various Indian methods of controlling discharge.

As regards your fourth question, as a rule the clitoris is a small, quite visible object, but this varies very greatly.

In answer to your fifth question, I should imagine that long absence makes your wife feel as though she were having a honeymoon, and that after a few months her desires would tend to decrease ... Yours very truly

13 JULY 1920, DERA ISMAIL KHAN: MR JR TO MCS. I have the honour to inform you that at a very large Public Meeting attended by the Zamindars and respectable citizens of Dera Ismail Khan, it was unanimously resolved to present you with a gold medal and an address for the most valuable services you have rendered to Science.

Will you kindly inform me when it will be convenient for you to receive this humble appreciation from the Public of the side.

Will you like whether the address and the gold medal should be presented by a deputation or by post.

Praying for your long life and increasing prosperity to serve your noble Mission to serve India with your zeal and devotion ... Yours very truely

7 DECEMBER 1920, LAHORE, INDIA: MR BC TO MCS ... I send you the following information:– A man after the first connection and discharge shd drink some milk and honey to restore his strength and without sleeping between the interval shd. have the second connection but shd. withdraw before discharge and wiping his organ dry with a soft cloth shd. go to sleep (undischarged the second time). Thus in 10 days he will acquire the power to hold on in sexual connection as long as he likes.

If a man counts his movements in the sexual intercourse until discharge and the next night does only half the movements and withdraws and every subsequent night adds one movement only to that half he can go on indefinitely prolonging the time he can hold on ... If the man puts either a little honey or a little soap or a little camphor mixed with soap or honey or his salive or a little attar of roses on his organ it gives great pleasure to the wife and she discharges soon ... With best wishes for the New Year, Yours sincerely

10 FEBRUARY 1921, LAHORE, INDIA: MR BC TO MCS ... Perhaps you will be interested to know that all doctors of the East say that shaving off the hair under the pit of the stomach and round about the sexual organ strengthens the sexual organ and increases sexual power as the blood-supply of the hair is absorbed in their stead by the organ when they are shaved off. They say that if a man will shave off the hair frequently the sexual organ will fatten and will become larger ... What is your opinion? I enclose stamped addressed envelope. Yours sincerely

1 APRIL 1921, PERSIAN GULF: MISS NB TO MCS. As I am given to understand that you are Authoress of many a books on

Matrimonial life, I intend to have some and as I am not in a position to afford to buy them, I beg of you kindly as a charity to favour me with same. I do not want the new ones, but all worn out will quite suffice. Should you like to have them back, I guarantee I would return them after perusal. I would not have asked you this favour if my maids have not told me about these books. I am engaged and my marriage will take place next September and hope fully by your renowned books I would be able to derive excellent benefit. I entirely leave the choice of choosing and sending the books to you as you are well acquainted. In conclusion, I shall be ever grateful to you and wishing you every success in all your endeavours. I beg to remain, Your deserving student

26 APRIL 1921, NAGPUR, INDIA: DR MD TO MCS ... My work here in India lies amongst the working classes and as abysmal poverty makes a continual appeal for curtailing the family and yet we seem to have no definite line of action. I am trying to start infant welfare work here in this city But I feel we dont want to much to reduce the Infant Mortality as to cut down the Birth rate – do some weeding. I have read your book Wise Parenthood – but I am wondering how can I put the means you advise at the disposal of these over-simple-minded, ignorant, poverty stricken people of this city – Yours sincerely

14 JULY 1921, BOMBAY: MR CD TO MCS ... I bought your book 'Truth About Venereal Disease' expecting it would at last tell me how such disease first came into being, what vice or violation of law was responsible for Syphilis and what Gonorrhea ... Such words as promiscuity, impurity, filth, beastliness, vice, ignorance etc as occur in your book do not enable me to understand what led to the appearance of gonorrhea and what to the appearance of Syphilis. I want to know whether Sodomy and intercourse with animals led to Gonorrhea or not, if not, what were its results. The prudery of medical writers makes them start with the mere fact that Syphilis and Gonorrhoea exist, and in general terms they condemn pros-

titution, promiscuity etc., but not a word to enlighten us on the above points. Can you favour an earnest student of religious philosophy with all the information you have on these points. Yours faithfully

8 MARCH 1922, ST PAUL, FRANCE: MR CM TO MCS. (*In 1920, alarmed by a falling birth-rate and the loss of so many men in the First World War, the French government passed laws making it a criminal offence to sell, advertise, or recommend birth control devices. The birth-rate went on falling, but the number of abortions rose. Monsieur M's suggestion here, of a 'baby farm', while prefiguring Nazi experiments, was at least novel. Marie Stopes replied conventionally, refusing to comment on his central idea.*) Well, I just read your book MARRIED LOVE and I can only sum up my feelings by saying that, as most Frenchmen, I thought I knew something about LOVE, and I realized – going through said book – that I *knew* nothing about it.

... Many propositions such as 'SCIENTIFIC MOTHER-HOOD' have been shown as necessary to raise our birth rate, better the race and, last but not least, give two millions of unmarried young French women the benefits of motherhood. Yet, none of these propositions has had any chance of being accepted by our Government, as none of them was economically possible. And there is the superiority of my scheme whose title COOPERATIVES MATRIARCALES shows all the program, i.e. an industry of any kind, let us say for instance a 'poultry farm', in which every member will be a woman between 20 and 30. Said members will receive shares of the business, and so become proprietors of it, every time they have a child, born in certain eugenic conditions. Every year, the capital invested will be amortized by means of profits, and after a few years the young women will entirely own the business and will live a happy life with healthy children, *without any cost to the State*.

I am looking for a patron to help me start the first cooperative, and once the proof is made that the scheme is sound economically, our Government will have to adopt it unless the race wants to commit suicide ... In any case, I am at your entire disposal to give my opinion on any point regarding man's feelings and experiences ... Yours respectuously

24 MARCH 1922, BRITISH WEST INDIES: MISS VR TO MCS. (*Miss R., age twenty-nine, a graduate of Sydney University, has had a vaginal discharge since the age of seventeen. It has defied all treatment – or even diagnosis – and she has now developed acute rheumatism, her hair has fallen out, and she is permanently ill. She hopes to marry later that year.*) ... A few weeks ago I ordered your books from London. My people disapproved very much, my mother said I shouldn't 'upset my mind with such things'. You must know that she has always forbidden us to ask questions on sex, and we have received no instruction of any kind – not even in Hygiene. Of course, when I woke up to things I lost no time in getting every bit of information that I could on the subject but I was 23 before I even heard of masturbation or of Venereal Disease ... In August last year I went to Bermuda. I had broken down at the end of term and remained in a state of appalling weakness for a month. Finally I saw a doctor and spoke to him about the rheumatism and he asked me if there was any vaginal discharge. I had grown tired of mentioning it especially as my doctor down here refused to take any notice. The Bermuda man took a specimen but when I asked for the result of the analysis said he'd rather not say ...

Since then I have felt very much worse and as if some change has occurred. The menses – after years of regularity – have become later and later and now are very clotted – I have a continual headache and a burning sensation over the region of the uterus – In addition the Rheumatism has now spread to the 'tailbone' and hips.

Last week I read your book on Venereal Diseases – and for the first time in my life heard that rheumatism could be the result of gonorrhea!

On Saturday I went to the doctor and demanded the analysis of the discharge – he said there were gonococci and 'plenty of them' – *and he has known for six months* and the Bermuda man knew and I have been infected all these years, and *never knew* – never dreamt such a thing possible . . .

You – above all others – can imagine what the news has been – I have looked forward to marriage all my life, I have craved for children all my life, I have tried to perfect myself physically and mentally for an ideal marriage.

I have a beautiful body – slight but perfectly formed – and I have always taken the greatest care of it – and once I had a superb vitality, once I had splendid gifts – and now . . . I have always been called a 'crank' because of my fastidiousness in washing and dressing. Yet as a child I knew nothing about the dangers in lavatories, in the use of towels etc . . . . I have moved about continually from chalet to boarding-house on train and steamer. On this island Venereal Disease is as common as a head-ache and children of all ages contract it – innocently – from nurses and servants or from one another. Nobody seems to mind . . . and now I am worried about my fiancé. You see I do not know that I have already infected him – could it be possible? Or – no – we have only kissed and loved a great deal – there has been nothing more but he has used my towels and basins. I have sent him to a doctor for a test and examination the doctor sent him to a bacteriologist here who says as there are no symptoms he can make no tests – and that blood and urine test are useless. Doctor, Can you spare a few minutes to advise me where to go in New York. I cannot risk inferior treatment or second-rate advice. I *must* be cured I am determined to fight this thing . . .

I am enclosing a snap each of my fiancé and myself – please don't think it foolish of me – as I said you inspire things of that kind. I am not always so ignorant and careless as I must appear in my letter – I am utterly tired and weak – and now I am beset by a horrible fear – Doctor, I *must* have my children – I want them for myself and I want them for my husband. Please forgive my writing, but out of the great heart and soul you seem to possess, help me if you can. Yours, with every confidence

12 APRIL 1922, MCS IN REPLY. Your letter is very pitiful

because I fear I can only have what you will consider bad news. Gonorrhoea such as you describe is practically incurable. You had better face it and get this grief over. It would be wrong of you to marry; it would be wrong of you to try to have children. The doctors may mitigate your symptoms but an absolutely reliable cure is almost certainly impossible . . . From what you describe it is certain that you acquired it quite innocently, probably from a school lavatory, the seats of which are very dangerous and have been the cause of many wrecked lives. If your infection had been caught at once, you might have been cured, but as it is of such long standing and from the symptoms you tell me, it will have penetrated beyond reach. You should never have physical connection with your fiancé; you should not think of a physical marriage, although there is no reason why you should not love him deeply and preferably give him up to another woman, which is the pinnacle of love under such circumstances . . .

All the love which you feel for children and for humanity you must now divert from selfish personal aims. Only when such a Society as ours is strong enough to combat treacherous opposition and the cloak of silence and the opposition of dirty minds such as you describe will the world be safe for children. I hope therefore that you will join our Society and try to make it something of a life work to fill the void which I fear you must find in your own private life. With every sympathy and good wish, Yours sincerely

16 JUNE 1922, BRITISH EAST AFRICA: MRS RC TO MCS. I am Australian born and at the age of 21 married a Frenchman. I thought I knew most things but soon discovered I knew nothing. For three weeks after my marriage I refused to allow my husband to touch me because of the awful pain it caused me, although several times I tried hard to stand the pain, but I could not. Finally I went to a doctor and told him; he examined me and said I was very small and that the internal membranes were extra sensitive. He gave me a cocaine and vaseline ointment to use for one hour before the act was to take place. With

the help of this I succeeded and had to use it for about two months ... I may say that never once in the whole of my married life did he once try to rouse me or once satisfy me. Before I go further I must confess to a rather terrible habit, which may help you to understand. Since I was a tiny child I had got into the habit of touching the Clitoris until a climax came and of course I liked it. My mother pointed out to me that I was committing a dreadful sin, but never told me why, or that it might affect my health. As I grew older I forced myself to stop it and I don't suppose such a thing happened more than twice a year. When I had found the husband enjoyed sexual connection, and fell dead asleep the next minute, I got tired of it and once told him what I had done as a girl. He replied that it was a dreadful thing to have done, and then one night when the act had been completed and for once had I suppose felt the need more than usual of the climax, I asked him to satisfy me, and he refused, so in desperation I commenced to do it myself. He caught me, flung my hand away from me and became very angry indeed ... through various causes my life became so unbearable with the husband that I left him and for three and a half years now I have earned my living and kept myself and my baby in this climate and, of course, now comes the tragedy of the whole thing. Another man has given me his love and I have given him mine ... He loves me and he knows that for some reason I cannot give myself to him as an ordinary woman should. I am 30 now, and now my desires are fully awake, he knows it and he does every mortal thing that a lover can do or think of to make me have a complete orgasm, but his disappointment and mine is this: I am awake, I want him, I am normally flushed, and moist, every fibre of me is just aching for the intimacy of the embrace, and all goes well until he enters me, and then, with all that, no natural movement or prolonged connection has the power to satisfy me inside ... I want to have it naturally and I cannot, I want the pleasure internally working up to the climax without artificial stimulation all the time, and I cannot.

He assures me he is normal, and I have no reason to disbelieve it, but I have tried to explain to him my married life, and the size of my husband's sexual organ, from which he has told me that the man is badly deformed. Perhaps you will understand the size when I tell you that the husband has never been able to put on a sheath without breaking it, no size being large or long enough being possible to buy ... I have even asked doctors, who promptly look at the other end of the room and say that it is perfectly natural that I should have no pleasure at all in the sexual act. What can I do, or how can I be cured, so that I can have sexual union happily and naturally with the man who loves me and whom I love?

11 JULY 1922, MCS IN REPLY ... I am really awfully sorry that I cannot help at such a distance, and knowing so little of your circumstances. Keep a brave heart, and do what is right, and perhaps your luck will change ...

6 SEPTEMBER 1922, WELLINGTON, NEW ZEALAND: MRS MN TO MCS. I saw the enclosed advertisement in the London 'Observer' of 23rd July and I shall be grateful if you can give me some of the helpful information ... sound practical advice on Birth Control in New Zealand would be warmly welcomed by most practical women. I know a woman 46 years of age, a dairy farmer's wife (I may mention that *he* is a German born) she is the mother of 17 children, she gets up at 3.30 a.m. and has to go to the cow shed and assist to *handmilk* 90 cows – then there is breakfast, housework, babies, most of them weakly and weedy, the older children are wild and void of morals – there is dinner to attend to, various outside duties that must be done, then several more hours of milking, then more meals to provide and after putting children to bed and washing up dishes she has the rest of the day to herself! ... Yours truly

11 DECEMBER 1922, SASKATCHEWAN, CANADA: MR AND MRS LR TO MCS. Your book *Wise Parenthood* was recently purchased by us and read with much enjoyment ... Here in Canada you can go into almost any bookstore and buy half a dozen books by different authors called 'Marriage Guides'.

They are in many cases written by cranks or abnormal people who picture things and advise ways that are absolutely impractical for ordinary people. For instance we have one of these books in our library which says intercourse should never be indulged in except to cause pregnancy, and that this should occur only once at about periods of about 3 years apart . . . Sincerely yours

20 APRIL 1923, DAVOS, SWITZERLAND: DR NW TO MCS . . . I have lately been consulted by a lady who has been doing the 'Cure' here during three winters for Tuberculosis of the Lungs. The disease is now adjudged to be closed and arrested, and she is ordered to live a normal but naturally a careful life. She is not allowed to have children. She is a lady of very highly developed sensibilities and for whom aestheticism or the contrary in the sexual side of her married life play a most important part.

The lady tells me that she has used a kind of sheath which has to be smeared with some micro-organism killing ointment, and introduced with forceps, it has to be removed immediately after intercourse and an irrigator used. She says that the process is so disgusting and unaesthetic that it takes all desire from her. She will not show me this sheath . . . She is rather a difficult person to question, and of course the subject is a very delicate one, but she also gives me the idea that she suffers from a very natural aversion to the express adjustment of an appliance *for the occasion*. The adjustment process seems to offend her in that it points out too brutally the clayey side of sexual desire. She would like that act to be the unpremeditated and unarranged-for culmination of a mutual flow of affection between herself and her husband . . . Very truly yours

6 JULY 1923, OUDH, INDIA: MR SPG TO MCS. I am very glad to receive your letter of the 30th May. It is really creditable on your part that you have spared no pains in seeking after Indian knowledge of this question for dealing on your subject to its utmost limit. For the last 7 or 8 years I am also working

secretly on the same lines. I have spent a lot of my time, energy and money in this research. Ultimately my efforts have been successful in possessing almost complete knowledge on personal union. But now I realize that my labour cannot bear fruit in this country. I am too famous so much so that among the distinguished and standard humourous writers I am placed on the top . . . Under such circumstances I tremble to publish a single line on sexual intercourse as it will at once drag me down into the mire of public redicule and contempt. I will be contemptuously pointed out as a notorious debouche. The more a man is famous the more he dreads the public redicule . . .

As regards the Indian works on the subject which you want to know . . . for practical use the 'Kok Shastra' by Pandit Koka is the best, because it has been written by a practical man, who wrote it after spending Rs. 30,000,000/- in debouchery. This work is written in Sanscrit poem and in figurative language, for the benifit of mankind and increasing conjugal happiness. But during the Mohamadan reign it fell into misuse. The licentious princes coveted this work most and used to purchase hand written copies of its Urdu translation for thousands of rupees. Since then the work became strictly secret for the sake of its value. But by its association with the licentious men its very name became horror to the ordinary public . . . The artists of Jaipur Rajputan somehow got that portion of it which contained the postures of intercourse and they drew pictures according to them and sold them at fancy prices. The original work contained only 21 postures, the Urdu translators made them 36, while the artists of Jaipur made them 84, combining the impossible with possible ones, simply to make money . . . Yours very truely

21 FEBRUARY 1924, VICTORIA, AUSTRALIA: MISS NO TO MCS. After many hours of thought I am writing to you for advice . . . It seems a hard and terrible confession for me to have to make; about the age of 14 I was friendly with a girl who showed me what I now know to be called self-abuse, I was a lonely child brought up in ignorance of those facts so

necessary to life, I regret to say this got a hold on me . . . when I got to the age of 19 I was told in an indirect manner, a certain amount of what happened between man and woman, it was then I began to realize what I was doing could not be right, and for nearly 12 months left myself alone, but during the next 12 months gave way again but only very rarely, and then came the hardest part, I met the first man and last in my life, one who loves me dearly, and I love in return, from that day for 2 years now I have left myself alone . . . A few months ago I read in a medical book that abuse unfitted the adult for married life, from then on my life has been one constant worry to me . . . I ask you Doctor, should I marry him? Would the necessary passion as explained in your book come to me? I must explain that in no ways do I feel cold towards my boy, when alone with him I feel, well the only way I can explain is, passionate and easily stirred. The only effects I notice are, dreaming once or twice a month and the nerve in the vagina getting on edge and constantly worrying me, accompanied with a weak feeling, tired, or in Australian 'Dopey' . . . Yours sincerely

24 MARCH 1924, NEW ZEALAND: CUSTOMS DEPART-MENT TO THE HON SEC CBC. Sir, Adverting to my letter No 24/43/21 of 7th Feb, 1923, with respect to the admission to New Zealand of the book entitled 'Wise Parenthood' by Dr Marie Stopes, I have to inform you that the matter has again been under consideration and it has been decided that this book is in future to be regarded as an indecent document within the meaning of the Indecent Publications Act, 1910. The import-ation of this publication will therefore in future not be permit-ted. I have the honour to be, Sir, Your most obedient servant

26 JUNE 1924, SINGAPORE: MR GAH TO MCS. My wife and I have read all your books and I have just completed 'Con-traception', 1923. *Please* help us if you can – You may consider we are fools to require help at our age. I am 51 and my wife is 46. We have been married 20 years. We had one child in the first year and have dared not have any since. Until 1920 I

served in the NE frontier of Burma, children would have meant the continual separation of myself and my wife and the upkeep of two homes ... Moreover the first child caused my wife so much suffering ending in a journey to England and an operation for prolapsus which crippled us financially for years. As a result of all this I have had no proper connection with my wife for 18 years and it has been positive *hell*. We have practised all manner of ways of satisfying each other but none of them we felt did us good ... My wife is healthy and strong and I, though appallingly thin, am very fit and must be wiry for I can follow the hounds on foot and have of recent years walked down men many years younger than myself. My wife and I are everything to each other. She is the best woman in the world and we both several times a month ardently desire connection but, for me, I lose all satisfaction once the sheath is donned ... would it be possible for me to undergo Vasectomy? Yours very truly

24 AUGUST 1924, VICTORIA, AUSTRALIA: MRS BT TO MCS. Please don't think it impertinent of me to write to you but I have read some of your books, *Married Love*, *Wise Parenthood* and *Contraception*, and I think you are the one person in the world to advise me.

My husband and I were in love with one another for years but owing to the fact that he went to the war and also has had to provide for his mother and I for mine we were not able to marry until May, 1922, when we were both aged 35 years. Even then we were not well enough off to afford to have a child besides which I was worn out with teaching music. So we carried out the instructions in your book, *Married Love*. In six months time our circumstances improved and now we are well able to provide for a child and we are just longing for one. I was examined by a Melbourne doctor who told me I was perfectly healthy and there was no reason why I shouldn't have a baby but when he heard that I had 'interfered with nature' as he called it, he said what else could I expect ... Yours sincerely

9 JANUARY 1925, PENANG, STRAIT SETTLEMENTS: DR VRS TO MCS ... While admitting that the particular method of control of conception recommended by you is the least objectionable one now available, I have to make the following observations in addition to those set out in my last letter: the female copulative organ is one of the most, if not the most, sensitive one intended primarily to give the most exciting sensation during the penetration of no other foreign matter but the male copulative organ. There are, of course, malpractices such as masturbation etc now prevalent among debased human beings and these abnormalities we must leave out of consideration. Now, if a foreign matter like the finger and the rubber caps enters the vagina every now and then, would not the highly sensitive tissues of the vaginal walls lose their pleasure giving sensation, which is a desideratum in the normal act of coition?

Had I sufficient training and material I would gladly devote my time in devising some means of preventing undesired conception, without the necessity of inserting the fingers often and often ... It is my ardent wish to give to humanity the benefit of my knowledge, imperfect though it might be, ere I am called upon to my last destination ... I am, Dear Doctor, Yours truly

23 FEBRUARY 1925, SINGAPORE: MR HTZ TO MCS. *This letter was headed* Re the Re-birth of King Solomon's Knowledge. *It read:* Further to my letter of the 19th November last I beg to inform you that after further consideration, in loving memory of my wife, I have resolved to give the above knowledge to the people of the British Empire, the Dominions, the Protectorates and the Federated Malay State, but I reserve my rights for the other nations.

I know for certain by giving this knowledge to them there will be more happy married life and more happy homes. Will you kindly submit my resolution to the proper authorities? Thanking you in anticipation, I remain, Yours sincerely

DIRECTIONS

Make the woman lie in the dorsal position and insert your penis into the vagina. Both parties then turn to their sides facing each other with your left arm under her right arm and her right arm around your neck and after assuming this position jerk your penis in such a way as to knock the Anterior wall of the vagina once every few seconds without oscillation of the penis; at the first touch of the glans of your penis on the Anterior wall of the vagina, her pupils will dilate with eyes opened wide and fixed, expression vacant and at every subsequent touch she will wriggle, then ask her to take the position of a man in the act of Coitus because she will be more comfortable. Repeat the knocks or tapping of the wall half a dozen times at an interval of a few seconds between each, then stop and see whether she will continue doing the act of Coitus without any effort from you. If she does then you remain quiet and allow her to continue wriggling until her passion is satisfied, if not repeat the knocking until she does and you will be surprised to learn that there will be no emission of your semen although she has satisfied herself. If the woman be very passionate you can easily satisfy her twice in a night or even more without emission of your semen or weakening consequence Less emission of semen means less loss of vigour and lengthening of a man's life.

(*MCS marked this 'No answer'.*)

5 APRIL 1925, UNIVERSITY OF LENINGRAD, USSR: PRO-FESSOR PL TO MCS. Being a member of Committee of Russian Eugenical Society and specially interested in the questions of birth control, I will deeply appreciate your printed or written information on this topic. Particularly, I will be much indebted for the description of methods and statistics of Mothers Clinic, maintained by your Society. Anti-conceptive measures in Russia are now officially recommended instead of free abortion, as it was before. Does Society sometimes make recomendations for the abortion on eugenical indications or not, exist or not any statistics on the frequency of miscarriages and abortions in England and which are judicial decisions in such cases. I remain yours very truly

25 MAY 1925, OHIO, USA: MR WR TO MCS . . . I hardly know how to tell you what I want but *please* believe that I need your help most dreadfully, in fact I have thought of suicide several times if I cannot get help from some source . . . I have had a very bad habit of masturbation ever since I was thirteen years old I am twenty one now. I am depressed and gloomy most of the time and don't seem to be able to get anything accomplished as my physical endurance is very poor. I seem to have no patience with anything. My nerves are in a very bad condition although not so bad as they were . . .

Some other things worrying me are that I have a hairsute growth clear up to the head of my penace which embarrasses me and makes it difficult for me to use a certain kind of preventative. The skin on the underside of my pinace is full of little hard bags of some secretion. What are those and what is the cure? It seems to be in the tendon under the head. Also there is a soreness around the head where I was circumcised last summer. When I masturbate or have intercourse these two places hurt me. What can be done for veneral warts Dr Stopes? I have had some small ones around the head of the penace for a couple years. How do you get them? That may seem a foolish question but I've just found out what they were lately. I don't ejaculate but little sperm tell me what to do to rejuvenate myself.

Please do not answer with a cooly formal letter Dr Stopes as I most fervently want you for a friend and confidential adviser I have all the confidence in the world in you . . . Yours very truly

23 JUNE 1925, PORT-OF-SPAIN, TRINIDAD: MR GWA TO MCS. I very humbly beg to write this letter to you and I am sure it will come as a pleasant surprise to you from so far away from England . . . We have nobody near to us in England now save some aged folk in Berkshire, and household articles in the matter of linen are difficult to obtain out here, owing to the very prohibitive prices put on them. We understand that it is not good manners to write to any distinguish person enclosing

a few coppers and asking 'Please buy such and such for us' that rather it is better form to beg outright. This being so, dear Doctore Marie, Could you do us the favour of sending us a good strong white linen sheet a couple of pillow cases not necessarily new? My wife is in a very poor way for underwear. I do not want to name the things. I'd rather she did herself for modesty is my motto, but she says I am a better writer, but I will stand my ground I won't write I will sketch [*here Mr A has drawn a pair of frilly knickers and a petticoat*] and any other old things that can be spared ... I remain Yours faithfully, an ex-soldier

11 AUGUST 1925, TRANSVAAL, SOUTH AFRICA: MRS LD TO MCS. Having read many of your articles on birth control, I wonder if you would be so kind as to tell me just a few particulars about that subject. I have been married 20 years or practically so, and in that time I have had 12 children. I know it sounds disgusting but, as I did not know of any prevention or help, I just had to go through with it every time. I don't mind having children but I just can't keep them and for the last years my husband has been afflicted with that dread disease – miner's phthisis, contracted through working underground in a gold mine. My last two children are puny little things, always ailing, and now I am told it is part of their father's disease which they have inherited from him. Miner's phthisis I may add is a form of consumption. so is it any wonder I dread bringing any more of these sickly little things into the world, and that dread is very real as I am only 35 years of age. I enclose stamped addressed envelope, so if you will be so kind to help me, I shall be forever, gratefully yours,

21 JANUARY 1926, MADRAS, INDIA: MR CSN TO MCS ... I am only a medical man of the Ancient Indian Medical Mystical Science. I have not read anything of the modern literature on the subject as I could not get any in my parts of the country nor could I abide to purchase all the publications in the line at the present. If you want the medicine I have to manufacture

and give. It is a very highly successful one, which I say after personal experience of mine for the last twenty years. In all the ways with perfect safety we can use the same. Can you give me the address of Mrs Margaret Sanger who has browbeat Mahatma Gandhi, who simply weaps over the subject without giving a practical solution, by her criticism and oblige. Soliciting for all the literature on the subject and an early reply, I remain, Madam, Yours faithfully

27 FEBRUARY 1926, MCS IN REPLY ... If you have any such drug as you mention and will tell me openly its name or send me a sample specimen, I will place it before our scientific research committee and have your claims investigated. You may be sure they will be very interested and assist you to publish the results openly, but for us you must understand it is not a good business matter at all as we have no interest whatever in the sale of such things, and I do not approve of helping any person who keeps such knowledge secret. Yours very truly

23 JANUARY 1926, BRITISH COLUMBIA: MR PS TO MCS ... It may interest you to know that in a Town of 1500 to 2000 people out here there is just one copy of your book 'Married Love'. It belongs to a lady friend of mine from Lancashire, and perhaps because of the vast number of paltry people around, she keeps your book in a brown paper cover marked outside 'The Way of an Eagle' and underneath this inscription large query mark. Funny! If the circumstances didn't bring tears ... Yours very truly

FEBRUARY 1926, CANADA: MRS AD TO MCS. I am English and am 25 yrs old. I am a married woman with 2 little ones, aged 3 and 4 years. I am a farmer's wife at least I should say a farm labourer's wife. We live 17 miles from a small town on the flat Prairie. I have been out in Canada 6 yrs only. I was a War Bride, my husband being a Canadian soldier ... I have been troubled with a lot of illnesses out here and I firmly believe that if I could have got advise from someone, I should have been saved from what I am now.

Well Dear Dr Stopes, the first year I was married I had 3 miscarrigges, each at 6 weeks–2 months. After the 3rd one I had to have an operation to set me right. Then I had my girl the next year, and the Boy a year after. When he was $1\frac{1}{2}$ yrs old I had another miscarrige and another operation. The following year I had another boy. He was born 8 months after my 2nd operation and he only lived 11 days fortunately. I went one year free from such things and again this last November I had the misfortune to have another miscarrige and had to go under another operation. Up to now I hope and trust I am alright, but I am almost worn out with worry and sickness. I only weigh 105 lbs and am so awfully thin. Sometimes I wish I were dead ... This last time I ask the Doctor to find out the cause of my trouble and he told me it was just some Local trouble. I ask him if he could not give me some instruction in Birth Control. He told me there was nothing he could tell me ...

I was all alone last year when my baby was born. Oh! Dr Stopes you have no idea how miserable and dejected I feel ... The doctors out here charge big fees, also the Hospitals and nurses. For a Maternity Case a Doctor will charge at least 40 dollars and a day nurse 3 dollars day. We are poor working people and my annual illnesses keep us poor. My husband is good to me, but just does not understand things. He asked me to write this in the hope that you could help us a little. The Doctors won't help as it does not pay them to do so! ... I shall be anxiously waiting to hear from you, Thanking you, I Remain, Yours Very Truly

20 FEBRUARY 1926, CHICAGO: MR JA MCL TO MCS. I have just finished reading (for the third time) your book entitled *Contraception* and considered the job incomplete without complimenting you on it. I must needs be discreet in my writing since this letter must pass through the U.S. Post Office with your name, and all that it means to what you very appropriately term the prudes. I think they are the hang-overs from puritanism. (They came to America to get freedom – and deny it to everybody else – Lloyd George.)

You deal with the cause – leaving the effect to be dealt with by the Salvation Army and other forms of humbugry. It would be comical were it not deplorable that any member of the C3 element that one might pick at random can give one mathematically accurate directions on how to go to Heaven . . . but know not the most rudimentary facts of their own miserable anatomy.

I had the copy bootlegged (smuggled) in from a publishing firm on the Pacific Coast. It cost me £3 4s 6d, but it would be cheap at twice the price. Trusting that you will be amply rewarded materially for your very worthy efforts, I remain very respectfully

16 MARCH 1926, MCS IN REPLY . . . I am extremely shocked and horrified that you should have to pay over £3 for it, its proper price is 12/6 which is less than three dollars. Do not imagine that I get any more because the public is made to pay a preposterously high price as you did. I get only a small royalty and it all goes to the firm who flourish and profiteer because of the repression and abominable effects of the American Comstock Laws; It is indeed deplorable for America . . . Yours faithfully

MARCH 1926, NEW ZEALAND: MRS WJB TO MCS. Would you be good enough to tell me your method of birth control, I ask more for the sake of other women less fortunate than myself. I have three living well grown loving daughters and have always had a reasonable rest between, thanks due entirely to my husband who never dreams of worrying me more than once or perhaps twice in a month . . .

I read your notes with interest in 'John Bull' and feel you are doing great work and would so love to help others here who seem to have the heavy end of the stick – I agree with you in saying the labouring class of man, has less consideration for his wife, than a better informed man and trust we shall soon have less, but better babies, the darlings should be blessed – In this country if a farmer's mare has a foal she is turned out to rear it in idleness, if his cow or sheep has a baby, it is given every chance to be a good one, but if his wife has a child in ten days or even less (evidently that absolute minimum time allowed to weakness) she does her own housework, milks perhaps ten cows night and morning, feeds calves, pigs, hens etc and suckles her baby. I would so much rather be a cow than an ordinary farmer's wife in New Zealand ... Thanking you for your great help to women. Yours sincerely

3 MARCH 1926, VICTORIA, AUSTRALIA: MR RF TO MCS ... I have only been married six years and have five children, and as I know of no positive preventive, the next few years seem to hold forth nothing to me but the prospect of a child a year. Had I unlimited income neither my wife nor I would mind but this is not the case. I enquired at a hospital where my wife was last confined and told the number of children I have and the time I had been married, and asked if they could advise me how to avoid further children. The answer was 'As long as a couple are young, strong and healthy, as you are, it is only right for them to have a large family.' This, you will agree, is not fair to the working class, when the moneyed people can pay a large sum and get any information they require ... Yours truly

6 APRIL 1926, STANTHORPE, AUSTRALIA: MRS MA TO MCS ... I was married in 1920 to a returned soldier to whom I was engaged before the war and whose record in the field is such as may be expected from a son of the Empire. He enlisted as a private, and returned, after 4½ years, decorated for gallantry and a Captain ... In less than five and a half years we found ourselves with 5 children ... In this mere 'spot' on the map of Australia, there is no doctor who can or will help me with the rubber caps you mention, and somehow I am unable to adjust those I have purchased in the city 500 miles away ... Yours faithfully

19 MAY 1926, AMRITSAR, INDIA: MR DKA TO MCS. I beg to be excused for taking the liberty of writing to you without acquaintance but as the subject of this letter concerns your

noble mission in life of which you are a world-wide leader and pioneer I dont mind doing so. Your welcome letter in the Times of India of the 12th May, 1926, has much encouraged me to write to you directly . . .

At the outset I would like to tell you that I am a married man of 34 years having 4 living children. Merchant, Banker and Landlard of both Bombay and Amritsar and quite well off, having nothing to grumble.

I am very much interested in the Birth control movement and feel that the salvation of mankind lies in its adoption. I very acutely realize that all the misery, pain, indebtedness, gloominess, sickness, ignorance, dirt, prostitution, war, litigation, underfeeding, poverty, child mortality, heartburning, misunderstanding etc are directly traceable to overbreeding.

The situation in India especially in the urban middle classes is getting intolerable, as you know this country of Hallowed Antiquity and Hoary Wisdom is very much caste ridden, custom ridden and priest ridden; so much so that it is a common sight to see a begger woman carrying 3, 4 childern in the street.

Where exists a greater and narrower religious prejudice and ignorance than here? It is needless to say that the people here are very much fatalist and are somewhat indifferent to the theory of cause and effect and the desirability of quality over quantity. Economic struggle is very acute, it being impossible for India to remain isolated from the world competition and factors. There is so much poverty and ignorance. Any how I am determined to do something and like to see birth control movement started in the Punjab. Am much cheered up with the prospect of your pamphlets and methods suitable for Indian condition . . . With Kind Greeting, Yours Truly

20 MAY 1926, NAGPUR, INDIA: MR VM TO MCS. I was very much interested in your letter, which was published in the Times of India, Bombay . . . In India girls are generally married at 11 to 14 among educated people, but in the labouring classes the marriage takes place even at 5. An average Indian

girl attains her puberty at 12 to 13. As soon as she attains her puberty she is thought quite fit to carry the burdens and res-ponsibility of a married life and she is rather forced to sleep in the room of her husband. It is thought a sin to keep a girl, who has attained puberty, away from her husband ... Thus as a natural course you may see thousands of girls of 13 to 14 bearing children, hardly knowing how to take their proper care ...

One of the chief causes why even the educated people do not resort to artificial methods of birth control is that Indian people are by nature very conservative and orthodox. They think it is a sin to kill the life-giving germs. This is because they do not know that nature itself kills thousands of these germs in its natural process. The other cause is that your methods of birth control, though very simple and effective, seem to these orth-odox people as uncomfortable and the womenfolk at the outset refuse to use them because they do not know how to fit them ... Yours sincerely

14 JUNE 1926, CONCORD, USA: MR BCD TO MCS ... we have been married now long enough (nine years) for the experiences of sex-union to settle down somewhat into a familiar method of procedure ... I had not known until I read your book that, for example, there was more than one position for coitus, that in which the husband is above his wife when he embraces her ... May I ask one other question? Can you tell me whether men and women usually experience these unions unencum-bered with clothes, in what seems to be the natural and most delightful condition, or whether it is customary for women (and men) to retain some of their night garments because of the instinct of modesty? I have a very strong, instinctive desire that there be no clothing at all, but some vestige of modesty in my wife impels her to retain her nightgown. Is such modesty normal? Or might I hope to overcome it?

14 JUNE 1926, MCS IN REPLY ... As regards your shorter and easier question about modesty, I think it is customary with most women to retain some sort of night garment, although I

think you are right in desiring complete freedom from clothing. Mostly it depends on the temperature, and I think in this country, where houses are not warmed, most people really need to keep night clothing on, but in your country, where you have central heating, that very mundane consideration does not come in, and there is no doubt that the ideal condition is complete nudity between the embracing pair. I think you may woo your wife to overcome her shrinking from it . . . Yours sincerely

26 AUGUST 1926, DELHI, INDIA: MR AHM TO MCS . . . Out in the West fortunately the sex problems are being more and more recognized – as basic, a solution of which only can lead to the lessening of divorces, happier matrimony, and strong home ties – the essential of virulent Nationhood. The Old time prudish ignorance of vital facts and questions and the taboo on vital organs is being surely though slowly raise.

Out in the East, however, conditions on the question are even more backward than what they were in Europe 500 years ago, so much so that the average woman may not eat at the same table with the husband, speak lovingly of her mate in the hearing of her older in-laws, or let the lady doctor examine her with female instruments. The use of cleansing aparatuses is the height of immorality and to be condemned . . . I shall be happy if you would be graciously pleased to allow me to collaborate with you by translating and publishing in Urdu only two of your wonderful books for the present: Married Love and Wise Parenthood; by communicating your assent at an early date you would be laying obligation on me, my community, my nation, my country the literature of my people and your own sex born and bred in this benighted land. I remain, dear Madam, An admirer of your great philanthropic works

22 OCTOBER 1926, BOMBAY: MR RDB TO MCS. Sweet doctor, I have the pleasure of having all your works on one of the shelves of my humble library. Shall I also have the pleasure of possessing your picture with these valuable works? Hoping

to be excused for wasting your precious time. Yours ever
sincerely

28 JANUARY 1928, NEW SOUTH WALES, AUSTRALIA: MR
TAA TO MCS. I have been reading your book entitled, *Wise
Parenthood*. You mentioned you would be willing to hear of
any feasable means to prevent conception for reasonable purposes.

You may not have noticed the method used by natives of the
arid part of this continent. They limited population on account
of the scarcity of food; perhaps not an original motive. Their
method is to make an insertion in the male organ, underneath,
near junction with the body. This cut is healed much the same
as perforation for ear-ring. They can fulfill all obligations except
propagate; as the seed is passed out at the perforation. We call
them whistle-cocks.

Their method must be a success, or else they would not have
practised it for many centuries. What is to stop an experiment
among civilization? . . . Yours

16 FEBRUARY 1928, HARIHARPUR, INDIA: DR FP TO H. V.
ROE. I beg to inform you of the following facts with a view to
ascertain any reasons you may be pleased to suggest:

I have been using the combination of three methods at a
time prescribed by Mrs Marie Carmichael Stopes, D.Sc.,
Ph.D., for birth control for the last few months. According to
instructions, my wife uses Pro-Race Check Pessary (solid rim).
Before fitting the Pessary it is being besmeared with Quinine
Ointment and then before cohabitation I thrust one Soluble
Quinine Pessary and satisfy myself both before and after that
the female cap is rightly placed and has not been displaced.

Now my wife's monthly course was delayed to 45 days and
on this account being afraid that she might conceive, I was
very very careful in the matter. I used her on the 9th day after
the last mense and the overy cap remained fitted for more than
48 hours. Then again it was inserted after a few days and it
remained there for about 8 or 9 days, during which period I

have thrust one soluble tablet each time before union. Thus I am taking possiblest caution, but to my utter disappointment, I find that she has at last conceived, for, up to this day 68 days have elapsed without the monthly flow and every symptom of pregnancy is daily becoming visible.

Under the circumstances I would request you to suggest any explanation about this, for I have prescribed this method recently to many others being myself a medical practitioner, and they will remark my failure, 'Physician, Heal thyself' ... Yours faithfully

17 MARCH 1929, AHMEDABAD, INDIA: MR NDS TO MCS. I have been using for the last two years your 'Pro Race' rubber pessary ... But I was very much surprised and also annoyed to find that my wife remained pregnant about three months ago ... What is your explanation? I am almost tempted to believe that one cannot depend either upon your pessary or the Dutch pessary and then the question is how to achieve contraception?

I hope you will fully realize the very difficult position in which we laymen are placed when advocates of contraception contradict each other in the way mentioned above and I hope you will kindly help me in my desire to avoid any further trouble next time. Hoping to be excused for the trouble, I remain yours truly.   P.S.   Some of my friends also report to me similar failures.

1 JULY 1929, STOCKHOLM, SWEDEN: MR LN TO MCS ... I am a man of 35, engaged to get married since 1920 but as a result of financial difficulties still unable to build up the home, which we both are longing for and which would give us right to settle down as a married couple ... We love each other whole-hearted and deeply – and we have not been able to resist the temptation to unite, when we are happy to meet. Dear Dr Stopes, do you consider we are wrong in doing so? Would it, do you think, tend to deprive us of our future luck and happiness when getting married? Although we don't think so and although we are married in our hearts with God as our only witness,

these are questions we making ourselves now and then. I dare say, that we ventured this step only since we had studied your book, 'Married Love' thus we have got into the habit of practising the quinine pessary method combined with a rubber sheath for the male organ, as under the circumstances my fiancée would not consent to get instructions of a medical practitioner ... Do you reckon these precautions safe? I am well aware of your objections especially against the 'condong' but do you think the harm due to this practice so serious, that it would be wiser to adopt abstinence altogether? For my part, I must confess, it would be a hard blow, as it is already nearly beyond my power to practice 'restraint' during the months we have to be separated. Although there are well-wise people argeuing in support of onani in cases such as mine, I dread to take to the undecent practice, but sometimes I am suffering something terrible from sleepless nights and spontaneous ejaculations. Have you no remedi but self-control to offer me? ...

... Dear Dr Stopes, I love my little girl so immensely; I adore her; I like to carry her in my arms for ever, because she is everything to me in this world and I worship the very ground she walks on! Oh! – it is heaven to kiss not only her lips but her neck, her bosoms, entire sweet little body and her little feet! And now to the point. I want to confess to you – because I have such a perfect belief in your integrity, experience and wish to help your fellow-creatures – something that I never would think of speaking to anybody else about. Sometimes when I bury my face in her 'lap' and feel the smooth skin of her legs against my cheeks and get intoxicated from the sweet, womanly mysterious scent of her beloved little body, I get such a wonderful indomitable longing to let her legs embrace my head and to – yes! – kiss her 'sanctuary'! I am not unaware that this sort of carresses are practiced by many men, and I would not hesitate for my own sake as I am certain I would not find it objectionable, but still – there remains a doubt whether I have the right to yield to my own selfish longing, if it is a proper and decent thing to do, or if it perhaps must be termed as even abnormal . . . Will I necessary have to conquer this yearning of mine? I am, Yours very sincerely

11 JULY 1929, MCS IN REPLY . . . I should strongly advise you to marry legally so that your love may be honourably owned up to the world. I see no reason why people should set up house together just because they are married. On the contrary I often advise young people to live apart for several years carrying on each their own occupation if necessary and spend holidays and weekends together. Once you are married, all and every embrace, even such as you describe, if agreeable to the bride, would be quite suitable; but this is a private mutual thing in which people's individual tastes vary and in this matter you should be guided by her feeling. With best wishes, Yours faithfully

5 SEPTEMBER 1929, ALLAHABAD, INDIA: MR JSK TO MCS. May I venture to be excused for intruding on your valuable and busy time. But being aware that you are constantly working for the improvement of human race, I make bold to request you for a suggestion.

I am 25 years old now. I married at the age of twenty to a girl of foreign extraction. We both were passionate then and she still is. But the difficulty arose when I read your 'Married Love' and found to my dismay that I was not acting properly. I had hardly a minute's retention . . . I discharge just within a minute. This has its natural consequences. Though due to mutual arrangement according to the two wanes in rise of passion I satisfy my wife to a very little extent indeed. She is generally cross. The Indian physicians advised me to use narcotics like opium, Cannabis Indica and cocaine, etc, which I greatly detest and I have never used so far. I am quite healthy and take lots of exercises and play all the games . . . Thinking that there is no better expert in the world today than yourself, I have ventured to approach you.

The next trouble is that due to masturbation when child, the penis is curved horribly and there is one great blue vein showing itself above the root of penis. This both my wife and myself horribly detest and not only that, this makes it impossible for us to practise other postures which we like. The Indian physicians advised to use Lion's fat and Bear's tallow. But I have refrained from using any lest it might cause eruptions and may dull all sensations altogether . . .

My organ, when erect and turgid is 5.6″. I am perfectly healthy otherwise. Never had gonorrhea and Syphilis because of your valuable 'Truth About Venereal Deceases.' My weight is 16 lbs . . .

I am popularising the Birth Control amongst my peasants. Please inform me if there is any newspaper which deals with sexual, social affairs. Hoping for a reply. Yours truly

11 SEPTEMBER 1929, ORANGE FREE STATE, SOUTH AFRICA: MR M MCD TO THE SECRETARY, RADIANT SOCIETY FOR BIRTH CONTROL. I am anxious to get in touch with you as it seems to me that there is great scope for your work in this country. Of course you have heard of the poor white problem here. There is a large proportion of the white population are below that of the native, Mentally, and of course they cannot compete economically with the native. The native can do more work and cheaper than the European. Unfortunately this class of European breed like rattlesnakes . . . the government are trying to solve it by employing Europeans at native wages, but of course a supernormal native is not going to endure for all time being bossed by a subnormal European and there is great trouble about this in this country. The European expects to maintain his superiority by machine-guns but I doubt very much whether he will be able to do so as mentality must count in the end . . . Yours truly

19 JULY 1929, MCS IN REPLY. The problem of the 'poor white' in Africa has been before us for some time. We have a few members in South Africa adhering to our main body and something has been done from time to time in rousing interest in sterilization which is more likely to deal with that problem than birth control, for the low-grade intellects will not take the trouble to use birth control. It seems to me that all low-grade

intelligence ought to be sterilized ... With best wishes, Yours truly

24 MARCH 1931, TORONTO, CANADA: REV TH TO MCS ... It seems to have fallen on my shoulders to be the protagonist of the Birth Control Movement in Canada. I lectured all through the Hinterland last summer (incidentally, I found doors and Halls barred against my lectures). That is a country where the most outrageous families are found. The whole gamut of human disaster is apparent on every hand ... So I got back to Toronto and did a bit of thinking. Of course I have been an advocate of birth-control for years but it had never occurred to me to become active in it. I started and wrote a booklet and devised a practical contraceptive device:

A cylinder about six inches long and one inch in internal diameter (it can be made in two sizes). There is a piston or plunger in it passing through a cork or stopper. The cylinder is open at the end. The sponge is slightly greased with the jelly and is compressed between the fingers and is pushed down into the cylinder. This is done with the utmost ease. It is pushed down far enough so as to admit of the right amount of jelly being placed on top of it in the cylinder. It is then inserted in the Vagina and pushed up gently until it comes in the region of the uterus and then the plunger is pressed with the first finger. Immediately the jelly is pressed out and surrounds the cervix and os uteri and it is immediately followed by the sponge that as soon as it emerges from the cylinder expands. The cup-like depression of course faces the cervix which finds itself thus protected by a double protection ... Yours faithfully (*A diagram was included in this letter.*)

CHAPTER SIX

THE ARMED SERVICES

A month after the First World War ended the British High Command, in an attempt to combat the boredom of troops awaiting demobilisation, urged the provision of education courses. These, related Guy Chapman in his autobiography, A Passionate Prodigality, *did not go down at all well – with one exception:* 'Our one success was a major from the field ambulance, who translated to a round-eyed audience the doctrines of Marie Stopes. A repetition of these lectures was requested several times.'

Officers serving at the Front were among the first to respond when Married Love *was published in March, 1918 (priced at six shillings, the book was beyond the pockets of other ranks). They bought it on leave, read it in the trenches, discussed it in the mess, and sent it back to their wives.*

Sexually the war left its mark – and not just in the increased incidence of venereal disease. Injury, mutilation, shell-shock and the mental strain of those four gruesome years resulted in many cases of temporary or permanent impotence in men, with the consequent breakdown of their marriages. An Australian, who had served two years at the Front, wrote to Marie Stopes: 'It is a dreadful thing to walk about feeling that your vigour is gone – and the spectre of an early crack-up haunts me. Will you help me? Please.' Marie Stopes replied: 'I'm so sorry I can't be too encouraging! So many men had their vitality sapped by the war and their wives have just to put up with affection minus coitus.'

She took a personal interest in such problems. Her second husband, Humphrey Roe, co-founder of the Avro aircraft company, had crashed while serving with the Royal Flying Corps in France. He jarred his spine badly and injured his legs. The effects remained *for the rest of his life, contributing to the gradual breakdown of a marriage which had started earlier in 1918 with such high hopes of the sexual and spiritual perfection which Marie Stopes had always sought. 'Modern marriage,' she wrote in 1935, 'is often undermined by one of the direct or indirect after-effects of the War, namely a lack of normal virility in men who pass, externally, for healthy specimens.'*

After the war, as her books began to be read all over the world and by all classes of people, the problems multiplied. Regular army officers serving in India would write about the effects of the climate, or of tough frontier conditions, on their wives' sexual needs. Their wives complained of frigidity – and of the fact that in such a climate soluble pessaries melted as quickly as their desire. Able seamen, after six months at sea, asked for help in controlling their passions on return, to avoid burdening their wives, ignorant of birth control, with yet another child to be brought up on inadequate pay.

Marie Stopes did all she could to provide help and information, inadequate though it might appear nowadays. As a major in the Royal Signals serving in India wrote to her: 'From reading your books you appear to be one of the few personalities with a really open appreciation of the human side and I do not think it any exaggeration to say that your books have meant the saving and happiness of a good many homes out here.'

7 MAY 1918, BEF, FRANCE: CAPT. JTP TO MCS. I have read with great pleasure your Interesting Book and am very much obliged for the valuable information given therein, a great deal of which I was entirely ignorant of ... I have been married 12 years and have two beautiful strong children, one a boy, ten years, and a girl of six years. We were hoping to have 2 or 3 more in good time, but of course the War came and I went off at once and have not been back since except at rare intervals ... Until about a year ago we never knew that a woman was capable of a full orgasm, and then I found it out by accidentally tickling her clitoris with my finger. I however did not like to do this again as she was so violently agitated that I thought it might be injurious to her. We then tried to effect the same

result by ordinary natural coitus but entirely without success, although we tried until she was so cramped in the legs as to be unable to bear it any longer.

In the last para of p. 46 you state that handling is injurious, or do you mean some more violent handling such as putting one's finger inside the channel of the vagina, which of course I did not do ... Things are going on well here with us and I hope to soon be Home again for good with the job finished. Yours very truly

22 JUNE 1918, MACHINE GUN CORPS, CLIPSTONE: LIEUT LD TO MCS. I shall be greatly obliged if you can more fully explain the term 'orgasm' referred to in your book *Married Love*. Also the paragraph re children. You quote the case of a couple having a child say born nine months after marriage and you go on to say that it would be better did they allow six months or a year elapse before a child were born. Do you mean that the sexual act should be withheld for a certain time? What I am not clear about is just this point – is it possible for the sexual act to be performed and no children born of it, and does it require any special thing to be done in performing of the 'act' to result in childbirth – in fact the whole point of 'conception' I am not sure of ... Yours faithfully

2 AUGUST 1918, IN THE FIELD, RAF, FRANCE: CAPT. SDJ TO MCS. I have just read your book which is being very largely read and discussed by married officers in France just now ... I have one child procreated in the second month of marriage. I was not able to get home for my wife's confinement and did not see the baby till he was nearly six months old. That is quite a common case now, of course. As my wife is terrified of having another baby whilst I am away the sex relations are rather abnormal between us and I have had unwillingly to practise 'coitus interruptus'. You see, we know so very little of scientific methods of regulating pregnancy and no one will tell us anything worth knowing ... I take the liberty of writing as above because I am afraid my wife would not have the 'nerve' to

do it! Wishing your book and work the greatest success, whilst admiring your courage and plain speaking. I remain, Sincerely Yours

3 MARCH 1919, BEF, FRANCE: BRIGADIER-GEN SDE TO MCS
... I am 41 years of age and married on Jan 4 last a widow who has already had two children. Her first husband died during the war after 8 years of perfect married life. They not only loved each other intensely throughout the whole period but he also appears to have been extra strong sexually and I think she must be too because he apparently had coitus with her nearly every morning and evening for some 3 months after marriage before settling down to about once a week ... During my three weeks honeymoon either from being run down from strain during the war or from possible abuse in previous life I was never able to get really passionate. That is to say that the penis never got possibly stimulated, i.e. stiff and erect. In the opening nights I had no inclination at all and afterwards I was only able with difficulty after systematically taking sex stimulants all the time ... Yours very truly

12 JUNE 1920, HMS PENELOPE, SHEERNESS: LIEUT SE TO MCS ... I and my wife have read your book and we have to confess that it was the beginning of our discovering the way to derive the highest communion and compensations from sexual intercourse. I have been married for just over two years, and up till about seven months ago, my wife had already begun to be apprehensive at the suggestion of the sex-act. I did not know this until we found the 'true way' and am extremely grateful to you for such knowledge as you have promulgated. But I would like your advice upon one little point ... Upon one occasion I unintentionally excited my wife upon the clitoris, from the *outside*. Prior to which she had not experienced sexual excitement. Both she and I thought that we had really and truly found the natural and happiest method. Upon studying my wife's behaviour at our periods of lovemaking I found that continuous working upon the clitoris induced in her an unusual

and, to her, deliriously joyous sensation. Now, I also possess 'Dr Foote's Plain Home Talk, and Social and Sexual Encyclopaedia' – a really splendid volume of formidable dimensions. In it, in the chapter for women, it dwells upon the *devastating* effects upon girls of the 'secret vice'. My wife and I got anxious and we think even now that we have after all not been indulging in the sex act in the right and profitable way, after all our study and seeking! ... We both concur heartily in your theories re the female sex-rhythm and wave-crests and I am very thankful to have learnt what I have. Whenever we have had intercourse within the past month, I have religiously refrained from playing upon the clitoris externally and have zealously tried, for the wife's sake, to excite and influence that organ from the inside extremity, with the male organ. Well, my wife does not have *nearly* the same degree of pleasure from the beginning of our love-play to the end; especially the end. In fact she tells me that she doesn't really know if she reaches the climax or not in our newer method. All this worries me as I want to know the method à la Nature – for both of our sakes. You see, I have converted my wife to the no-corset method and also persuaded her to diet herself with plenty of milk and eggs, and she is a thorough fresh-air girl and performs her daily Swedish exercises. Otherwise, I shrink to think of what she would have become had she lived a different sort of life if we had continued to use the 'outside' method ... Yours respectfully and gratefully

17 JUNE 1920, MCS IN REPLY. I am enclosing the printed slip which most people get from me now, but your letter rather interests me ... As regards your question, the external stimulus such as you describe is often necessary to complete the orgasm with a woman. As you may imagine the relative sizes and shapes of people vary very much, and it is only a fortunate chance which brings together two people who fit so exactly that the simple internal penetration results in the complete orgasm. In my opinion, the local stimulation if followed by the complete union and ejaculation of semen does no harm at all. It is apt to leave a woman exhausted if it is done too frequently, or if, on the other hand, it stimulates to a point and then misses

the completion – nothing is more exhausting than that. Then also exhaustion follows if the semen is not sufficiently long in contact with the vagina. I should strongly advise you to remain together as long as you possibly can after the orgasm . . . Yours very truly

22 AUGUST 1920, INDIA: MAJOR RD TO MCS . . . I have now been married for eighteen months and whatever may have been the case at first, it is now only too plain to me that my embraces no longer have any attraction for my wife. Since I have read your book I have come to the conclusion that this is probably due to the fact that I have too quick an ejaculation and that I am smally made by nature. India as you know necessitates wife and husband being separated for a protracted period each year as it is incumbent to send one's wife to a hill station during the hot weather. This gives rise to a considerable amount of what I fear is only too often well founded suspicions. This is the situation I now find with regard to my wife and I am therefore most anxious and distressed about it. I shall in consequence be eternally indebted to you if you can by some means indicate first a really efficient method of checking too hasty an ejaculation and secondly if there is any means known to medical science by which I can increase the size of my congenital organ . . . Yours faithfully

18 SEPTEMBER 1920, MCS IN REPLY . . . As you are in India you are at the very source of native information about this matter. Perhaps you despise and do not know many of them, but if you do you will find the average Indian knows a great deal about the art of prolonging the act, and that there is in India more than one form of a type of structure which is added to the penis in order to enlarge it, which I suggest, though I hardly like to advise, you might find out about and use to advantage, as your difficulty seems one that is very prevalent in that country . . . Yours very truly

4 APRIL 1921, CEYLON: LT-COL BWK TO MCS. I have just read with much interest your two books *Married Love* and *Wise Parenthood* – alas too late to be of any use to me – Had

they been written 17 years ago and had they been read by my wife and I before we married, much unhappiness might have been averted, and our married life might not have been broken up as it is.

So many Englishwomen look upon sexual intercourse as abhorrent and not as a natural fulfilment of true love. My wife considered all bodily desire to be nothing less than animal passion, and that true love between husband and wife should be purely mental and not physical. This naturally caused a split in our married life and we are now separated . . . Like so many Englishwomen she considered that any show of affection was not in keeping with her dignity as a woman and that all love-making and caresses should come entirely from the man and that the woman should be the passive receiver of affection . . .

30 JULY 1922, JSL TO MCS . . . Most young men on entering the marriage state are even more crassly ignorant and misinformed than you imagine, and I can only regretfully confirm your faithful description of one's helpless bewilderment and agonizing impotence to do the right thing, with and by, one's even more ignorant and innocent girl-wife . . . I am a ship's officer. My wife and I dearly love one another: we have been married since 1914. No war-time marriage, mark you, I courted my wife long before that.

My wife, having been delicately brought up, was quite innocent of any knowledge. I – I am not boasting, many things contributed towards it, the chiefest of all, of course, being my Mother, and my ideal of loved and loving woman – I had never had any connections with any woman. After the first two nights of misery, I went out and purchased Stoll's books, previously thought indecent, and together we tried to grope our way to a right understanding. I think that I may honestly claim to have at all times tried to have been the thoughtful and tenderly careful husband that you so rightly instruct one to be. For instance, I honestly thought, as do most clean-living men, that one ought NEVER to have connections after one was aware that conception had commenced. I went further than this; I thought that at least one year should elapse after childbirth . . . I found the restraint increasingly difficult. I found that to keep my resolve, I had to refrain from being demonstratively affectionate, and this of course gave rise to the added misunderstanding that I was growing cold and indifferent, even thought to be jealous of the child that I had longed for. Then came a spell of sea-voyages. After a six-months voyage, I was as you might imagine unable to restrain myself any longer! and to my horror suddenly found conception commenced again. I have always felt that I was at fault somehow, but then you see I honestly thought that to use preventatives was:

(1)   morally wrong

(2)   Physically dangerous and Harmful to the Wife

(3)   Indecent, and therefore a subject I dared not touch upon with my dearly-loved wife . . . I hope you will tell me if our odd, and as I term it, 'spasmodic' form of married life can provide you with any further data. Married life to the sailor man is somewhat like a sandwich: large chunks of bread and butter earning, with only a very thin smear of the honey of life between! . . . Yours truly

2 AUGUST 1922, SCOTLAND: LT-COL STP TO MCS . . . Might I ask if you consider it right, or advisable, for a girl before marriage to have her hymen removed by a doctor?

The reason I ask is that I came across a case in France, in September 1914, of a young girl (17) who had been raped by two Germans – whose hymen was so thick and tough ('like a football bladder' – so the French doctor who examined her described it) that without some such operation she could never have had children. One of the two Germans was caught, in a curious psychical way, not long after, and paid the penalty. I know of at least two cases in which the honeymoon was quite spoilt by troubles connected with the hymen. Among savage tribes which look upon a marriageable girl as being worth so many cattle or sheep, the importance of its presence can be understood, but nowadays I imagine that any means that tended towards making a marriage happy should be resorted to ... Yours truly, I am a married man with a small son.

18 AUGUST 1923, CO. ANTRIM: MAJOR KTS TO MCS ... We are most anxious to have a child but are not able to manage it in the usual way owing to my suffering from malarial poisoning to the heart contracted in German East Africa during the war. This has affected me so that I am unable to have an erection and to perform the operation in the usual way.

I married in 1918 and was then able to perform the usual functions, but my wife and I rode and hunted on horseback – this seems to have upset matters each time I came home on leave ... My wife is 44 and I am 54 so we are afraid that unless we are able to bring about the desired results soon it will be too late ... What I want to know is *can I collect the semen and inject it into the vagina* by means of a syringe and thus enable my dear wife to have her heart's desire and become pregnant? If this can be done where can I procure a syringe of the necessary type – a very blunt nosed one which would not lacerate or hurt the organ?

In case this can be accomplished I presume the vessel in which the semen is collected and the syringe should be kept at 'blood-heat' and that the operation should be expeditiously performed so as to form as nearly as possible a quick and continuous operation – while the female organ is still 'tumescent'? Yours faithfully ... To add to my troubles, this cold and inclement climate has given me lumbago.

27 FEBRUARY 1924, INDIA: SERGEANT WS TO MCS ... My trouble is this. My wife came out here to marry me a month ago. We are passionately fond of each other but after several tries to have sexual intercourse we have failed. As far as I can make out, I am too big for her thing. I know I am fairly big but I always thought my penis would go into any woman's organ ... Night after night my wife and I show our forms and our 'things' to each other in the hope that we shall both get excited and get the 'horn'. Pardon the expression but I do not know

the technical word. Well the culminating point was reached three nights ago. My wife and I laid naked together and made love to each other. I laid on top of her. I followed your advice in *Married Love* and I kissed and sucked her nipples. She was quite ready to receive me as she always has been and she took hold of my stiff penis and endeavoured to insert it but couldn't. Well in this exasperating process the gentle touch of her hand was sufficient and naturally I couldnt help it but I came in her hand. I really couldnt help it. She at once became offended and smacked my face and pushed me out of the bed. She has not spoken to me since and she alleges that I done it on purpose. Well please if you can tell me what *can* I do. Well Doctor I enclose Rupees 10 and I beg you to put your answer to my question in the Times 5th April personal column. Preface your answer in the Times with the word 'Harry' and I shall know it is my answer. In enclosed envelope I send the size of my penis when erected. It doesnt seem too big, but dear, oh dear! Yours faithfully

1926 (OTHERWISE UNDATED) PORTSMOUTH: MRS AEB TO MCS. I am writing to ask you to kindly enlighten me on the Subject of Birth Control. I am 23 years of age, and have two children, one age 3 years and baby age 9 months. It is not that I am afraid of having children, but that I cannot afford to keep any more, as I have a terrible struggle to make ends meet with two babies. My husband is an A.B. Seaman in the Navy and until he is 25 years of age I am not entitled to 'Marriage Allowance'. He is 23 years of age now and my 'Allottment' from my husband is 24/- a week, also I am living in one upstair room, and there seems nowhere else to be able to live, especially with two children. My husband went away on a cruise in September 1924 and now writes saying they will be in England soon, and instead of being excited about seeing him I am really dreading him coming home, because I shall be sure to become pregnant again and I dont know what I should do with another baby, here in one room, and he has not seen this baby either, yet ... Yours faithfully

6 MAY 1927, INDIA: MAJOR CGC TO MCS. My wife was married in 1914, at the age of 17, to a man many years her senior. She had no intercourse with him owing to his impotence during the whole of their marriage. In 1921 she obtained a decree of annulment.

We were married in 1923 and passed that year in England. Our life was perfectly normal and happy. We had intercourse once or twice a week, save for a month or two when I was seedy with stomach trouble. During intercourse I used a sheath but my wife always experienced a full and satisfying orgasm and was in good health.

On returning to India in December 1922, we had a bad time in tents on the Frontier and intense cold. This resulted in my wife having very severe gastric trouble and general upset. She got over this, though by nature very delicate, but when fit enough to resume normal intercourse, she found herself becoming less and less capable of effecting an orgasm at all. The desire for intercourse remained but the physical power to effect an orgasm and all local sensation went . . . The sheath of course shuts out semen from the walls of the vagina (as well as from the womb). You mention in *Wise Parenthood* that semen has a vitalizing effect on the woman. I am wondering therefore whether absorption of semen in this way would eventually effect the cure . . . Yours sincerely

25 JUNE 1928, MCS TO MAJOR LCB (*the letter to which this was a reply appears to have been lost*). Dear Major B., . . . As regards your problem about the fur, I confess quite frankly that it is definitely a minor abnormality which you ought to try in a way to overcome, but I can quite understand that after so long having these feelings, it may be difficult or impossible for you to do this.

I do not know if you would like to show this letter to your wife, but if so, might I tell her through you that I think she should humour you to a certain extent. Why should she not have a pretty nightgown with a pretty strip of fur on it or a little fur collar in bed with you. Let her look upon you as someone injured in the battle of life who needs assistance. If you had broken your leg, although she might hate it, she would allow you to have a crutch; if you had injured your sight in a motor accident, although she might hate it she would allow you to wear glasses but would love you just the same. Let her consider therefore that you have been injured in a subtle kind of way and that she has got to let you have this assistance. That seems to me the simple, straightforward, common-sense way of dealing with it. Yours sincerely

17 APRIL 1929, CHELTENHAM: MAJOR MSB TO MCS ... I felt it my duty to let you know that when I was serving in India 1896–1904, it was then a commonplace that the natives we had to deal with made a practice of prolonging a single act of coition for eight hours or so, an 'all-night job' in fact, by the use of Opium suppositories, by the male of course. In the hope that this will help your research, Yours faithfully

CHAPTER SEVEN

THE MIDDLE CLASSES

It was largely to the middle classes that Marie Stopes owed her pre-eminence as an adviser on sexual technique and birth control. Herself the product of a staunchly middle-class upbringing, she was, by 1918, when her first book on the subject was published, only too well aware of the problems created by prudish middle-class morality. Though she wanted her message to reach the lower classes – some curtailment of their breeding, she felt, was essential to the improvement of the human race – she aimed Married Love directly at the middle classes.

It was a time when most members of that section of society boasted a servant or two, and dressed for dinner (thus giving women, as Marie Stopes suggested, the opportunity to insert their diaphragms comfortably in advance of coition). Should they be feeling a little under the weather sexually, they might, she suggested, take a month or two off in Switzerland, eating oysters and drinking stout to restore flagging sexual powers.

Critics instantly pointed out the narrowness of her approach. Of what use, it was asked, were oysters, holidays and a diaphragm to working-class women burdened with unwanted children, usually living in one room with a drunken husband? 'I must first of all make birth control respectable, then I will tackle the working classes,' she replied to one such critic.

Her instinct was right. Married Love was published in March 1918, and within six months had sold 10,000 copies in Britain, and by 1923 the reading public (virtually all middle-class) had bought 210,000.

Such a response was important at several levels. It engendered financial support for the clinic she set up two years later for working-class women. It ensured a steady stream of encouraging letters to the press, thus stimulating controversy and the creation of an atmosphere in which sexual matters could be openly talked about. It also gave her, through the thousands of letters she received from the middle classes – by far the largest group among her correspondents – further material for her research, and support for those theories she had advanced with insufficient scientific evidence.

Like the clergy and the medical profession, the middle classes had to a large extent learned how to limit their families, either by abstinence or by the use of contraceptives to which their superior education and income had given them access. Their letters to Marie Stopes, unlike those from the lower classes, were therefore largely concerned not with birth control and requests for abortion, but with the problems created by a sexually repressive society.

In her first two books on the subject, Married Love *and* Wise Parenthood, *Marie Stopes asked for readers' own experiences. She was overwhelmed by the response. To take just one example, in* Married Love *she had tentatively formulated her 'discovery' of a peak of sexual desire in women roughly halfway between the two monthly periods. This was based only on her observations of herself over a period of several months, and on those of one other woman. The hundreds of letters she received after publication corroborated her theory and gave her the confidence to go on, despite the sneers of established medical opinion.*

14 JUNE 1918, WESTMORLAND: MRS MA TO MCS. My husband sent me *Married Love* which I received from France today. I am writing to tell you how much I have enjoyed it, how true it is, for many of your conclusions I have proved in my own experience.

But why I particularly write is that I should like to confirm what you say as to fortnightly recurrences of desire. My husband is a medical man and has been in the army three years: for the last six months he has been in France. I live a very quiet life in the country with very little excitement or means of stimulation and I imagine I am just the average woman: and in my case it is perfectly true that, as you state, about ten days after menstruation, comes the desire of male companionship, which recurs for some days; and within the last six months this state has come about with such clocklike regularity that it has at last attracted my notice, and I made a mental note that halfway between each period I must expect a few days of restlessness. I only write this because in your note you have asked for information. I am, Faithfully yours

8 AUGUST 1918, BELFAST: MR WA TO MCS. My wife and I have read your articles in this and last week's *Sunday Chronicle* with very deep interest inasmuch as our case is a tragic example of the need for the reforms you advocate . . .

We had been married 17 months and our ages are 25 and 24 respectively. A month or so before we married my wife had a very nasty sore on her lip. As it did not disappear with ordinary home treatment she went to a Manchester doctor about it, who gave her medicine saying that 'her blood was out of order and that she must continue to attend him.' In a week or so the sore disappeared, and as the doctor's remarks had not led her to believe there was anything very serious wrong with her, she discontinued to attend him. Shortly afterwards we were married, and about two months after that date her throat became very sore and small painful sores appeared on the private parts of her body. She accordingly went to a doctor here in Belfast, who after examining her and learning of the sore she had had on her lip, stated that she was suffering from syphilis and that she had got it by kissing some syphilitic person, or from a teacup etc. We were naturally astounded and much troubled to learn this, because by this time my wife had conceived – I made it my business to visit the doctor and asked him if in view of the circumstances he would not do anything to prevent her bringing into the world such a child. Needless to say the reply he gave was decidedly negative. She was put under mercurial treatment (3 grams a day) and has remained under it ever since.

Seven months ago our child was born. At birth he weighed

3½lbs and in spite of all treatment, today he weighs a little over nine pounds, does not notice, is ruptured and in consequence of all the trouble we are having with him, our lives are a misery.

Added to all this my wife is now a week late with her menstruation, we fear she has conceived again and we are faced with the dreadful probability of having another child like the present one. Needless to say if we knew how to prevent it, we could not have the slightest hesitation in doing so, for I consider it would be a lesser sin than to allow another such child to be born . . . Yours faithfully

21 AUGUST 1918, MCS IN REPLY. In reply to your letter, I must first express my sympathy with your case which seems an extremely hard one . . . As regards your present anxiety about your wife, I fear very little can be done. She must on no account take the various quack drugs that are on the market. The only thing I can suggest is that she should two or three days before the next menstruation is due, take several good doses of epsom salts and the very hottest baths she can stand. Operations for abortion are illegal you know and though in her case I am sure it would be justifiable I really do not know any doctor who would do it for her. Let her take plenty of good iron pills, every day (Widow Welch's are the best) and then try the hot baths at each menstruation period. I think there is a reasonable hope that you need not fear a birth . . . Yours very truly

1 SEPTEMBER 1918, CHESHIRE: MR FS TO MCS . . . The question with me is that I am now nearly 35, unmarried and living with a widowed mother and helping to support the home. Though earning sufficient to keep myself I have never felt that my income was sufficient to ask the kind of girl with whom I could live happily to be my wife. To me it is hateful to see a girl of good education and upbringing turned into a household drudge. I have seen such cases – girls doing all the work and possibly looking after one or two children. Their work was so arduous that when finished they were too tired to take an

interest in any of the higher things of life, the things that really make life worth living, art, literature, etc . . . I have always felt that if I could not have a wife free from this kind of thing it was fairer not to marry at all. Yet no man can reach my age and remain pure without a terrible struggle. The sex appeal is insistent and if continually repressed I am sure that nature takes a strong revenge. Up to the present, in spite of very strong temptations I have remained pure for I have felt that it was not right to sacrifice another even for my own benefit but I am coming to the conclusion that it would be better for England were we freely and openly to recognise the Japanese system where sexual relations are looked upon as a proper and natural thing instead of something debased and sinful and degrading . . . You say I could marry a girl and she could go on working but do you think that any girl is willing to do that? . . . I should be very grateful if you could give me any ideas or offer any solutions to my difficulties. Yours very truly

2 SEPTEMBER 1918, MCS IN REPLY. In spite of your arguments (which, by the way, are misinformed about Japan, I have lived there) there is nothing *right* for you but marriage.

Let me know more of your circumstances and send your photo. I know one or two most suitable and nice girls – willing to work after marriage for some years at least. If you are good enough for them I might bring you together! From your letter you seem a thoughtful and nice man with whom a girl should be happy. Yours faithfully

(*There was a postscript to this letter from H. V. Roe. It read:*) My wife mentioned your letter to me, I should think a girl who works would suit your temperament better. Personally I always dislike the idea of a girl marrying as an 'occupation'. If she is clever enough to be able to keep herself, you are more assured that she marries you because she really loves you.

22 JUNE 1919, CHESHIRE: MR FS TO MCS. You may perhaps remember that I wrote to you last autumn . . . You answered that sexual relations without marriage were wrong and that you thought there were girls who were willing to marry and at the same time go on with their work and thus augment the

husband's income. You very kindly put me in touch with a Miss E K, another correspondent of yours. You explained that you had not met Miss K, but only knew of her through her letters to you. A very interesting and animated correspondence sprang up between Miss K and myself and I invited her to stop here last January. We both understood that if we liked each other physically as well as spiritually we would become engaged. You will remember that Miss K was receiving at the time £20 monthly from her father in Germany; he was of German parentage.

When I saw Miss K personally I did not quite like her – not nearly as much as I did her letters; but she was all impetuosity and rushed the engagement forward. Quite contrary to what you surmised the actual proposing and arrangements were done by her and looking at the matter with absolute frankness, and without conceit, there is no doubt that she liked me far better than I liked her. I accepted with strong reservations. One was the father must be favourable and continue some allowance; otherwise we could not get married ... It would have been quite impossible to keep Miss K on a small salary. She had not saved a penny out of her allowance – all of it had been spent on clothes, amusement and theatres. When she came here in January she had borrowed money from all her friends and before leaving asked me for several pounds as a loan, to pay her return fare to London. She actually came here without the money to return to her work in London ... Miss K wrote an enthusiastic letter to her father telling him she had met in me the man of her choice.

In answer to that he wrote back one of the most grossly insulting letters with reference to myself that it has ever been my lot to read. The letter seemed to contain all the beastliness of the German mind; one felt nauseated after reading it and no longer wondered whether a filthy spirit could exist in a German. I was looked upon as a dirty mercenary adventurer, a ravening wolf taking away a helpless lamb, etc ... The gist of the matter was that if his daughter married me she would be cut off from him and the family for ever and never a cent more would she get . . . Will you again put me into touch with a nice refined girl with whom I could correspond, if possible a Britisher? You will remember that Miss K was of German descent and had also adopted a baby. These two things would have been very difficult to live down. I trust you will help me again. With many thanks. Yours sincerely

25 JUNE 1919, MCS IN REPLY . . . I am sorry that the responsibility is too great for me to carry it any further. I should advise you to join a literary or other society associated with your church or local clubs. You are sure to be able to meet nice girls if you make a little necessary exertion. With best wishes, Yours very truly

11 OCTOBER 1918, DEAL: MISS SLR TO MCS. I am writing to you because after reading *Married Love* I feel sure that you will be able to help me in my present difficulty. My mother died when I was four and since then I have spent my time between strict boarding schools and at home with my Father and an elderly housekeeper so you can guess that I am as ignorant as unfortunately many girls are. For the last two and a half years I have been engaged to a boy in the army and he is very anxious for us to get married. I should like to do so but for one thing and that is the fear of having a child until we have a house of our own . . . I spoke of this to a girl friend of mine and she lent me your book. I must say it is awful the way girls get married having no knowledge of married life. You speak on this subject in Chapter 9, but I can't understand how people can be married for a year or two and have no children without injuring their health. Rather than do this and perhaps lose the great love we have for each other I would prefer to wait for some time but he has had such hard times since the war that I hate to keep refusing him. He agrees with me that we cannot have children until after the war when we have a house of our own but he does not know how very ignorant I am on such matters. If I asked any married women they would not tell me I know and that is why I write to you and ask you if there is any book I could get . . . Yours truly

8 DECEMBER 1918, LONDON: HS TO MCS. I have just read
your book *Married Love* which I am sure will be very helpful to
young married people. I have been brought very much into
contact with cases of 'unmarried love' in my professional
life and my experience has led me to think that much more
thought must be given to the sex problem than has been
meted out to it in the past. I should be glad to hear your
views on some aspects of it and I should be pleased to give
you the benefit of such experience as I have had ... Yours
faithfully

11 DECEMBER 1918, MCS IN REPLY. Dear Madam ...
The points on which your experience might throw light are:
(a) the most frequent age at which women have illegitimate
children; (b) whether or not they have confessed to you to
direct consciousness of the need for the sex life; and (c)
whether they are conscious of definite dates in the month at
which this desire becomes acute. If you have any information
on these points, I should be extremely interested to know of it.
Yours very truly

13 DECEMBER 1918, HS IN REPLY. I am a man! My job for
nearly a quarter of a century has been to interview all mothers
who are confined in the workhouse of illegitimate children and
I have had hundreds to see. But I have also in my practice as a
lawyer had experiences which have led me to seriously recon-
sider the code of morality which has fixed a father's responsibility for his child at 5/- a week and has made a pariah of the
mother, often driving her into prostitution. My experience
leads me to predicate the following:

    (a)   The normal man's sexual passion is stronger than the
normal woman's.

    (b)   It is constant whereas the woman's is intermittent.

    (c)   It lasts longer in life than a woman's.

If I am right, how can we, with justice, apply the same test of
morality to man and woman, and is it not because this has been
done that we have the horrible canker of prostitution in our
midst ...

To deal with your points:

(a)   I have kept no statistics, but they are mostly under 22, maybe under 20.

(b)   Very few admit any desire, on the contrary, they say they only did it to please the man. It is quite the exception for one to admit the desire or any gratification from the act.

17 DECEMBER 1918, MCS IN REPLY . . . Your answer to (b) that very few admit any desire, confirms my general opinion that it is only to a woman – and to a particularly sympathetic woman – that the truth is ever told, particularly by women in such circumstances as those among whom you work.

As regards your own points :–

(a)   I do not believe that the normal man's sex needs are stronger than the normal woman's. The *average* man's undoubtedly are, owing to the utterly false repression of the woman's and the utterly unnatural stimulation of the man's which have been current for so long, and have created a mental atmosphere . . .

(c)   I quite disagree that it lasts longer in man than in woman. I think the reverse is the case. What has been happening in the past is that the interlude of one to four years which is common in a woman between 40 and 50 is taken to be the end of all things, both by the woman and her husband, and when she settles down into her later normal life and desire is renewed, she is either ashamed to confess it, or in some way or other it has been driven under ground. I have first hand evidence from many women that desire is much stronger when they are old than at any other time . . . Yours very truly

30 JANUARY 1919, LINCOLNSHIRE: MRS BC TO MCS. I have been reading your book *Married Love* and want to know if you can tell me what is wrong if after intercourse, the semen always returns? I have not been married long – but am anxious to have a child and don't see how I can – if this always happens. I do not always have much of the feelings which it seems I ought to have, but even if I do, it is always the same . . . I wonder if you *could* tell me what is wrong – perhaps it ought to happen like that sometimes? Or perhaps directly he has finished he should withdraw himself, so that the passage closes up again . . .

2 FEBRUARY 1919, MCS IN REPLY ... The return of the semen is not at all unusual, and as such a minute speck of it is sufficient to impregnate it may make no difference at all to your power of conception ... You might find it advantageous to turn over and lie on your face for an hour or so after union, if you wish to conceive ... Yours truly

18 APRIL 1919, NORFOLK: MR LW-R TO MCS ... I was married in 1914 and came to England from South Africa on my honeymoon and joined the army on Sep 11, 1914. I have not seen my wife and family for four years ... You say in your chapter on Mutual Adjustment that it may take as much as from 10 to 20 minutes of actual physical union to consummate her feeling, while two or three minutes of actual union often completes it for a man. In my case, seconds would be nearer the mark. Now why is this, and how can I control myself so that there shall be a mutual crisis to love? My wife and I are both of an affectionate disposition and she likes to be fondled and caressed but its such a strain on me and if I don't actually have intercourse with her I am sure to lose a certain amount of vitality which is surely harmful to me. Loving her is like sitting on an uncovered barrel of gunpowder smoking a pipe, a single spark will set the whole thing ablaze – a little movement on her part and the damage is done. Just before I joined the army I went from the 1st to the 11th Sept without intercourse but I am sure I lost some vitality in the process. Of course I have never practised the control that I mean to practise when I get home again. I knew nothing about sex tide. Rigid control will probably help but will it be sufficient? I do wish I could meet you and have a heart to heart talk on this supremely important subject ... Yours gratefully

20 JUNE 1919, CAMBRIDGE: MRS PE TO MCS ... Seeing from your photographs how handsome and well-developed you are it may be difficult for you to enter into the feeling of a less fortunate woman who is undeveloped. Since my marriage my lack of bust has been a great upset and grief to me because I can see it is a great disappointment to my husband and I am

afraid it will estrange his love for me. That being so, I would do anything short of injuring my health to increase and enlarge my bust. I enclose particulars of a treatment I have seen advertised but am afraid to try it in case it should prove injurious . . . Yours very truly

23 JUNE 1929, MCS IN REPLY. I realise that the desire to enlarge your bust may be very serious with you, but I can assure you you are simply wasting your money on these advertised products. So far as I am aware, they are harmless, but for a couple of shillings you can obtain much more useful remedies – a simple laxative and a tonic. Keep your bowels acting regularly, your outlook happy, and take exercise in the open air. This will do far more to give you a good figure than any of these absurd advertised treatments. Massage the parts, sometimes that helps.

10 AUGUST 1919, EXETER: MISS ND TO MCS. I have been reading the correspondence lately in *The Challenge* on birth control and the sex instinct and I see that further correspondence is to be addressed to you. Writing from the standpoint of an unmarried woman I wish to know 'Is there any legitimate means by which an unmarried woman can satisfy her sex instinct?' If monogamy is right there must be unmarried women. *The Challenge* in one letter quotes St Paul, 'It is better to marry than to burn' etc but what about those, especially women, who can't always marry, I should be grateful for an answer as soon as possible. Believe me, Yours faithfully, A Seeker of Truth

19 AUGUST 1919, MCS IN REPLY. I am at present dealing with the most difficult question of the unmarried. In reply to your letter however, if a woman is young and strong, and prepared – as she should be – to do household work to some extent, she should go to Western Canada, *not* to the cities like Toronto. She would then, I think, very soon find that marriage was possible.

On the other hand, if she is quite unsuited for such a life, and marriage is really impossible, I do not know how the sex instinct can be legitimately fulfilled, except by deflecting it into sound work.

At the time of conscious need of sex, really hot baths are good in dissipating the electric energy which accumulates.

The problem you raise is, of course, one of an increasingly urgent nature since the cruel devastation of the War, and it is one which I fear individuals must solve for themselves at present. Yours very truly

30 JANUARY 1920, BIRKENHEAD: MRS LD TO MCS ... I have one *great* fear of having no child. May I tell you as briefly as possible? When I was about 8 years old I discovered by riding astride on a merry go round that I could derive the most wonderful sensations – I practised certain movements in a chair at home and soon found that I could get the same wonderful feelings. Every spare moment when I was alone I devoted to this pastime – and hardly missed a day – not till I was 24 did I realise that it was complete orgasms I was getting each time – I have never felt any apparent bad effects from it except for the terrible longing of getting an orgasm with my husband which seems *impossible* – I am not of morbid temperament and have only felt my nerves since I married three years ago, having no baby, and getting no orgasm except as usual alone – But I greatly fear I may have overdone it and that this is the cause of my having no children – three other women I know are the same, so can it be so abnormal?

If you, dear Dr Stopes, who are so wonderful and have the power to speak of these yet unspoken things with the 'tongue of angels' could *warn* parents to watch their children what a lot of unhappiness could be avoided! ... Yours most gratefully. p.s. Two of the other women mentioned have children.

20 JUNE 1920, LONDON: MRS LS TO MCS. I have read your book *Married Love* with deep interest and feel that your wish is to help anyone who is earnestly endeavouring to grapple with the sexual problem raised by our state of civilization. I have a son of 15 years of age, now at public school – he is very

developed for his age, he is very affectionate and should, through inheritance, have a passionate nature. Since his baby-hood we have been frank with each other about sexual matters and I know that he has been free of any sexual indulgence – can this continue until he is able to afford to marry, probably at 26 years of age at the earliest or will this self repression be bad for his mental balance just as over indulgence would be? If this is so, can you suggest an alternative – what am I to advise when the time comes, when he asks my advice? ... Yours sincerely

MCS IN REPLY (NO DATE) ... Healthy exercise, plenty of cold water cleanliness, keeping his mind off the subject and knowing that his women folk expect him to keep straight until his marriage are sufficient to keep a well bred man clean for his wife. I should encourage early marriage. Yours very truly

25 AUGUST 1920, KIDDERMINSTER: MR LW TO MSC. I am engaged to a girl, and *very* much in love with her. I have been engaged for over a year. (Through the war I am only *now* nearing a position when I shall be able to marry.)

Lately I have felt a sexual longing when sitting on the couch with my fiancée. I often get this feeling. It is as if, although both are fully dressed I long to get near her. You probably understand better than I can explain.

Am I normal and natural to feel this sexual longing or am I abnormal? I suppose I should try and smother my sexual feeling?

Since feeling the sexual feeling I have occasionally had a discharge of semen when asleep at night, although up till lately I have not had a single discharge for years ... Yours truly

2 SEPTEMBER 1920, MCS IN REPLY ... From what you tell me you are quite normal. It is indeed the usual result of a long engagement and one of the strongest arguments in favour of a short engagement once you have found the right person. I should advise you to marry as soon as you can and to follow the advice in *Wise Parenthood* if you cannot afford a child during the first few months. With best wishes, Yours very truly

25 AUGUST 1920, DORKING: MRS LN TO MCS . . . I should be much interested to know whether you believe in co-education. I was for five years at a big co-education school and feel both from my own experience and from observing others that such an upbringing is enormously helpful in maintaining a right attitude between boy and girl and man and woman.

I would like just to add that, although a healthy normal couple, we are both 'revolutionaries'! We do not think you show enough sympathy with those who want to bring about radical changes in the distribution of wealth and the conditions of production. Science has yet to be applied to the economic organisation of society. Vested interests and traditional prejudices are the enemy in this field just as in medicine and hygiene. Surely we ought not to be satisfied with things as they are, and may not the spirit of unrest be the spirit of progress? . . . Yours truly

9 SEPTEMBER 1920, MCS IN REPLY. P.S. . . . Yes, I certainly believe in co-education. I note that you are 'Revolutionaries', but I hope you will not forget that manual labour always has been and still is grossly overpaid in comparison with what it produces, while brain work always has been and still is grossly underpaid in proportion to what it produces, so that if wealth were rearranged in proportion to the contribution to humanity, there would be a small number of brain work multi-millionaires and a world of starving labourers. Yours very truly

10 OCTOBER 1920, CHESHIRE: MR B MCD TO MCS. (*To summarize part of a very long letter, Mr McD is a clerk earning £4 a week. An Irish Catholic now living near Liverpool, he has already visited several doctors, who prescribed bromides for his 'nerves' and eventually a psychiatrist, who diagnosed sexual repression and told him that 'Nature takes no notice of morality'.*) . . . although I am sure that you have dealt with some curious cases in your time I venture to think that mine may prove to be the most unique of all . . . I am a Catholic and all this [i.e. what the psychiatrist said] is contrary to my beliefs. I really don't know what to do or think, for Gods sake Dr please tell me. Now

I must tell you I cannot marry for various reasons. I do not know any girls well enough to ask them to marry me and I know *positively* that I am too grumpy and unsociable ever to make any girl tolerably happy even. But it is all on account of my fearful 'nerve trouble' as the doctor persists in describing it. And in any case there is a worse difficulty than that. I am sure I could not retain my fluid until I came in contact with my wife . . . I was close on 20 years of age before I understood the process of human reproduction. That is God's truth. I was born in a remote country district in Ireland and I always thought that if you talked too much with girls or made chums with them too much God would send a child. When I left home to go to business in Belfast I was only a very short time there till I was learnt the habit of generating an erection etc. I have been practising the habit on and off ever since I am sorry to say. Often at night indeed it is the only sure way of getting off to sleep. My erections are so strong and over-mastering that it is all but impossible to resist seeking relief.

I kept company with only one girl in my lifetime and she broke it up two years ago. I met her shortly after I came here from Ireland. The doctor says that precipitated the crisis. And now I want to tell you why I believe actual physical sexual union would be impossible for me after what Dr W. told me I would have been glad of sexual union anyhow only for fear of venereal disease. I walked out with a girl a few times in London and when we were sitting in the park and when my penis became turgid a slight movement I made to adjust it caused an ejaculation and the mere reading of your books caused me to be so sexual that I was afraid to move for fear of ejecting. Now that is continually the case. You know the results if I did marry and this were to happen. Would you advise me to seek physical union *somehow* first . . . Do you know of any place in my district where I could have sex union without danger of infection by disease. I ask you this in all earnestness and seriousness doctor, believe me, come what may I cannot suffer the subtle horrors of my present state indefinitely . . . Of course

I have to bear in mind that if I did have physical connection now outside marriage I should have terrible remorse and I would feel guilty if I came to marry afterwards. Nevertheless I feel that if I had the opportunity of securing a real satisfying union with the danger of infection by disease eliminated I should unhesitatingly accept it . . . Yours faithfully

13 OCTOBER 1920, MCS IN REPLY. One of the effects of such difficulties as you have is to make the sufferer feel that he is unique and to despair. I can assure you that I have much more difficult and peculiar cases than yours to deal with. Your type of difficulty is indeed quite common in a strongly sexed young man who flouts nature to the extent of not getting married . . . You should not think even once of having an illicit connection such as you feel yourself driven to. There is absolutely no guarantee of safety in them and they are morally deplorable . . .

Now as regards your marriage, you say you have four guineas a week, and this should be ample for you to marry a nice sensible girl who does not desire to set up housekeeping right away, but will do her share to help you along in the first few years. There is no need to have children for five or six years yet. You should get your wife to read *Wise Parenthood* and take the necessary steps herself . . .

You tell me you spend much time crying, feeling fear and dread and that you have drunk hogsheads of bromides. Do you not know that bromides are most terribly lowering and that if I drunk even a pint of them I should be weeping all day. Stop them at once.

If you do not know a nice sensible girl you could really love in Liverpool, I do. I happen to know a girl who, in every way, would be suitable and well worth winning. If you care to give some further guarantee about yourself, I might put you in touch with her, but, of course, only on the basis of an immediate marriage or as soon as you have won her affection. The only bar to marriage would be that you are inclined to the Catholic religion, but I hope, as the Catholic religion is so negligent of bodily health and moral needs of its devotees that you will drop that religion and take life on bigger and sounder lines. With every good wish, Yours very truly

15 OCTOBER 1920, MR MCD IN REPLY. I am much obliged for your letter of the 13th inst, and if I did not feel very sure that your advice was kindly meant I should be much offended by the remarks you made in the last paragraph of your letter. You do not know what it is to be a Catholic, or what the consequences of 'giving it up' would entail ... I consider it unreasonable to blame Catholics wholesale as it were for something (undefined) that you do not approve of. I will tell you candidly that as far as sex matters are concerned my views are – more elastic shall I say – since my interview with the London specialists and after reading your books. But I do not understand your reason for advising me not to have children for six years or so ...

With regard to the girl you know in Liverpool I have thought the thing over carefully and I think I would like to meet her if you do not give her to understand definitely that I am going to marry her ... I would certainly not mind marrying a Protestant provided I liked her well enough. I am afraid I would not be able to ask her here to my digs for tea or anything like that because another gentleman shares the sitting room with me – and he stops in and reads mostly ...

18 OCTOBER 1920, MCS IN REPLY. You say that you would not object to marrying a Protestant but any Protestant woman in her senses would object to marrying a Roman Catholic. Most Catholic laymen seem to know very little of the tenets of your Church. They prohibit the use of proper hygienic Birth Control methods preferring that a woman's health should be entirely ruined and that she should bring forth feeble, dying or imbecile infants rather than that proper hygienic methods should be used. If you remain a Roman Catholic you must solve your difficulties for yourself. I only wrote you as I did thinking from your letter that you were perhaps ready to leave the Church. Yours very truly

19 OCTOBER 1920, MR MCD IN REPLY. I have just received your letter and I am truly pained by the bitter tone in which it

is written ... I am very much surprised at a lady of your intelligence for being so bitterly hostile. I assure you I do not say that disrespectfully. I want to assure you of one thing, however. My mind is absolutely made up that I will not bring children into the world recklessly whenever I do get married. My mind has been made up on that point ever since I learned that birth control was possible. I have reasons for this that have more influence with me than the teachings of anyone. I myself have seven brothers and five sisters and how my poor mother brought us all up successfully I do not know. But I want you to take note of this fact. My brothers and sisters are all big strong healthy boys and girls. My mother is still strong and active, although she is 56 ... Please give me an introduction to the young lady you know in Liverpool if you will. Yours sincerely *(Marie Stopes did not reply to this letter; nor did she reply a year later when Mr McD wrote, rather cheekily, asking her to find him a job, lodgings, and a girl in London.)*

I NOVEMBER 1920, CROYDON: MR PE TO MCS *(after reading* Married Love) ... My first surprise was in following the eulogizing and glorification of the physical aspect of marriage which, however romantic and poetical its mental and affectional concomitants, seems to me in itself nothing but a sordid and bestial function of our animal nature. Indeed we always speak of it in terms of disgust and abhorrence in any relation but the legitimate one, and since mere legality cannot convert an essentially abominable and filthy action into a pure and holy one, by thus referring to it we contradict and stultify ourselves ... Admittedly it is essential to the continuance of the race, or at any rate it is so, failing a scientific method of exogamous inoculation, but so are many other animal functions, and it seems to me you might as well rhapsodize over defecation or micturition, both of which afford a pleasurable sensation, as that which is essentially the foulest and most revolting of all. As my late young wife remarked: 'Well if God invented such a coarse method of propagation as this I do not see how he can be so pure and holy as he is supposed to be.'

You represent also husbands as being for the most part so considerate and gentle with their wives, whereas by far the larger proportion are brutal and unscrupulous to the last degree, though this does not seem to be particularly distasteful to many women, who, to use their own phrase, 'like to be taken by storm'. I was determined to be scrupulously regardful of my wife's wishes, and as a matter of fact we had been married two years before, at her own insistence, I first exercised my marital rights. This scrupulous consideration, however, hardly seemed to be appreciated and indeed she more than once whispered, 'Do not ask me, I like to be caressed without being asked.' In the end, in fact, this indulgence and yielding to her every wish or whim instead of rendering her reciprocally gentle and considerate of my desires, only caused her to be increasingly exacting and imperious . . .

I am surprised at your sanctioning such frequent intercourse as you specify, even to the extent of three times a week! Theoretically I should think the ideal was once in two years, or only when offspring is desired. Once a week or once a month I should have thought plenty, although I am bound to say my wife would have been pleased with much more frequent embraces . . .

As for your proposals for birth control, I consider them both unnecessary and immoral, also revolting as providing the man with opportunities for indulging his lowest passions without the natural result which alone justifies it . . .

1 DECEMBER 1920, MCS IN REPLY . . . I am sure you will not realize it, but I think that your nature shows signs of a complexity which verges on the abnormal and, therefore, your relation to women is not as simple, straightforward and happy as is the case with the majority . . .

20 JANUARY 1921, MR E IN REPLY. Esteemed Madam, If by 'abnormal' you mean a man whose mind dominates his body instead of vice versa (pronounced wee-kay wairr-sah) I certainly am abnormal . . . But very few people, especially women, can believe this of any man. Thus when dining with my daughter at the house of a Scotch lady, she remarked, 'Oh, I

suppose when you were young you sowed your wild oats the same as others', to which I replied, 'If, Madam, by that you mean that I associated with loose women, I absolutely repudiate your vile insinuations' . . . Yours

4 DECEMBER 1920, LONDON: MRS DR TO MCS . . . I have been married 7 years. I am 42 and my husband just 50 . . . I am rejoining my husband in India this week after 4 months separation and I am writing to ask you whether you would be so very kind as to tell me if there is any other reason than that which you mention why I should *sometimes* remain awake, as you describe wives do. Neither my husband nor I know any reason, both being under the impression that a climax has taken place. Indeed my husband is usually longer than I in a way. I hardly know how to describe it, but I mean he likes deferring the climax so as to prolong the time, whilst *I* feel it more natural somehow to be uninterrupted and go at a gallop to the finish! So this seems not to coincide with what you say in your book. The sleep which perhaps usually does come is so blessed and life-giving I would like to know how I might always get it. *He* certainly always does! . . . How grateful I should be if you could make some suggestion, for I am not at all strong and have a great deal to do in India, so many sleepless nights are rather a serious thing.

7 DECEMBER 1920, MCS IN REPLY . . . I should think possibly that your sleeplessness might possibly be due to the fact that you need a second orgasm or even a third; some women do. On the other hand, it might be that your impulse has been thwarted by the orgasm completing itself too soon before your husband. If the latter is the case you should endeavour to defer to time with him. If the former you should have a second or a third . . .

18 APRIL 1921, SHEFFIELD: MR SF TO MCS . . . If a woman has the hymen unbroken at the time of marriage and she should decide to follow your advice as to the use of the rubber cap, fitting it unknown to her husband on the first evening of their

married life, would not the fact of the cap's insertion break the hymen in the same manner as would the entrance of the penis? If so, you may imagine the unhappy state of mind of a loving husband anticipating the slight pain spoken of on page 88 ('Married Love') and finding no obstruction. In such a case the whole happiness of the lovers may be imperilled for lack of understanding. Would you be so good as to inform me if it is possible for a woman to be actually a virgin and yet have the hymen broken? . . . Yours faithfully

26 APRIL 1921, MCS IN REPLY . . . I deliberately omitted from my books instructions for the first few weeks of marriage. Before marriage the wife cannot and should not attempt to insert the cap. For the first few weeks of marriage the husband should wear the sheath, after which the wife should wear the internal cap such as I advise in *Wise Parenthood*. Yes, in these days of athletics, it is quite frequently the case that a virgin has the hymen to some extent broken. The absence of pain in the first union should not cause distress to the husband but he should rather rejoice. Yours very truly

9 MAY 1921, DORKING: MRS CH TO MCS (*refusing an invitation to a meeting about birth control*) . . . there is something to be said on both sides of this very thorny subject of birth control. Of course there are very great dangers that it might lead to even more widespread immorality . . . from my own experience in such cases I have often known the child to be the salvation of the girl mother, it has awakened her to love and the feeling of responsibility. If she knew methods whereby she might sin and could evade the consequences it might lead to deeper degradation. Yours faithfully

2 JUNE 1921, LONDON: MRS BR TO MCS . . . I have read all your books with great interest and attention and when your book *Wise Parenthood* came out both my husband and self felt that if true in practice it would simplify the difficulties of married life very much indeed.

We were married in 1916 – in Dec, 1916, our first child was

born – after this we did not wish to have another child for at least 2 years, and then the question of a preventive arose; we both disliked the idea of a sheath being used and decided on a well known make of pessary – this failed after 9 months, and a second child was born in 1918. We still wished to avoid using a sheath, and this time my doctor prescribed a method – however our third child was born in 1919.

By this time your book *Wise Parenthood* was published and we read it with great relief, for the rapid increase in our family was a very serious matter for us.

I bought check pessaries of all three sizes to make sure of getting one which would fit accurately, and quinine pessaries of a well-known make. I renewed the check pessaries every 3 months for additional safety. All went well until Sep 1920 when I became pregnant once more. We could not believe it possible and in fact went to see a specialist about it – he confirmed the pregnancy and asked me what preventive we had been using; on being told he said that several women, who also employed the above methods, had been to him for the same reason! Unless you have received other letters on the same subject you will naturally say 'Ah yes, yours is an exceptional case' – but unfortunately it isn't.

Three other women have to my personal knowledge used your methods –

(1)   The wife of a doctor who fitted her himself – after 3 months, not being aware of pregnancy, she had a miscarriage: – this woman already had 3 young children.

(2)   First child born April 1919. Fitted afterwards with check pessary by a doctor, 2nd child born June 1920.

(3)   Medical student, newly married, no children, fitted self with pessary 18 months ago, and method still successful.

From these four cases you will see that only in the case of a newly married girl with no children has this method proved successful.

In view of the statements published in your book these are very serious facts and I think you will agree with me that they should be brought to your notice ... I much regret the necessity of writing this letter. Yours truly

16 JUNE 1921, MCS IN REPLY ... I should be glad if you would kindly send me the cap which you say failed you. There are many inferior articles on the market, and I cannot even have you suggest my responsibility for failure if you have been using the wrong thing. Kindly also let me know the price charged you for it, and whether you were using quinine at the time as I advise. Yours very truly

18 JUNE 1921, MRS BR IN REPLY ... I much regret you should think I hold you responsible for the failure of the method of birth control used – if you read my letter carefully you will see that as far as possible all personal references have been left out – the whole question is much too important and serious a one to be treated personally ... I am unfortunately unable to send you the cap used, for as I have been pregnant for nearly nine months I destroyed it long ago. The cap was bought by me at Messrs Allen & Hanbury, Wigmore Street, and was the best procurable, costing 3/6 ... The cap was carefully examined before every insertion, and also smeared inside and out with a quinine ointment as a further precaution – in addition a Rendell's quinine pessary was used at the same time. If in spite of all these precautions failure occurs so readily the method seems much less reliable than suggested ... I have, I think, stated all the facts I know as fully and clearly as possible, and I must beg of you once more not to treat them as personal reflections. If a satisfactory method of birth control is ever to be discovered then surely all the facts relating to the subject must be carefully recorded and considered ... Yours very truly
(*Marie Stopes did not reply to this letter.*)

25 JANUARY 1922, LONDON: MRS LD TO MCS ... I am a practising Roman Catholic, but am perfectly convinced from a very practical experience – that some sort of Birth Control is *absolutely essential* – and *is* practised by all *thinking* Catholics – I have discussed the subject with both Ecclesiastical and Lay Catholics – and found that many Lay Catholics imagined that by

taking large monthly doses of medicine they were safe guarding themselves from too frequent birth, and still keeping the letter of the law! and were most surprised that I deplored this method, if successful, as miniature and early abortions, and advocated preventative methods of some kind . . . Personally I married at 19, both ignorant and innocent of sex altogether – in the first 6 years I had two 3-month miscarriages and three births – then I came across your books M. Love and Wise Parenthood and of *course* – realized the misery I might have been saved – the joy I had *not* experienced – I informed my confessor I was fully convinced it was wrong to continually 'be having babies' – and that having discovered a method which was harmless – I intended to have no more children till I could afford them and wanted them – I was refused the Sacrament, this for a long time I submitted to – then I thought the matter over and came to the conclusion it was solely a matter for one's own conscience – and I changed my confessor and in future did not mention it . . . Yours sincerely

21 MARCH 1922, SUSSEX: MRS RBE TO MCS . . . You do not approve of corsets and I agree, but find it difficult to find a suitable suspender support which does not pull at the waist. Yours

28 MARCH 1922, MCS IN REPLY. P.S. Yes it is awfully difficult to keep up stockings. I have never yet succeeded in finding a proper suspender and I always wear loose garters below the knee. When I was 19 I went to see a doctor to find out if there was anything better, and he said that he did not know of any satisfactory suspender. Yours very truly

14 SEPTEMBER 1922, YORKSHIRE: MISS MM TO MCS . . . I am unmarried but the sex instinct is tremendously strong in me and your theory of the normal sex cycle in women is absolutely confirmed in my own case.

I feel that desire is absolutely right and natural and the normal heritage of every healthy woman whether married or not.

But I am not quite sure whether even under strong sexual desire it is ever *right* to induce excitation of the clitoris and the wonderful thrill which is the outcome of such an action? It is intensely difficult for an ardent woman to always refrain even when she deliberately diverts her thoughts into other channels. Do you think that an occasional indulgence viz two or three times a month is detrimental to health – or disloyal to the highest and best we know?

Personally I feel physically better for the occasional relief of desire, but if it really means a denial of the best and impoverishes for marriage in the future, relief must surely be firmly denied – always. If in the midst of your busy life you can let me know your thoughts about this I shall be truly grateful.

It may interest you to know that I am 41 years of age and only realised the possibility of self satisfaction at 32. Yours very sincerely

16 SEPTEMBER 1922, MCS IN REPLY ... I think for young people action such as you describe is very harmful, but for women over 30, if they understand it is dangerous, and control the use to not more than twice a month, it is *sometimes* beneficial.

26 SEPTEMBER 1922, SURREY: MR WM TO MCS. The recent loss of my own wife, as a direct result of our ignorance of suitable contraceptive methods, has convinced me that it is high time the subject of birth control was brought before the masses. In my own case the doctor who told me my wife must not have another child fobbed me off with a jest when I asked him to tell me how to obey his mandate; and ironically enough she had been dead a fortnight when your little book *Wise Parenthood* was brought to my notice ... Yours sincerely

16 OCTOBER 1922, MR CBD TO MCS ... One feels that unless the influx of low-caste foreigners especially from Eastern Europe, is checked, they will fill up the gaps and mongrelise our English and Scotch stock. Like the rats, these low-caste

foreigners have large families and are industrious workers and have strong tribal instincts, but compared with our people they are cunning, bloodthirsty and cowardly . . . Yours faithfully

6 MARCH 1923, LONDON: MRS PW TO MCS . . . I was married two and a half years ago – when I was 23 and I don't think two people could be much happier than we are – but we do long to have a baby and so far there has been no marital relation between us. My husband has been to see his doctor who says there is nothing wrong and has given him tonics and pills which have had no effect. He is a very hard-working solicitor and I believe too much brain work does make men incapable but, to my mind, it is more a question of ignorance than anything else. He is of a very sensitive nature and has therefore never discussed sexual questions with either his parents or other boys – nor has he ever indulged in sexual intercourse. It isn't as if we never feel the need for conjugal relations but at the moment of contact the desire vanishes with both of us, so I feel sure something must be wrong . . . Yours very truly

8 MARCH 1923, MCS IN REPLY . . . Hard mental work often has that effect on men who are not very strong, it must be very sad for you. I should think by far the best thing for you to do would be to take your husband to the Swiss Mountains somewhere high like St Moritz for two or three weeks, you would find the effect almost magical. Get him also to eat oysters drink stout and eat oranges . . . With every good wish

11 MARCH 1923, GLASGOW: MR LB TO MCS . . . I feel that I cannot tell you how greatly I appreciate your courage, your ability, and your resourcefulness in writing such a helpful book and your insight into human nature amazes me. Somehow I have always had the idea that women who were so very highly endowed intellectually, especially on the scientific side, would be inclined to look slightingly on sex love, and so I feel your book is all the more refreshing. How anyone can take exception to it I cannot understand. To me the reading of it brought a feeling of tender regard for women generally; the same feeling

which I remember having as a young man when I first came to know about the monthly periods just after I was married.

Please allow me to say how sorry I am for you that you have so much misunderstanding and opposition to contend with, but I do trust that you will yet come out on top, and that your noble efforts will be appreciated at something like their value ... Yours faithfully

(*This is only one of many letters of encouragement and support Marie Stopes received after judgment went against her in her libel action against Dr Halliday Sutherland earlier that month.*)

19 SEPTEMBER 1923, LONDON: MRS KS TO MCS ... I will state my case as briefly as possible. I married very young, when just 22, knowing scarcely anything of life; my husband, an Irish Catholic though 10 years my senior appeared to be equally ignorant on sex matters – the result was that the marriage was never properly consummated. I was very unhappy owing to his excessive drinking. In fact, after a few months he never came home sober. Things went from bad to worse – he lost his jobs, got into debt and meanwhile I was getting very nervy ... Before I was 26 I ran away to my mother's and began earning my living as a pianist in ladies' orchestras. After about a year I had neurasthenia and was 10 weeks a patient at a nerve hospital. My husband, so I am told, lives anyhow and anywhere, has D Ts every now and then and so it goes on. Now, I am 31, a few months off 32, and have known a most charming man for the last 18 months. We are both deeply in love and wish to marry, but it seems I can't get a divorce for incurable drunkenness alone – adultery on his part I can't prove and doubt if it exists ... Yours faithfully

15 JANUARY 1924, REPLY-PAID TELEGRAM FROM SCOTLAND TO MCS. Would you kindly tell me if you know of any nurse or competent person in Aberdeen or Edinburgh who would fit Pro-race cap I find my middle finger too short.

2 MARCH 1924, NORFOLK: MRS MP TO MCS. I have recently been reading those very fine books of yours on married life etc

and in one of them ('Radiant Motherhood' I believe) I came across the lines 'little, laughing messenger of God'. They struck me as exquisitely rhythmical. I was at once tempted to write the inclosed verses and I am sending them on to you as a small tribute to your own beautiful thoughts . . .

BABY SOULS

Baby souls in your far off haven,
Are you waiting for mothers to hold you close?
Waiting for bosoms so soft and tender
And oceans of mother love to unloose.

If you come down here there is mist and coldness
And cruel thorns for your baby feet
The path to earth is thro' woman's anguish,
And yet you would find her love so sweet.

Yes, we of the shining, far off Heavens,
We baby souls of the realms above,
We want to come to your dreary earth world
And by pain's pathway find its love.

We answer the call of the mother-hearted,
We feel the yearning of waiting breast
And so in the flesh of manhood's making
We would nestle up close in innocent rest.

We have lessons to learn in your cold, grey planet,
Lessons which cannot be learnt up here,
And so we are patiently waiting our summons
Ready to start when the call comes clear.

29 MARCH 1924: MRS BL TO MCS. (*Two days earlier, at the age of forty-three, Marie Stopes had given birth by Caesarean section to her only surviving child. Ill as she was, she still managed to make some response to the nation's sexual ills.*) First let me offer my sincerest congratulations upon the birth of a son – I hope he will give you cause to be proud of him as you have given him cause to be proud of you. At such a time as this in the midst

of your great happiness, I feel dreadful intruding my troubles upon you, so without wearying you with the whys and wherefores may I just put the following bald fact?

(1)   I have 2 little girls – ages 4 and 5 years and we cannot afford to rear more.

(2)   I have been to your Clinic, learnt how to use the pro-race etc, but

(3)   My husband will not let me know when he wishes to have intercourse and will not let me get out of bed to insert the pro-race. Consequently twice I have become pregnant and had the greatest difficulty in bringing my periods ... Gratefully Yours

(*Marie Stopes scribbled over the letter 'Answer: put in cap early in afternoon and take out next morning'.*)

15 APRIL 1924, BRIGHTON: MRS LEC TO MCS ... I am now just 48.   I was married just before I was 18 by arrangement to a man I have never known before, after an engagement of six weeks – I had had no thought of marriage and no wish for it and this event was so sudden as to be a shock – but although I resented the whole terrible plan and fought against it as much as I could, I had to give way to please my mother – my father was a most charming man but an inveterate gambler who ran through everyone's money. That was why my marriage was arranged – I had only loved one man – whom I loved and admired chiefly because his violin playing appealed to me ...

My husband had led an absolutely pure life and when I met him he was 30 – I don't remember all your opinion on this subject, but as far as I was concerned, the man's terrible ignorance made the first union into nothing short of a tragedy for me. Sexually, so little did he understand that I think that was part of the cause of all the misery ... The tragedy of all started at its worst I suppose somewhere in 1914 or earlier, and it became terrible to go on trying to live in harness. My husband had his sexual needs and in order to try to satisfy these I went through *hell* time after time ... It seemed as if he wanted so much to be done for him, in a sense as if he were incapable through nervousness or some other cause, as if I had to give the bodily love of two people instead of one and receive nothing myself except misery heartbreak and repulsion – it was *terribly* revolting and lowered me in my own estimation. I used to clench my lips and pray to God to help me through, all of course hopeless – I am very passionate and know I can love and have needed that love I have never had . . . I felt I must not leave home. During five years my husband on one hand going on like a raving maniac, chasing me all over the house at times (on only three occasions I refused him intercourse. I felt I *could* not and my son so ill with shellshock that in the dead of night he was smashing furniture and all day I had to try to protect him from his father, whose own nerves were so dreadful, they made my son ill.) Two years ago, after I had months of all this added to hard housework through my being servantless, I found it imperative to go away with my daughter for a fortnight. I had not been gone long when I heard from my husband that one of the lady servants I had secured was his mistress . . . all the time scenes went on and things were unhappy. I needed sexual intercourse in the usual fashion – but I never seemed to have it – When through the advent of this woman my services were no longer needed, I felt a thankfulness and a relief, but with it all a great sadness and loneliness hard to describe . . . but I have more to tell you. A year ago my daughter met an old schoolfriend of her brother's – She liked him very much and in the midst of this nightmare of a life we have led in a house like a prison, this friend came to see us. He had distinguished himself in the war and is a most charming kind and delightful man. He felt very sorry for us all and almost at once seemed to take the place of a dear son and friend to me and of a very sweet brother and more to my daughter. Then when I had not known him more than perhaps ten weeks, he behaved to me as a lover and offered me what perhaps he knew I have never had – a real man's love. He probably said it half in fun, but he said that he meant it and that he admires me more than my daughter. I could never treat such matters lightly, I objected and spoke of my daughter, of my age and so on – He said he wanted me and from then until now I have felt for the first time in my life I know what it is to love with one's whole heart and soul and body. The latter has had no part in all this except that he kisses me. It is a tragedy . . . I am sorry to say that at times he takes more alcohol than he should – but I have felt years younger and happier since I knew him but in between times I have done nothing but weep morning noon and night, feeling what that love which cannot come near me, would mean to me . . . He can't love me in the way I love him, for as he is thirty and I am 48, it would be unnatural and wrong – but he understands meantime I feel as if I shall sometimes go mad. I feel as if I had never *lived*. And all this came first when I read your book . . .

My daughter and he have planned that they and I shall live together and do farming, but I wonder how this can be possible as I feel too intensely . . . Years back when I was in distress I was advised to read Married Love – I read it about a year ago. Every mistake and every tragedy and everything that has led to trouble in my life is accounted for in a marvellous way in your book. But the cure has come too late. The man whose touch of the hand draws sympathy from you is there, but I have to choke the sympathy and love and hide them in tears. Do tell me what can be done if you will be so kind . . . Yours sincerely

p.s. I have had a certain disillusionment in this friend. Who has lost money, and whom I have helped – only a little as my means are now small – but a great deal for me. To find there has been on the whole a good deal of ingratitude and that a good many things which might have been done for my daughter or for me, have been done for others – though I am owed everything for at least six or seven weeks, including the entire use of a car, which he will have on loan for another three months. All this hurts me, when one has done all one can for a person, out of absolute affection. I think alcohol warps all the finer feelings.

2 NOVEMBER 1924: MR CD, FOUNDER OF A NUDIST COLONY, TO MRS BOOTLE, MCS'S SECRETARY . . . Our movement is suffering from just the same apathy and obstructionist tactics that yours did at the start, but we are slowly forging ahead . . .

Could you send me some of your pamphlets for distribution among our members, we are introducing a 'Birth Control' section into the Sun Ray Club, in fact we want to introduce a section on all progressive movements, so that the Sun Ray Club shall eventually represent the great progressive social movement towards complete emancipation from the thraldom of humbug and hypocrisy. Do you think it possible that Marie Stopes would consent to be President of the Sun Ray Club? Yours sincerely

22 NOVEMBER 1924, BILLERICAY: MRS R TO MCS. Lying here, one of the nurses, thinking to help me, lent me two of your publications . . . I am 38 years old, married sixteen years, and have nine children aged 14, 13, 11, 10, 9, 8, 4, 3, 1 year 7 months. I had, in the Dr's words, 'an extraordinary miscarriage' five or six years ago. I menstruated slightly about the fourth month of pregnancy and then three weeks later, slight menstruation started and continued, with but a few intervals of a week or so for six months. Being very worried at this time with exceptional family affairs, I put off sending for a Dr thinking it was nothing serious. Then one day without warning, I 'flooded'. Ten hours after it occurred again, and the Dr had to perform an operation there and then. He found the child wedged firmly in the mouth of the womb. The doctors declared it was a unique case and the 'child' was preserved and sent I believe to London. Six weeks ago I came in here, because being four months pregnant, menstruation started suddenly. Again the doctors found everything dead, and performed an operation . . .

I was very strictly brought up and when I married knew nothing of sex relations, realization coming as a dreadful shock. My husband was well off then and both of us very, very fond of children. Although a public school girl, with a 'finishing' abroad, I had a rooted conviction for years that contraception *of any kind* was immoral and indecent. Hence my large family. When war came my husband's income went and for years I have had to struggle against unaccustomed poverty, quickly recurring pregnancies, ill health and the housing problem – made still more difficult because of my numerous family.

In the first years of married life I travelled a good deal, and during a holiday in Germany I had occasion to render a small service to an old woman who hailed from the Black Forest. She came to me one day to thank me, and after saying the family knew of things unknown to others (her appearance was very much like the popular idea of a witch) she said as a slight return for my help she would give me a secret that would bring me happiness and wealth. To my utter amazement she told me the following. I give it in her own words, a rough translation. 'If you would desire boys, then you must to your husband give instruction that *his* pleasure comes first, if girls you desire, *you* must have *your* pleasure first.' Altho' I thought her mad at the time, I did not forget, and I have subsequently found her advice true. Only twice have I failed to *know* what the sex of my coming child would be, and the correct date. I know for a fact that upon the three occasions I conceived my girls, I had a complete orgasm . . .

Altho' utterly unable financially to bear the expense of my younger children, I can honestly say that they are all clean, healthy, well-developed, mentally well balanced children; and their upbringing has been the joy of mine and my husband's life. I have always been an advocate of the 'natural life'. And they have never worn hats, shoes or more than four garments (until they reached the age of ten) except in winter for out-of-doors. Their diet has consisted chiefly of fruit, vegetables, eggs and cereals, with milk and barley water with lemon juice as their drinks. Twelve hours sleep, plenty of cold water. Not being able to get other quarters when we were made to leave our little farmhouse, to make room for employees, we did the only thing left to us. We hired a large tent, and pitched it in a field, and all through the summer the children have grown and thrived, taught by myself and as happy and healthy a young family as any mother could wish to possess. My husband, a public school man, ex-service and formerly tutor in highly-placed families abroad, has in some way offended 'headmen' and they have retaliated by turning my children out of the tent (there six months) and into the Workhouse. My tenderly guarded, refined little ones! and not satisfied, have published in the local papers an account stating 'the children were found in a state of neglect, barefooted', etc. My God. Madam, as a public worker and one who knows the world and understands so well the human mind; can you imagine the hell, purgatory that I am going through. I see another of your books is entitled *Radiant Motherhood*. It seemed to mock me from the printed page. Yours gratefully (*MCS marked this letter 'No Answer' – perhaps for once defeated by the severity of the lady's problems.*)

4 DECEMBER 1924, B— SCHOOL: MR KR TO MCS . . . I am on the staff of this school, aged 37, my wife being 15 months my junior. As usually happens, our daughter was born in the following June, the healthiest, bonniest child you can imagine. I am devoted to children, and long to increase my family, but a Doctor's bill of £20 and trained Nurse £25 is more than I can possibly afford a second time. Consequently we have had no union since the child was conceived over five years ago. My wife has firmly resisted any attempt on my part on the score of expense, and I am most unwilling to make any demand against her will. So on reading your books I bought her the preventive you recommend: she declined to ask for such a thing! That was in July last; and I cannot get her to make any attempt to use it for she admits now that she is frightened of it . . . I am very puzzled about it all. I haven't the smallest doubts about her devotion to me, but I don't think she can have any very strong sex feeling. I have failed to discover any wave crests recurring fortnightly. Yet if I were better off I feel sure she would be delighted to be the mother of another or two more children. What am I to do? Must I deny myself entirely for another five years? . . . Very truly yours

(*Seven years later, after Marie Stopes had advised him, failing his wife's co-operation, to use a sheath, Mr R wrote again*)
FEBRUARY, 1931: I have been reading again your beautiful book, *Married Love*, and it has filled me with intense sadness.

For it has made me realize all the joy of marriage that I have missed . . . on your advice I used a sheath. But that was only for a couple of years, for I found my wife more and more reluctant to receive me. So it is now more than four years since we have had any intercourse. I tried every occasion I could, but have never succeeded in discovering any time when there is in her feelings that 'high tide' that you speak of . . . Four years ago when I inherited my parents' estate, we agreed that we would try and have another child, for I have a great longing for a son. But from that day she has flatly refused any sexual intercourse. There is my case. I am not seeking advice, for I feel that none would avail. But I simply had to tell some sympathetic and understanding listener all about it. Forgive my wasting your time. Yours truly

21 JANUARY 1926, CHESHIRE: MRS SL TO MCS. I have read your articles in *John Bull* with deep interest and I venture to ask you for your counsel and advice in my case. I hope you will not judge me too harshly. Unfortunately, my husband has been detained in a mental institution for the past $18\frac{1}{2}$ years leaving me at the age of 22 (I was married when only 19) with a baby boy and three months pregnant with another. Since that time I have hoped and prayed for his recovery, but the Doctor's reports are always the same. 'No improvement mentally, quite well physically.'

Nearly two years ago I met a widower now the friendship has grown to love and I confess intimacy has taken place of late. How can we avoid an increase in family as it is impossible to marry as the law stands today. In fact I don't want to start again as my son and daughter are quite grown up, but my friend has five children, he losing a good wife and mother over childbirth. It has been a long, hard and lonely life for me, and I have been strictly chaste up to meeting my present friend and a new life appears to be opened to me. But I am afraid of being damned by trouble, although we try to be careful . . . Yours sincerely

(*This letter was marked 'No Answer'.*)

2 FEBRUARY 1926, SOUTHSEA: MRS CR TO MCS ... I would like to ask if you have considered matters from every point of view before advocating birth control. It seems a *tremendous* responsibility to take on oneself preventing of other human beings being born into the world, if it goes against God's plan, simply because in our blindness *we* cannot understand what that plan is. Were there not poor and sick and halt and blind in the time when Christ was on the earth; were they not shown all love and tenderness by Him. One would think the disciples would have suggested that such afflicted creatures should not be sent into the world, or that the Master Himself, seeing all the suffering, would look to it that such a state of affairs should not go on ... There are other ways out than birth control, but it is the easiest way and calls for no self sacrifice, that is its great recommendation, but it seems to me the birth control advocates have got hold of the wrong end of the wedge. What we should insist on is that all these foreigners who are allowed to come and take the bread from our poor working people, should be sent out of the country ... It is easier to try and cast aside that which God ordains, than to alter the luxurious habits of the rich, even for the sake of helping the starving ... Yours sincerely

16 MARCH 1926, MCS IN REPLY. I have indeed considered birth control from every point of view. I must ask you to read my book *Contraception*. You will find there that people objected to chloroform just as they are objecting to birth control and for the same reasons – ignorance and prejudice. I can assure you that for the world as a whole birth control is the greatest help and will not prevent the birth of any child who is desired by its parents ...

19 MAY 1926, LONDON: MR RB TO MCS. As no comment is made in *Contraception* as to probable stamina, health etc of a child whose conception may be the result of an accident such as perforation or break in either a condom or Pro-Race cervical cap, and as my knowledge of contraception is only superficial I shall be glad if you can supply me with some information

as to probable vitality physically and mentally of a child conceived under above circumstances. I understand that in ordinary connections without contraceptive measures being taken, the strongest sperm survives, and matures, but in the supposed instance the sperm being so extremely limited, there would of course be no competition, and the escaped sperm may probably be the weakest ... the possibility of a weakly child mentally or physically due to reasons stated above would be a matter of very serious self-reproach to the writer and should be extremely reluctant to take the risk or responsibility of being the author of an immature child ... Yours truly

29 MAY 1926, MCS IN REPLY ... In reply to your question, I think that you may have no anxiety that if a spermatozoon penetrates through a perforation in the condom that it will be a specially weak one. In a full ejaculation there are something up to six hundred million sperms, and even an almost invisible drop of spermatic fluid contains thousands. After penetrating the condom the sperm would have a long distance to travel which would naturally test its vital powers. The chances are, therefore, that any sperm which succeeded in fertilizing the ovum under these circumstances would be an unusually healthy specimen.

13 JUNE 1926, STOCKPORT: MRS TN TO MCS ... I wondered if you could help me in my difficulty or if you had an instrument applicable to my case. I have only one child – a daughter of 15. I had a very terrible confinement and was quite an invalid for 13 years. Two years ago a Danish Doctor treated me with electrical massage light rays and violet rays together with certain remedies and now I am able to run or walk and in excellent health. My trouble is this – I was badly torn outside and inside also womb torn and in the struggle the two doctors present at my confinement tore out the smaller pair of lips. I am therefore very very open the opening extending almost to back passage. For the 13 years, intercourse could take place as the torn womb and dropped ovaries helped to block up the passage and assist at intercourse. Now, since the womb has been drawn back into

place the front passage is clear of any organ and therefore very large. My poor husband can't have intercourse because I can't retain his penis. He is naturally a very affectionate man and requires intercourse two or three times a week. For the past two years, this being impossible, he has had to relieve himself as best he could and now his nerves have broken down and he is in a very nervous state and I am wholly to blame I believe. Oh Dr Stopes, this means so much to our married life and I can't explain all this to a man doctor so please can you help and advise me and have you some instrument I could arrange inside to fill up the opening a bit . . . Very sincerely yours

15 JUNE 1926, MCS IN REPLY. From what you tell me, you must have been most wickedly handled at the time you had your baby. My heart fills with rage at the way women are treated, even by expensive medical men. To put you right now, I fear there is nothing that I know but an operation, but I believe you could still be partly helped if you would consult one of the dearest, nicest men possible, who is the expert gynaecologist at Guy's Hospital . . . Yours sincerely

16 MARCH 1927, BELFAST: MISS M TO MCS . . . I have been friendly with a young man for some months back and we are in love with each other and would indeed be married only that he hasn't a big enough salary.

About once in six weeks, he has, when making love to me, stood facing me in a suggestive position – is this right? He is a very good chap and would never do anything wrong, I know, but is it necessary for him to relieve his feelings in this way. It is about three months since he has stood like this now and I would like to refer to the matter to him even if he did do it again. Would you be kind enough to tell me if I ought to allow this once in a way like this or ought I to move to another position or scold him about it . . . Yours gratefully

24 SEPTEMBER 1927, HARROGATE: MR NW TO MCS. I very earnestly beg of you to read this letter and to kindly reply. I am a clerk on the L&NER Company and my age is 19, at which age

a youth should be feeling the joys of youth – healthy, strong, jolly etc. but I deeply regret to say I am feeling the entire opposite owing to incessant self-abuse of 4 to 5 years standing and sexual intercourse. As a result I am very pale and awfully depressed, I cannot interest myself in anything. I am unfit for my work, sometimes I feel so depressed that I wish I was dead. I am perfectly certain that my present condition is due to my awful folly ... My chief ailments are: unceasing headache, aching eyes, and I have a throbbing in my body which seems to make my whole being give a little automatic jump, the jump keeping exact time with my pulse and veins ... Yours very truly

7 NOVEMBER 1927, BURNLEY: MR GL TO MCS. I received your letter for which I am grateful. I will do my best to give you all the information I can.

1.   I have been married for 9 years.

2.   My wife is, and has been during our married life, in splendid health. She is in fact a typical healthy country girl.

3.   Sex Union. This is a very irregular function sometimes as long as two and even three weeks between the acts but generally about once a week. She is sometimes very much against it and I can only refrain for a time until she recovers. Here I might say that it almost appears to be a state of mind caused by an indecent assault made upon her when she was nine years of age ...

4.   She does not enjoy it in any way in fact she almost hates it, although sometimes she hates it less than others. As far as feelings go I have irritated the nerve centre at the mouth of the womb it is effective but only so long as the nerve is irritated.

5.   Withdrawal. Yes, I used withdrawal but only for about two months.

6.   Wooing her is very difficult since she is so very lapathetic. I did my best, but lately I have just allowed her to practically choose her own time in the hope that she might become normal. I hope I have given you all the information you need to help us, or rather I should say me, for she does not mind so long as I am

prepared to carry on but it seems such a degrading and debasing thing to have intercourse with her in her present state that I almost feel I would rather abstain altogether ... Yours sincerely

11 NOVEMBER 1927, MCS IN REPLY. I am glad you have given me further details ... As regards withdrawal, if you have only used it for two months that ought not to have any remaining bad effect. Of course, it is very difficult for a woman who is apathetic; I can quite understand that, but it is up to your wife to try and make a joy and pleasure of it. She should try to notice her own rhythm, studying the *Married Love* chart rather carefully, and seeing whether her own times coincide with that, or whether she has a different rhythm, and she should go a little out of her way to be charming and pleasant at these times. One thing about human nature which scientists are discovering is that if you pretend to feel an emotion, it does help the internal juices to be secreted almost in the same way as if you really did feel it ...

When she has found by a careful study of her self her own rhythm, let her then be charming to you and pretend she is acting the part of a charming woman who is happy with her lover, and it will be so delightful that after a few times, she will find she is no longer acting but really doing it ... I do not know how your circumstances are, but if you can afford it, encourage her to eat oysters occasionally, whitebait and oranges. They all tend to improve the general stamina in a special way which is valuable to sex life.

If she has any lingering dislike of the union, try to eradicate it by a careful study of *Married Love* and tell her to believe that the woman's part in the world is very largely to give, and that by being charming at these times and giving happiness to her man, she will find, after a little while, she gains very much herself. With every good wish, Yours sincerely

16 MARCH 1928, LONDON: MR MRS TO MCS ... Is it natural for two exceptionally sensitive and highly-strung people to suffer a violent and inexplicable revulsion of feeling towards

one another after sexual satisfaction? This will last for several days and causes doubt as to whether our love is pure, so much so, that knowing that we will always suffer in this way we have parted on the eve of marriage. Would it be a normal adjustment for us to marry and resist all sex instincts for the full benefit of our spiritual happiness or is nature warning us that we are not compatible? Yours very truly

22 MARCH 1928, MCS IN REPLY . . . As you tell me you are not married, I can quite understand the incomplete sex experience in which you foolishly indulge before marriage may cause revulsion. Before marriage, beyond kissing the lips, there should be no sex experience. If you doubt your love, you should certainly not marry, and even if you love, after marriage the conduct of your unions is very important. You should follow the advice given in my book *Married Love*.

29 MARCH 1928, MANCHESTER: MISS DM TO MCS . . . I am getting married in July this year. We are both very anxious to have children, and only wish to consider contraception for the purpose of spacing births.

I really want your advice about this matter. I have an idea that among Jewish women, an operation before marriage is usual, involving the rupture of the hymen, and so presumably enabling the first experiences of sexual intimacy to be complete. I do not know if this is ever done for English women, and if there are any reasons why it should not be done. I should very much like to know what is your opinion. I should like to undergo the operation myself, judging from my present-knowledge. It seems much more sensible . . . Yours truly

4 APRIL 1928, MCS IN REPLY. As regards your question about an operation before marriage to rupture the hymen, I personally think this is revolting, and a very unfortunate recommendation recently put into circulation. It is certainly a matter about which you should consult your future husband if you propose to do it, as most Englishmen would hotly resent their bride having been tampered with before marriage. If you find, after marriage, that the hymen is so tough that it cannot

be broken, an operation could then be performed, but I confess that anything of the sort seems to me to be an unfortunate second best ... Much of course depends on the degree of romantic feeling which lies between you and your husband, but knowing as I do the attitude of so many middle-class men on this subject, I am perfectly sure that the vast majority would not dream of their fiancée being touched before marriage. With all good wishes, Yours very truly

2 MAY 1928, DAGENHAM: MR PRN TO MCS ... May I be permitted to ask your kind assistance for my family of 7. We owe £3.10.8 rent and two months on our furniture hire. My youngest girl is 8 years, others are 3 girls and 2 boys. Last week I earned only £2, a sum I am sure you will agree will not meet our needs. We have had a lot of illness with our children and that is the cause of all the trouble. Trusting you will be able to do something to help us, I am, Yours Obediently (*MCS marked this 'Begging letter. No reply'.*)

22 NOVEMBER 1929, LONDON: MRS MH TO MCS ... After five years of marriage, we have no children, though we both earnestly desire them. I went to a gynaecologist who examined me and said I was perfectly normal and she could do nothing more but my husband must be examined. He went to a specialist who examined him and his seminal fluid was tested and although the spermatozoa were there they were lacking in vitality. My husband was told to go for a 6 months holiday without me and eat oysters and drink stout and probably things would come right. We are not well off so of course he couldn't leave his work for all that time and he hates eating oysters. Trusting you will help us, I am Yours truly

25 NOVEMBER 1929, GLASGOW: MRS KA TO MCS. I am wanting a 'Corrective' and enclosed is a sample of tablets that have been supplied to me to be taken in doses of 6, 8 and 10 following hot baths and hot drinks of Hollands Gin.

I should be obliged if you would give me your opinion if this would be a safe and effective remedy. Yours truly

28 NOVEMBER 1929, MCS IN REPLY. The thing you are attempting to do is criminal and the methods you are recommended are swindles. Yours truly

2 JUNE 1930, GRIMSBY: MISS WED TO MCS ... I am single and 29 years of age this August, absolutely obliged to earn my own living and am entirely struggling along and battling for my existence because my Mother brought me up so strictly and in such a narrow-minded world, and now, through negligence on her part I am become the victim of innocence and have fallen through no fault of my own ... it is hardly necessary for me to explain that I hold a position of trust and am respected by one and all in the Department only to be robbed of same now by some unknown cad of a commercial fellow who I shall never set eyes on again or even find out who he is ... I have been more or less trapped and am now left stranded to face the consequences with not a friend to stand by me or even advise me as to what steps I can take to save me from the snares of hell ... I am just asking if you will advise me as to the best and correct methods of trying to carry out a preventative treatment ... Trusting to receive a favourable reply in the hopes that you will be helping to save one more sweet life from the very depths of hell. Believe me, Yours faithfully

Marie Stopes sent on this letter to the Daily Express, *with a covering letter to the Editor.* Dear Sir ... what the young woman is asking is a criminal offence and in a sense you and your paper are responsible because you have sneered at and barred proper decent discussion on the subject of control of conception and sound sex instruction would have prevented this young woman ever placing herself in such a position. I do not know why you imagine that if you ban decent sex instruction and birth control you will get a properly moral population – you won't – criminal abortion is the alternative of the work for decent sex attitudes which I am carrying on ... (*The Editor of the* Daily Express *replied, refusing to publish Marie Stopes's proffered articles on abortion and birth control.*)

CHAPTER EIGHT

POLITICS

In the 1920s, birth control was not a political issue, except negatively as a possible vote-loser. Nor was there any significant party alignment. Right-wing Conservatives compaigned against birth control on conventional lines. Equally, Communist-oriented Labour MPs fought it on the grounds that it would reduce the number of dissidents prepared to fight against the established order – and also that Socialist measures, anyway, were of more importance in creating a just society than the mere application of birth control measures.

Contraceptive advice was not available at the ante-natal and maternity welfare clinics that had already done much to reduce infant and maternal mortality. Yet when Ernest Thurtle, MP for Shoreditch, moved in the House of Commons in 1926 that local health authorities should be allowed to give birth control advice, the motion was defeated, 167–81, on a free vote. Of Conservatives who voted, 33 per cent were in favour of his motion, 38 per cent Labour, and 23 per cent Liberal. Significantly, of the four women MPs who voted, only one – Ellen Wilkinson – supported the motion.

In the same year, Lord Buckmaster, former Lord Chancellor and a Vice-President of the Malthusian League, introduced a similar motion in the House of Lords. It was passed by 57 votes to 44 – a tribute both to upper-class philanthropy, and to the free thinking encouraged by a legislative body without power, but without the shackles imposed by having to cater to popular prejudice.

It was not until 1930 that the Ministry of Health, encouraged by Buckmaster, Marie Stopes, Dora Russell and many others, grudgingly consented to allow local authorities to give contraceptive advice.

Well into the Thirties, prejudice persisted. Just before the Second World War Hannen Swaffer, about to give a lecture on birth control, asked Sir Winston Churchill what he should say. 'Tell them,' Churchill replied, 'to breed up to quota, or they'll all be wiped out.'

3 MARCH 1921, 10 DOWNING STREET, LONDON: MISS FRANCES STEVENSON TO MCS. (*Frances Stevenson, secretary and mistress to David Lloyd George and later his wife, was herself in favour of birth control. Though she dealt sympathetically with Marie Stopes's letters and visits to 10 Downing Street, however, she was unable to persuade the Prime Minister to give any support to the movement.*) I spoke to the Prime Minister about the matter upon which you approached me the other day, and after deliberation he regrets that he does not see his way to giving his name as a patron of your Clinic.

I am so sorry that I have not been able to secure your request, but I expect you will realize the difficulties in this case owing to the Prime Minister's position.

1 JULY 1921, LONDON: SIR MS MP, TO MCS. I am sorry that I do not see my way to become a Vice President of the Society you are about to form. The reason is that I have been bombarded with attacks from all kinds of people because my name appears as a patron of your clinic. I have not the time to answer all these attacks and in many instances I do not think it wise to do so for it may lead to unnecessary controversy. I had no idea there was such an amount of opposition. Yours faithfully

25 NOVEMBER 1921, 10 DOWNING STREET, LONDON: MISS FRANCES STEVENSON TO MCS ... Mr Lloyd George wishes me to acknowledge the receipt of your letter and Resolution which you sent to him on behalf of the Society for Constructive Birth Control and Racial Progress. In reply he wishes me to say that although he fully appreciates the fact that your Society is

working with a real desire to improve the conditions of the working classes, he feels that the suggestion contained in your Resolution would be bound to provoke controversy and that he would not be able to see his way to advocating it . . .

Mr Lloyd George wishes me to assure you that his decision does not arise from the fact that he deprecates in any way the work you are doing, but he feels that at the present time it is better for you to continue this work as an independent Society without the support or acknowledgment of the Government . . . Yours sincerely

4 NOVEMBER 1922: BERTRAND RUSSELL TO MCS . . . As I am a vice-president of the CBC and am addressing it the day after the poll, I hope you will suggest to any members you may have in Chelsea that they should support me. My views on the subject are known and will lose me much of the Roman Catholic vote, so it is only fair that they should support me, and that I should gain the vote of supporters of Birth Control.

THE PARLIAMENTARY QUESTIONNAIRE

Shortly before the general election of November 1922, Marie Stopes sent out a questionnaire to all parliamentary candidates. The response was disappointing. With high unemployment, an acute housing shortage and the apparent threat to the established political parties from the 'Red Clydesiders' few candidates were much interested in the vote-catching possibilities of birth control. There were only ninety-one signed, returned copies from Labour candidates, thirty-seven from the Liberals and twenty-three from Conservatives.

One difficulty may have been the woolly wording of the statement candidates were asked to sign and return to the Society for Constructive Birth Control and Racial Progress. It ran:

'I agree that the present position of breeding chiefly from the C3 population and burdening and discouraging the A1 is nationally deplorable, and if I am elected to Parliament I will press the Ministry of Health to give such scientific information through the

Ante-Natal Clinics, Welfare Centres, and other institutions in its control as will curtail the C3 and increase the A1.'

It was obvious from the comments sometimes accompanying the returned statements that not everyone understood its implications.

LABOUR CANDIDATES

Coventry . . . I am not sure that I am entirely at one with you, as I think that the improvement of the conditions of the people through the economic changes proposed by the Labour Party will be more effective in securing a better race than the selective breeding which seems to be implied in your declaration which you asked me to sign.

Stretford, Lancs. I agree with the object but disagree with the method. I do not know whether the disadvantages of using clinics for this purpose would outweigh the advantages. No Roman Catholic would use the clinic if the subject were made a part of the MOH's duty.

Derby. Could your Society give me a little financial help we are badly in need of funds. Any donation however small would be very acceptable. As I am only a working man.

LIBERAL CANDIDATES

Glasgow. I think the person who framed the above resolution must have had a C3 brain. Why can't you state exactly what you propose to do?

Suffolk. I think your question to Parliamentary candidates is very funny and trust you do not take this matter too seriously. The laws of Nature work very wonderfully and are rather beyond human control.

We are all, I take it, opposed to 'breeding chiefly from the C3 population'. If we assume that we are A1 ourselves, and it is without prejudice to our own individual rights, I think that the idea you have that things will be better if they were better is one to which each of us can subscribe, but how any Institution is going to tell millions of people that they must not breed, or how you are going to get physical and mental deficients, who sometimes are returned to Parliament, to vote for the extinction of their rights, and to reflect on their parents by passing an Act of Parliament, I do not know.

I know several of your Vice-Presidents, though I do not know of their reproductive success, but I see at least one of very unbalanced mind, some cranks and some who are childless. They may be quite right in their estimate of the undesirability of increasing the population from their stock.

London. If the proposition put up by your Society is as simple as it looks from the form of your question, then I can most heartily subscribe to it. If, however, it involves anything in the nature of a Malthusian doctrine or artificial birth control, then I must withhold my support.

No address. I can accept no responsibility for the accident of your birth.

CONSERVATIVE CANDIDATES

Macclesfield. I am in receipt of your letter, and do not propose to reply to your questions. It is not a suitable subject for a Parliamentary Contest.

London. I have signed your statement. At the same time I am at a loss to understand how the Ministry of Health is going to regulate this matter – and would *certainly never* lend my name to the use of preventives.

Birmingham. In reply to your circular letter, I am in agreement that there is much in this difficult subject that requires much consideration, but at the same time I am of the opinion that the public have not yet been sufficiently educated and I am not myself prepared to express an opinion at this juncture.

At the same time, nothing but good can come from the

circulation of knowledge that has for its end the improvement of the English race.

*

7 MARCH 1923, ASHINGTON. At a meeting of the women's section of the Ashington Labour Party the following resolution was passed: .

That we express our gratitude to Dr Marie Stopes for her work amongst working women in relation to birth control, also for her splendid fight in the recent law case and express our gratitude for the publicity given to this vital matter. Her books we would recommend to all married people and feel that the reading of such will contribute to mutual understanding on fundamental relationships.

12 MARCH 1923, MCS IN REPLY . . . I am indeed thankful that all the trouble and anxiety of the last weeks have at any rate resulted in the spreading of the news among the very people that I most desire to help. Yours very truly

I MARCH 1924, MANCHESTER: MARY STOCKS (LATER BARONESS STOCKS) TO MCS . . . We are now violently at war here with the R.C. Bishop of Salford, who has called upon his flock to 'hound us' with 'hue and cry' out of the district. How would you call that but incitement to violence? And what would Joynson Hicks say to a Communist who indulged in that kind of exhortation? I got Josiah Wedgwood to air the matter in the House on Tuesday evening. Meanwhile we are advised that should any violence occur we can hold the Bishop responsible. It *would* be fun to prosecute an R.C. Bishop for incitement to crime. As a matter of fact, Mrs Pankhurst and Christabel got three months without option of a fine, for precisely the same thing in 1910! Yours sincerely

3 JULY 1925: THE SOLICITOR-GENERAL TO MCS. I regret to be unable to accept your invitation to become a Vice-President of your Birth Control Association. The acquaintance which I

have with your publication leads me to think that there is a great deal that is thoroughly objectionable mixed up with possibly legitimate propaganda. Yours faithfully

22 MAY 1935, LONDON: SIR MF, BT, MP, TO HON SEC, CBC.
Will you be so kind as to cancel on your mailing list the copy of the Birth Control News. It is not the kind of document that I care to have in a mixed household. Yours faithfully

CHAPTER NINE

LITERARY

28 AUGUST 1918, PENLEE, DEVON: GEORGE BERNARD SHAW TO MCS. Aylmer Maude has lent me your book on Married Love, which I failed to get in London from, I suppose, shortage of paper. It is the best thing of the kind I have read.

However, I do not write merely to announce that not very surprising opinion. I want some information which you can perhaps give me.

Among my friends is a married couple. The woman wants a baby. The man, in consequence of a rupture, is impotent. The reason seems to me inconclusive: he is to all appearances a normally virile person; and I suspect that in competent medical hands the difficulty could be removed. But the ordinary medical practitioner knows nothing about this department of his business; and the only specialists I can name are in America ... I shall be here (at the Fabian Summer School) until the 7th. Ever

30 JUNE 1921, GEORGE BERNARD SHAW TO MCS. I have to make an iron rule against Vice Presidencies, Patronships, and all the rest of it: otherwise I should be V.P. of everything under the sun. Also I cannot take on Birth Control just as I cannot take on India and psycho-analysis and lots of other things. I am particularly bothered about B.C., because the method most commonly employed changes genuine intercourse into reciprocal something else that I know by actual experience of both to be different and that I greatly distrust as to its effects. I really don't know what to say about it except what I said in my America article. Someday I shall tell you of one or two cases

that have startled me. For the present you must write me off as useless. Ever

20 SEPTEMBER 1921, SIR ARTHUR QUILLER-COUCH TO MCS (*refusing a vice-presidency of the Society for Constructive Birth Control*) ... I fear that in practice, and in other hands, your teaching will be dreadfully perverted. The objection you mentioned at the Queen's Hall – that the publication of preventive methods will teach the young that unchastity can be combined with security – *is* an objection ... But a stronger objection, to my mind, is that the majority of honest lovers *start* married life with no desire – rather a disinclination, to have children. They simply haven't the wherewithal to understand the holiest and least explicable bliss in the world, that of having a child in common ... So poor things, while instinct is pushing them towards the best thing in life, they will go on thwarting it (having learnt the appliances) until it is too late ...

1922 (NO OTHER DATE), NOEL COWARD TO MCS.

> If through a mist of awful fears
> Your mind in anguish gropes
> Dry up your panic-stricken tears
> And fly to Marie Stopes.

> If you have missed life's shining goal
> And mixed with sex perverts and Dopes
> For normal soap to cleanse your soul
> Apply to Marie Stopes.

> And if perhaps you fail all round
> And lie among your shattered hopes
> Just raise your body from the ground
> And *crawl* to Marie Stopes.

26 OCTOBER 1923, KING'S COLLEGE CAMBRIDGE: J. M. KEYNES TO THE TIMES. I am informed that the enclosed advertisement, after having been accepted for insertion by the *Times* was refused and the cheque returned. As a Vice-President of the Society against which this discrimination has been

exercised, I should be grateful if you could let me know what special circumstances led to this unusual decision. I am myself aware of none, and would wish, in view of my association with the Society, to be aware of them if they exist. Yours faithfully,

31 OCTOBER 1923, THE TIMES IN REPLY. Replying to your letter, the small advertisement announcing the meeting to be addressed by Dr Marie Stopes was refused as it was not considered by the Management to be suitable for insertion in *The Times*.

2 DECEMBER 1924, AYOT ST LAWRENCE, HERTS: GEORGE BERNARD SHAW TO MCS (*following the House of Lords decision – the final court of appeal – against Marie Stopes in her libel action against Dr Halliday Sutherland*). The decision is scandalous; but I am not surprised at it: the opposition can always fall back on simple tabu. The subject is obscene: no lady would dream of alluding to it in mixed society: reproduction is a shocking subject, and there's an end of it. You may get a temporary success by luring the enemy out of that last ditch into the open where there is no defence but argument; but the only result is to drive them back into the ditch; and then you are done: the tabu is impregnable. Huxley had to leave reproduction out of his textbook of physiology; and you are as helpless as Huxley. I wonder what the Lord Chancellor will say to your last appeal! And WHAT has this business cost you? ever

18 DECEMBER 1924, MCS TO NOEL COWARD (*after seeing his play* The Vortex). Oh, my dear Noel Coward! It is now eleven hours since I parted from you and the play exists: that is to say the play that I told you in your dressing room that we must write together, you and I. You see what a vitality your play must possess, thus instantly to procreate a successor. Your play is, of course, tremendously fine and interesting, but the position perfectly beastly . . . The one I have just done should resolve the abominable tangle and achieve ultimately a happy ending . . . Anyhow I have got it. Perhaps there are fewer tantrums, but I think it contains as much dramatic interest as in your first great beginning.

Is there any reason why plays should not be serialized and the vital interest created by your living characters carried on in a second complete play? Now tell me, before I trim up the dialogue, shall we collaborate? Is it to be a play by Noel Coward and Marie Stopes, in which case the same characters . . . I think the continuity of interest in a completely fresh play about the same characters, with the further intensified dramatic situations which my play creates is by far the best scheme and would give such advertising value to them both as would insure a vital interest . . . Yours sincerely

(*Noel Coward did not respond favourably to Marie Stopes's attempts to rewrite his plays with a happy ending. She wrote to him again when, following the financial crash of 1929, her clinic began to suffer from lack of funds.*)

29 JUNE 1925: MCS TO GEORGE BERNARD SHAW. I am humbly following in your footsteps and having a row with the Government over the iniquity of the Marriage Tax in the form of supertax. We have a clear and good fighting case for 1919, in which year owing to losses my husband was not liable to supertax and neither was I if we were both treated as separate individuals, but our incomes being added together we are liable for supertax which we are refusing to pay on the grounds of morality as I consider in a Christian country it is an immoral and outrageous act to tax me because I am living in Holy matrimony instead of as my husband's mistress.

We are to be before the Commissioners in the middle of this week and I shall be extremely obliged if you could let me know whether you succeeded, as report says, in defying the supertax people on the grounds that you did not know your wife's income and could not force her to tell you? I was told that for years you did not pay them anything and they did not dare to make you. Is that true or have they got some dodge to get round you? If you could tell us anything that would form fighting material I should be enormously grateful, as I think it is about time this iniquitous imposition was stopped. With kindest regards, Yours sincerely

I JULY 1925: GEORGE BERNARD SHAW IN REPLY. You have no case. There are many ways in which a mistress has advantages which a wife forfeits, though on balance the wife would not change places. The principle of taxing the family income is sound enough, though it is monstrous that the man should be accountable for the woman's taxes, even to the extent of having his body taken into execution and imprisoned for life, when he has no power to make her do more than keep him out of the workhouse.

What happened in my case was this. I was called on as usual to declare my wife's income. I went to the Revenue people and explained that I did not know what her income was; that I had no means of finding out, as I made her keep her separate banking account and solicitor when we were married; and that all the Suffragists were refusing to disclose. I said I was perfectly prepared to pay my wife's taxes, or any other of her debts, so far as I could ascertain them . . .

As they were convinced of my good faith, they passed an Act, which I called the Bernard Shaw Relief Act, enabling husband and wife to make separate returns; and we now do so, though the incomes are added to one another to fix the Supertax graduation. But I am liable. If I were not, my wife would have to pay Supertax at a much higher rate than that proper to her income.

All the stories you mention about my refusing to pay and so forth are fables.

The Commissioners will tell you that your remedy is to get divorced and resume cohabitation as a mistress. They cannot possibly let you off for 1919: the law is the law and they have no power to break it . . . ever

26 APRIL 1926, MAX GATE, DORCHESTER: THOMAS HARDY TO MCS. (*Thomas Hardy lived twenty miles away from Marie Stopes's holiday home, the Old Lighthouse, Portland Bill, which had figured in his novel,* The Well Beloved. *His letter here refers to Marie Stopes's autobiographical play* Vectia, *which she had sent him to read. The play – refused a licence by the Lord Chamber-*

lain – deals with her unhappy first marriage to Reginald Ruggles Gates, dissolved on the grounds of nullity.) . . . It seems to me that the situation and events are improbable for art, which must keep far within actual truth. I cannot conceive a young woman not an imbecile who has been married three years being in such crass ignorance of physiology, especially with a young man through the party wall ready to teach her. If she had been married only three days, or even three months, it would not have thrown such a strain upon one's credulity. However, taking the case quite seriously, the position of the pair is painful without reaching to the tragic . . .

25 MAY 1926, 13 HANOVER TERRACE, LONDON: HG WELLS TO MCS. It's a great and selling idea to write a book on *The Change of Life*. But I don't find much in the book . . . I am 70. I suppose I have been through the Change of Life somewhere and I don't find a single thing about men in your book that tallies with my experiences. I have never been able to detect any lunar periodicity in my life although I kept a very careful private diary for two or three years. I don't think there is any male equivalent to menstruation or the menopause. Yours ever

28 OCTOBER 1928, 4 WHITEHALL COURT, LONDON: GEORGE BERNARD SHAW TO MCS . . . I have had another shot at you in an interview which I have just given to the American Press, which included a question about Birth Control. I think you should insist on the separation in the public mind of your *incidental* work as a scientific critic of methods of contraception with your main profession as a teacher of matrimonial technique. People do not yet understand that there is such a thing as a technique of marriage, and that a would-be violinist taking up a fiddle and expecting to get music out of it without instruction is not more absurd than a husband taking a wife, or a wife a husband, in the same darkness. You are really a matrimonial expert, which is something much wider and more needed than a specialist in contraception. You should make it

clear that you are a doctor, not a Malthusian nor a trader in sterilizing devices.

The recent books about Dickens call for some public comment from you. Imagine a husband and wife 'pleading incompatibility' after 23 years together, when the difficulty was clearly the result of the woman's chronic pregnancy with an enormous family, mostly of good-for-nothings . . . ever

28 NOVEMBER 1929, LONGMEADOW, STREET, SOMERSET: LAURENCE HOUSMAN TO MCS . . . I think you misunderstand my attitude towards birth-control. All I said was that artificial methods do not appeal to *me* personally. I prefer another course, which, however, I have no wish to impose – either as more 'moral' or more 'natural' or more 'hygienic' – on others.

I am entirely in favour of those who like to use contraceptives being allowed to use them, and also of everyone being allowed to have free knowledge of *all* methods. I am in favour, that is to say, of full liberty. But that does not make me an enthusiastic backer of devices which I don't want to use myself . . . The only people who make my hackles rise in the matter are the theologians – to whom I say 'Damn your eyes and damn your arguments!'

20 SEPTEMBER 1932, HEATHERBANK, HINDHEAD: MCS TO NOEL COWARD. I'm always thrilled by your repeated success and feel the warmest sympathy and delight in it – remembering you told me mid-Atlantic how determined you were to win it for your mother's sake . . . Herewith is a book of mine (I want you to *read* – dear Noel, *do* please) and let it touch and wring your heart for other mothers. See in it but a tiny fraction of the agonies they pour out to me over 12 years. I respond and respond and respond beyond my strength and means till my private purse is empty . . . so do be an angel and send me £3000. It would have been so little for me to do myself a few years ago before I'd spent ten times that on the work. I pray you may thus help me to help other mothers. Yours ever cordially

27 NOVEMBER 1934, 4 WHITEHALL COURT, LONDON: GEORGE BERNARD SHAW TO MCS. I dictate this from a sick bed against the doctor's orders. Weep for me.

Betty Ross, who sent me her bundle of congenital inaccuracies, is threatening to publish a letter of yours in which you go characteristically off the deep end about my views on motherhood.

I have given every possible publicity to my obligation to my mother, and have been duly reproved for not playing the conventional good son. I have also, in comparisons of the nonexistent infant mortality on the mud floors of Connemara with the appalling death rate in the beautifully equipped Kaiserin Augusta House in Berlin, placed myself beyond all suspicion of advocating institutional treatment for infants. So you must be careful not to give it the credit of my support.

What I have never said, and what you must not elicit from me in public, is that to call my mother a bad mother would be unjust only because from your point of view she really was not a mother at all. The fact that I am still alive at $78\frac{1}{2}$ I probably owe largely to her complete neglect of me during my infancy, because if she had attempted to take care of me her stupendous ladylike ignorance would certainly have killed me. It used to be a common saying among Dublin doctors in my youth that most women killed their first child by their maternal care. I, fortunately, was left completely in the hands of a very decent Irish Catholic nurse, and subsequently in those of Irish country girls at a standard wage of £8 a year.

On the other hand you must bear in mind that if my mother had been an ideal Marie Stopes mother she would have been hopelessly incapable of earning my living at the North London School or anywhere else except perhaps at a children's hospital.

On reflection, you will see the importance of insisting on the fact that motherhood is not every woman's vocation. As far as I have been able to make a guess founded on the experience of welfare workers, mothers may be divided roughly into three classes. The first class consists of naturally good mothers who know better than the welfare workers how to handle their own children and everybody else's as well. The second class, the largest, consists of women who can bring up their own children quite well enough with good guidance. The third class is so completely hopeless that even the worst institution could hardly be more mischievous to children than maternal care.

You will see that the publication of your letter by the irresponsible Betty would only create misunderstandings as absurd for you as for me. You must always assume that I am always right; and then you will never be wrong. Yours, dearest Marie

(*This letter evoked an angry outburst from Marie Stopes against Betty Ross, a journalist whose book* Heads and Tales *included interviews with Shaw and Marie Stopes. In her reply she asked him publicly to repudiate the parts of his interview she disapproved of, offering in return to withdraw her letter to Betty Ross about Shaw. The letter had been written, she explained, 'in the heat of my indignation on behalf of the race'. She ended with a conciliatory expression of hope that he was now strong and well again.*)

13 DECEMBER 1934, GEORGE BERNARD SHAW TO MCS.
Nobody pays the smallest attention to Betty; but they would if we contradicted her. Never advertise an idiot. I am NOT strong and well again: I am barely alive. How unfeeling you are!

12 JULY 1939, HOVE: LORD ALFRED DOUGLAS TO MCS.
(*Lord Alfred Douglas – the 'Bosie' of the Oscar Wilde scandal – being a Catholic who had often attacked birth control, Marie Stopes posed as 'Mrs Carmichael', mother of a young family, when she first sent her poems to him for criticism in 1938. She was fifty-eight, Douglas ten years older. She eventually admitted her true identity and the two became friends. Douglas spent many weekends at Marie Stopes's home, Norbury Park, and she helped him, financially and emotionally, through the last few years of an increasingly lonely and embittered life. At the time, he was writing a book about Oscar Wilde.*) . . . I am beginning to think I cannot possibly do it, as I find that when I begin to remember all the

details of the old tragedy and the frightful experiences I went through, it upsets my mind and causes me a tremendous amount of mental disturbance and distress, on my own, as well as Wilde's account . . . It seems to me that if I do the book at all, I shall be *forced* to go at length into the whole question of homosexuality. I am very reluctant to do this. I *hate* the whole thing myself and wish to God I had never even known or heard anything about it. But there it is and fairness to Wilde would compel me to say that he was cruelly and vulgarly treated, because people who have that attraction for their own sex ought not really to be blamed for it . . . Now if I say all this in a book it will be difficult to avoid appearing to defend homosexuality (I mean the acts, not the instinct, which no one can help, if he or she happens to be 'built that way') . . .

2 AUGUST 1939, MCS IN REPLY. My dear Bosie . . . I'm thinking much about your chapter on the horrid homosexual problem and I wonder if you would let me see it before it goes to the publisher? It is a very terrible scourge of modern society and I have a good deal of inside knowledge about it. A lax attitude towards the older and corrupting partner is very wrong, for young people's lives can be, and often at present are, absolutely ruined by it – yet the Wilde case shows up how wrong too great severity is . . .

(Included with the letter were Marie Stopes's notes for his chapter on Homosexuality): Homosexuality, like other acts, varies in its nature with the contingent circumstances, e.g. two adult men, congenitally abnormal in this way, living together, commit no social crime, only 'sin'; but an adult who corrupts and uses young normal boys commits a social crime of a revolting nature and may most probably destroy soul and body of those boys rendering them useless as adult husbands and fathers. Hence by this crime the State is deprived of useful citizens for two generations and their potential progeny are destroyed.

I know from my social work that this is so and therefore punishment by the State must be meted out to adults who corrupt normal boys in this way. The punishment however should not be vindictive, only to prevent the spread of what tends to become epidemic and a real social disease. In the sentence on Wilde vindictive and unsuitable punishment was meted out – the hard labour a real brutality.

21 AUGUST 1939, LORD ALFRED DOUGLAS TO MCS ... I agree that corrupting boys is a terrible thing but when I say that homosexuality is 'no worse' than adultery or fornication, I mean that *per se* it is no worse. Circumstances may of course make it worse, but that equally applies to other things. For example, would you say that it is worse for a man to corrupt an innocent boy than for the same man to seduce an innocent girl and put her 'in the family way'? I wouldn't think so myself . . . ever yours affectionately

STATISTICAL
APPENDIX

The survey was carried out on a total of 300 letters from the period 1918–29. The letters were taken from four of the sixty-five boxes of general correspondence in the Stopes-Roe collection, arranged alphabetically by surname. As far as it is possible to tell the boxes have not been tampered with and are probably as MCS left them. It is possible, though, that she removed particular letters, or categories of letter – as she occasionally did for the purposes of book compilation – thus making the contents of the boxes not wholly representative of the total correspondence. Only personal letters from that decade were studied, and if the correspondence continued for more than one letter only the first letter has been used.

As might be expected, more women than men wrote to MCS, though not overwhelmingly so – 56 per cent as opposed to 44 per cent respectively. 88·3 per cent of the sample were writing for themselves while 11·7 per cent said they were writing for their spouse, a friend or a relation. 15·7 per cent of the correspondence received came from overseas, the remainder from the British Isles; a more detailed breakdown is given below:

Geographical Distribution		*number of letters*
London and the South East	41·3	124
Wales, Midlands, East Anglia	11·7	35
South West	8·0	24
North of England	14·3	43
Scotland	6·7	20
N. Ireland, Eire, Channel Islands	2·3	7
Overseas	15·7	47

Correspondents wrote for a wide variety of reasons. Not surprisingly most had sexual, medical or contraceptive problems, though some wanted to know where to get books by Marie Stopes, or to arrange a personal consultation.

Interestingly, though MCS claimed to have had many letters from those strongly opposed to her work, the sample shows that 41·7 per cent of correspondents expressly supported her work, 57·3 per cent were non-committal, and only 1 per cent actively disapproved of her ideas.

The number of letters received varied considerably from year to year. The variations can be partly correlated to the propaganda activities of MCS in this period:

1918	*Married Love* and *Wise Parenthood*	18
1919	*A Letter to Working Mothers*	39
1920	*A New Gospel* and *Radiant Motherhood*	32
1921	Opening of Britain's first birth control clinic. *The Truth About Venereal Disease*	39
1922	*Early Days of Birth Control*; 10th ed. of *Married Love* (191,000 copies sold) and of *Wise Parenthood* (170,000 copies sold)	24
1923	MCS's libel action, widely reported, against Halliday Sutherland	40
1924	Libel action appeal in the House of Lords	29
1925	*The First Five Thousand* (report on clinic)	9
1926	*The Human Body, Sex and The Young*	25
1927	Organization of first travelling birth control caravan	13
1928	*Enduring Passion*; *Love's Creation*	22
1929	*Mother England*	10

(One explanation for the relatively few letters in 1925 may possibly be that MCS herself abstracted a number of the letters arising from her series of articles in *John Bull* that year, filing them separately for subsequent use in her collection of letters from working-class women, *Mother England*.)

Of the correspondents 246 gave some indication of their

initial impetus to write. In 91 cases, there was more than one reason for their writing:

Genesis of letter

Married Love	154
Wise Parenthood	95
Other publications	24
Newspaper items, letters, articles by MCS	35
Libel action, 1923–4	14

Significantly, given MCS's contempt for the medical profession where sexual and contraceptive matters were concerned, eight correspondents wrote to her because their own doctors refused to give any advice. In three cases, the doctor concerned admitted ignorance and himself advised an approach to Marie Stopes. In four other cases, friends or relatives of the correspondent had suggested writing to her.

I also noted age, marital status and family size of the correspondent if stated in the letter. Of those who gave their age (37·3 per cent did not) 85·6 per cent were between twenty and forty years of age. Just over half (55·7 per cent) of the correspondents were married and had been married for some years; of this group, only half were men. 17·3 per cent were newly married and 14 per cent were about to marry (here there were almost twice as many men as women, asking for advice). Very few (3·3 per cent) were single, and most of these claimed to be inquiring on the behalf of friends.

The majority – 63·3 per cent – gave the number of children in the family. The family size of those who gave details is perhaps smaller than might have been expected:

Family size	No.
0	104
1–3	67
4–6	19
7–10	2

In most cases it was possible to make an estimate of the social class of the correspondent. This showed that 39·3 per cent were working class, 60·7 per cent upper and middle classes.

The subject matter of the letters falls broadly into six categories, and a total of 59 (19·7 per cent) correspondents asked for help with two or more of these problems:

		No.
Sexual		
satisfaction, frigidity, impotence, premature ejaculation, masturbation	19·0	57
pre-marital sex and first night problems	6·7	20
Birth Control	39·0	117
pro-contraception	3·3	10
abortion requests	7·0	21
advice on sterilization	2·0	6
requests for advice on eugenic advisability of having children	2·7	8
General medical problems	7·0	21
Theories and experiences	4·0	12
Requests for consultations, books	20·0	60
Letters of encouragement, etc.	7·7	23

Most of the correspondents were writing for themselves, or themselves and spouse; 4·7 per cent wrote asking for information for their spouse, 4·7 per cent for help with friends or relations, and 1·7 per cent asked for information for groups of people – medical patients, for example, the poorer classes, or men serving in the army.

Several interesting facts emerge from the study. All the 0·3 per cent of correspondents writing about premature ejaculation were men – one of them a captain anxious to answer questions his troops put to him. Of the 21 correspondents asking for advice on sexual technique, there were twice as many men as women. Nine correspondents asked for help with frigidity – but only two of them were women.

Similarly with first night problems: of the 6·7 per cent expressing doubts about how the hymen should be pierced, or what contraceptive should be used in the first days of marriage, there were twice as many men as women. However, the women accounted for the majority of requests for, and advice on, abortion – 5·7 per cent as opposed to 1·3 per cent of men. The abortions were asked for mostly on economic grounds – lack of money, and threat of eviction should the number of children in the family increase.

CHRISTOPHER STOPES-ROE